NOTHING LEFT OF ME

ALEX WALTERS

BLOODHOUND
— BOOKS —

Copyright © 2024 Alex Walters

The right of Alex Walters to be identified as the Author of the Work has been asserted by them in accordance with the Copyright, Designs and Patents Act 1988.

First published in 2024 by Bloodhound Books.

Apart from any use permitted under UK copyright law, this publication may only be reproduced, stored, or transmitted, in any form, or by any means, with prior permission in writing of the publisher or, in the case of reprographic production, in accordance with the terms of licences issued by the Copyright Licensing Agency.
All characters in this publication are fictitious and any resemblance to real persons, living or dead, is purely coincidental.

www.bloodhoundbooks.com

Print ISBN: 978-1-917449-4-65

For Helen

CHAPTER ONE

It's strange what goes through your head when you think you're about to die.

My first reaction, funnily enough, was embarrassment. I'd screwed up. Others must have screwed up too, but no one would rush to admit it. The buck would stop with me. Especially if I wasn't around to pass it on.

Danny Royce dragged me into the open. Before I could offer any resistance, he threw me down onto the paved path in the centre of the garden. He stamped his boot on my chest and raised his shotgun.

I was armed myself, but that was a fat lot of good now. All it did was give Royce a justification for killing me. He couldn't know I was a copper. I was just an intruder with a gun. He couldn't take any chances. I could hear him saying it.

Even Royce probably wouldn't get away with that. But that's the thing about people like Royce. They don't care. They don't think about the consequences. Nothing would stop him pulling that trigger. All I could do was close my eyes and hope the end was quick and painless.

When I heard the roar of the gunshot, my first thought was

that Royce had somehow missed or was playing with me. It was only when I heard the thump of his body hitting the ground that I realised it hadn't been Royce who'd fired.

I opened my eyes. Sean Critchley was leaning over me, smiling faintly. 'You okay?' There was a mocking edge to his question, maybe not unreasonably.

It was a moment before I felt able to answer. The most I could say for sure was that I wasn't dead. I dragged myself to a sitting position. 'Sore back. A few bruises. Other than that, I'm okay.' I waited a beat. 'I didn't know you were there.'

'You weren't supposed to.'

'That right?' Critchley was goading me into asking more. Bugger that. If anyone wanted to tell me what was going on, they'd do so soon enough. I managed to get to my feet. Royce was on his back, his chest a bloody mess, a dark pool under his body. 'Well, thanks anyway, I suppose.'

'Just doing my job, bro. Though now we'll have to go through the balls-ache of an enquiry.'

That was the moment I finally decided to jack it all in. I'd been contemplating it for months in a half-hearted way. I felt jaded, tired, older than my forty-odd years. I'd seen it all and didn't want to see any of it again. I needed a change.

That moment in Royce's garden crystallised my discontent. It wasn't even that I'd narrowly escaped being killed. It was more that the price of survival would be endless bureaucracy, and at best an earnest bollocking, another blot on my career copybook. Standing there in the small hours in the glare of Royce's state-of-the-art security lights, I knew I simply couldn't be arsed.

I wasn't sure how my resignation would be received, particularly given my track record, but it was accepted with no question or objection. The enquiry went ahead, though there was no suggestion either I or Critchley had been guilty of any misconduct. The only question was how Royce had discovered me, with the implication that I'd been negligent. Maybe I had been. I didn't know quite what had happened in those critical minutes before Royce dragged me into the open. I might have literally dozed off. Understandable, when you're stuck on what seems pointless surveillance for hours on end, but not smart and not acceptable.

That didn't explain how Royce had known I was there in the first place. I'm pretty sure I'd done nothing to give myself away. There wasn't much point in speculating on that, or why Critchley had been so conveniently on hand. All that was above my pay grade.

I was long gone before the enquiry concluded, but I heard on the grapevine that it had panned out as expected. Another operation that had gone tits up. No one really to blame, though there'd possibly been some failings on my part. Some bollocks was concocted to explain Critchley's presence. The shooting had been necessary to protect a fellow officer facing imminent risk of death. Above all – though the report didn't say this in so many words – no one gave a flying one about the fate of Danny Royce, a mid-range gangster and thug.

That was months ago. Apart from the odd phone call, I've not been in contact with anyone since. As far as most of my ex-colleagues are concerned, I've vanished off the face of the earth, and I'm content to leave it like that. I thought I might miss some of it – the excitement, the adrenaline rush, the satisfaction when an operation comes together – but I was never tempted to look back. I've never been one for living in the past.

But I have learned that sometimes, usually when you least want or expect it, the past comes looking for you.

CHAPTER TWO

I'd never intended to stay up here. Not for long, anyway.

My first thought, once I'd handed in my warrant card that final Friday, was just to get away. I didn't really care where as long as it was a long distance from Glasgow. I'd been thinking about heading back to England, maybe to the Peak District or Northumbria, places where I'd spent enjoyable holidays with Maddie years before. But that connection in itself was enough to give me second thoughts. Another part of the past I didn't want to live in.

I first came across Gus through one of the guys at work. We'd been chatting about my plans after leaving – most of those I spoke to seemed astonished and slightly horrified that I'd actually taken the plunge – and I'd told him I just wanted a break. I wanted to get my head together and think about what to do next. I had some savings so I could afford to take my time.

It turned out the guy's wife was from the Highlands and that she still had family up there, including a brother, Gus, a crofter on the east coast. Gus owned a couple of cottages he used mainly as holiday lets, but he was happy to accept longer-term rentals, particularly after the end of the tourist season.

It was an area I knew hardly at all, but it sounded idyllic and certainly fitted my key criterion of being nowhere near the central belt. I made contact with Gus, who seemed an amiable enough individual, and arranged a viewing the following week.

I fell in love with the place on first sight, which is more than I've ever managed with a human being. It seemed exactly what I was looking for. The cottage was on the fringes of Gus's land, with spectacular views over the hills, the Cromarty Firth glittering in the distance. It was sufficiently remote that I was unlikely to run into anyone except through choice, but within reasonable striking distance of Dingwall and Inverness. It was a place that would undoubtedly restore my sanity, if it didn't drive me utterly crazy in the meantime.

The cottage itself was stone-built, a converted outbuilding. It was only a small place – a bedroom, bathroom, living room and a small kitchen – but plenty large enough for my purposes. It was basic inside, but I knew I could make it comfortable.

'It's booked off and on till the end of September,' Gus said as he showed me round. 'I've been holding off taking bookings for next year as I'd rather get a longer-term tenant if I can. If you're interested, it's yours from October for as long as you want.'

That suited me perfectly. It was mid-August, so that gave me time to sort out letting my flat in Glasgow. The income from the rent – likely to be much more than I'd be paying for this place – would help cover my living expenses till I decided my future. 'I'll take it,' I said without hesitation.

Gus had looked surprised. 'You're sure about that? It's one thing being up here in the height of summer – or what passes for summer in these parts – but it's another being here in mid-December. You might want to think about it.'

No one had ever taught Gus the fine art of salesmanship, which is one reason I'd warmed to him. He'd systemically pointed out the shortcomings of the house as well as highlighting its more attractive features. 'I've thought about it,' I said. 'I want to take it.'

He grinned. 'As long as you don't come complaining if you get snowbound. I use the tractor to keep the tracks as clear as possible, but there's usually a day or two in the winter when we have problems.'

'I'll cope,' I said. 'A bottle of decent whisky, the log stove and I won't want much more.'

He looked sceptical. No doubt he'd encountered his share of visitors with romantic notions of the Highland winter. 'Well, if you change your mind, I'll understand. Otherwise, I'll get the paperwork sorted out.'

At that point, I thought I'd probably rent the cottage for a couple of months – Gus was happy to be flexible about the tenancy, which was another attraction – just to give myself some breathing space. Three months later I was still there with no desire to move on. I'd even talked to Gus about buying the place. Everything seemed to have worked out better than I could have hoped, at least on that front.

Even the winter hadn't been as bad as I'd feared. It was a relatively mild one – or so Gus insisted – and we hadn't yet had sufficient snow to prevent me getting down to the main road. The cottage itself was well-insulated, the log-burning stove sufficient to keep the place as warm as I needed.

I'd moved up here as agreed during the first week in October. I'd let my flat as furnished accommodation, so I'd left behind pretty much everything without a personal connection. The rest I'd easily fitted into the back of the car – books, some records, pictures, and a few other items with sentimental value. The stuff I'd need to make the cottage feel like home.

Gus had been there to greet me on arrival and had helped me unload the car. He'd even left me a box full of foodstuffs.

'Just the basics,' Gus said. 'Keep you going until you can get to the shops. I hope you've not had any second thoughts.'

I turned and gestured to the landscape behind me. 'How could I have second thoughts about this place. It's idyllic.'

'Aye, for the moment.'

'Why do you say that?'

'Ach, probably just because I'm a grumpy middle-aged man who hates change. But nothing's perfect, even up here.' He gazed at the open fields and moorland around us. 'I mean, take this land. People think that because it looks like a wilderness it must be unspoiled common land. But most of it's owned by a small number of landowners. Sometimes the same families who've owned it for generations. But they're selling out to overseas investors, conglomerates, developers.'

'Does that matter?' I felt naive even asking the question.

'It depends. Sometimes not so much. For some of the Middle East investors, it's just a status thing. My Scottish estate. But even that can be damaging. They come here once or twice a year grouse hunting, then let the property out to overpaid merchant bankers to play at being landed gentry. In the meantime they've got staff damaging the environment, illegally killing supposed predators, burning the heather, just to make sure they've enough grouse to kill.'

I'd been vaguely aware of these issues, but I was surprised by how vehemently Gus was expressing his opinions. 'I hadn't realised.'

'No, well, people often don't, unless they live here. And that's not the end of it. There's only so much you can do with a stretch of moorland. But if the land can be developed, there are bastards who'll try to squeeze every penny from it. And it's not usually affordable residential property, which would be welcome. It's high-end leisure resorts, gated private communities, yet more bloody golf courses...' He trailed off as if embarrassed at how much he'd allowed his feelings to show.

'I've not seen much sign of that,' I said.

'We've been lucky so far. But I reckon our luck's running out. You've heard of Gregor McBride?'

'The Laird of New Jersey?'

'Aye, so the wee gobshite styles himself. He's been buying up property in these parts.' Gus gestured towards a wide area further down the hill where the land flattened out into a patchwork of fields. 'That whole stretch down there, for example. All his, apparently. Plans to turn it into some kind of huge golf resort. Imagine what a bloody eyesore that'll be. And that's just one of several in the Highlands.'

It was difficult even to imagine the kind of development Gus was describing. Anything like that seemed like an intrusion from another world. All I knew about McBride was the little I'd read in the media. He was a brash US businessman who'd inherited wealth and invested it mainly in property and leisure interests with varying degrees of success. He had a high profile in the US media, originally because of a series of 'fly on the wall' documentaries which featured him pontificating boorishly and at length. He had strong if largely uninformed views on everything from deal-making to sex to politics, all of which could probably be summarised as 'I do what I like, and I get what I want'.

Whatever else he might be, he was a successful self-publicist. He'd made an unsuccessful attempt to run for President as an independent in the previous election. Most people had assumed his sole objective was to raise his profile still further. Whatever his original motives, there were rumours he was considering running again, this time on a Republican slate. Polling suggested he might even be in with a chance of winning the primaries and possibly the election itself.

'He always strikes me as a nasty piece of work,' I said.

'He's that all right. Doesn't care who he tramples on. When he was building his golf course and resort in Perthshire, he had numerous tenants evicted, sometimes almost literally overnight. If anyone tried to fight back, they were subjected to a campaign of harassment. He didn't care about the law. He didn't care about planning or building regulations. He had enough friends in high places to get away with it even in the face of huge local opposition.'

'You reckon he'll do the same up here?'

'It's already happening. Quietly so far, because he's kept his land acquisitions largely under the radar. But I know of tenants who've suffered.'

'That won't affect you?'

'I'm safe enough, as long as I can scratch a living. This land's been in the family for generations. But there are plenty who won't be.' He shook his head. 'There's some local opposition growing, though. We've set up a campaign. I've persuaded a guy called Cameron Fraser to act as our figurehead. Another businessman. Not exactly in McBride's league, but with enough money and influence to make himself heard. Knowing Cameron, he's probably more interested in protecting his own interests up here than in safeguarding tenants or the environment, but you have to find your champions where you can.' He laughed. 'Sorry. Just blethering on. Like I say, middle-aged man who's not keen on change.'

In fact, he was probably only five or so years older than I was, but that afternoon as he helped me move my stuff into the cottage, he felt like the big brother I'd never had. After we'd finished moving boxes, he produced a bottle of Glenmorangie and poured us both a celebratory dram, raising a toast to me. '*Fàilte!*'. If I'd had any lingering doubts about my decision to move up here that was when they melted away.

Even so, it took me a week or two to settle in properly. Part of that was getting the house the way I wanted it. As Maddie would have been the first to tell you, I don't always have the highest domestic standards, but I like to feel at home. It's one reason why I'm happy living alone. I can create a space that suits me. With winter coming, I wanted the cottage to feel cosy, welcoming. Somewhere to keep the outside world at bay.

In the event, that wasn't too difficult. The cottage had been cleverly converted, with large windows to capture the available daylight, increasingly welcome as the days shortened. At the same time, there were heavy curtains to keep the heat in once the sun had gone down, and the kind of warm décor that made you feel that nothing outside these walls really mattered. All I had to do was add some of my own pictures on the walls, a few ornaments and personal knick-knacks around the place and I felt more comfortable than I'd ever felt in my Glasgow flat.

The other part of settling in was getting to know the area. Dingwall was a twenty-minute drive away, a pleasant old-fashioned town that, apart from a handful of familiar chain stores, looked as if it hadn't changed much since the 1950s. There were some empty shops, but it was good to find a place with proper butchers, greengrocers, a traditional hardware store, even a couple of bookshops. I suspected I'd be coming here to do more than replenish the fridge. Inverness was larger and had more to offer, but I wasn't sure I'd need to venture there too often.

Apart from that, I spent those early weeks driving round the local villages, heading up and down the coast and over on to the Black Isle, visiting Dornoch, Tain, Cromarty. I made a couple of trips over to the west coast, visiting Ullapool and Plockton, and out along the shores of Loch Ness to Fort Augustus. More locally, I took Gus's advice on walks in the vicinity of the cottage, and discovered that it was possible, within only ten or fifteen minutes, to find myself in what felt like an utter wilderness.

I wasn't even sure why I was so keen to do this. I just wanted a sense of the place, an idea of what it had to offer, a feeling for how it all fitted together. That doesn't generally interest me too much when I'm visiting a new location, but this felt different. I was going to be living here, at least for a few months, maybe for longer. I wanted it to feel like home.

Looking back now, I'm not sure my behaviour was entirely rational. Maybe I was still suffering from shock, maybe even PTSD. After all, there'd been a moment in Danny Royce's garden when I'd been absolutely certain I was about to die. That might explain why I was so keen to get away and why I worked so hard to establish a new life elsewhere. I don't suppose it matters much. Within a few weeks, I was settled and, possibly for the first time in years, I might even have been happy.

CHAPTER THREE

Christmas came and went. Gus had been concerned about me spending it alone. He was heading south for Christmas to stay with his brother and his wife in Stirling, and he felt uncomfortable leaving me on my own. I told him it was exactly what I wanted – which was true – though I'm not sure he believed me. As I'd expected, it was fine. I didn't make much of the day itself other than treating myself to a decent bottle of wine with my dinner and a more expensive than usual bottle of single malt for afterwards. I went for a walk, built up the log burner, stuck on an old Watersons record that felt appropriate to the season, and spent the rest of the day and evening reading. It might have been the best Christmas I'd ever had.

It also felt like a symbolic moment. The turning of the year. Time for new starts and all that. And, fittingly enough, it was at Hogmanay that I first had an inkling about where life might take me next. Gus and some other local crofters had established a tradition of hosting a Hogmanay party for their friends and acquaintances in the surrounding area. Despite the remoteness of the region, they managed to attract a surprising number of guests and, according to Gus, the evening would be a lively affair, growing increasingly raucous as midnight approached. 'You're very welcome to join us,' he'd said, in his usual diffident manner. 'It'll give you a chance to get to know some more folk locally. You might even meet the legendary Cameron Fraser.'

I was reluctant to accept. I was afraid I'd feel out of place, an outsider among a group who knew each other well. I'm not always the most sociable of individuals, and I could imagine myself isolated in a corner, counting down the minutes to midnight, while a crowd milled about me.

'It's not like that,' Gus had insisted. 'We get all sorts coming along. Half the people living here are incomers. We welcome everyone, even ex-coppers.' He grinned. 'Anyway, I'll be deeply offended if you don't come. You don't want that.'

So I went along, unsure what to expect. What I found was A large group of guests – it was difficult to be sure how many because some came and went across the evening – every bit as diverse as Gus had suggested. Gus hosted the party in a converted outbuilding adjacent to their main steading. He generally used the building as a workshop, and over the preceding days I'd helped him clear it out and prepare it for the party. He'd hired some industrial heaters, though as it turned out the weather was relatively mild. We'd set up some trestle tables along one wall for the food and drink, and Gus had booked a DJ for the night.

This year, Gus was also using the event as an opportunity to promote the campaign against the new McBride development. He'd set up a small stall in the corner of the room, with mocked-up images of what the development would look like and graphic descriptions of its impact on the local community and environment. There was a petition and an opportunity for people to sign up and donate to the campaign. Gus had organised various activities across the evening – a raffle, an auction and some other competitions – to help raise funding.

'Not entirely festive,' he'd admitted. 'But most people here will be behind the cause.'

Some technically savvy mate of Gus's had put together a video, running in a loop on a computer monitor on the stall. It was an unflattering montage of clips of Gregor McBride, the self-styled Laird of New Jersey. There was McBride hectoring a crowd during his failed Presidential campaign, stabbing his finger like a bargain-basement dictator; McBride spouting a stream of misogynist nonsense during a board meeting filmed for his 'fly on the wall' series; McBride at the formal opening of his Perthshire resort, looking baffled at the hostile reaction from the local residents.

I watched the video in fascination. It had clearly been edited to show McBride in the least complimentary light, but he cut a grotesque figure. Overweight, ungainly, a man manifestly ill at ease in his own body, his dyed black hair slicked back, his lips seemingly pursed in permanent disapproval. His speech was a sometimes barely coherent deluge of self-aggrandisement that concealed his evident insecurity as successfully as the dyed hair hid his advancing years. The whole effect ought to have been simply risible, but somehow it was chilling. Something about McBride seemed genuinely malevolent, the sense of evil rendered oddly more potent by the absurdity of its manifestation. It was hard to envisage a figure less suited to the relaxed, good-natured hospitality of this gathering. The devil walking into a *cèilidh*.

I'd gone along early in the evening to help with the final preparations, and I watched as people filtered into the room. Some of them clearly knew Gus well. Others looked as nervous as I was feeling. To my surprise, particularly after the first couple of beers, I began to enjoy it. I wandered round the room, finding people to chat to, discovering that they were genuinely a mixed bunch. A few were English like me, some who'd moved here for work or family reasons, others who'd chosen to retire here. There was an American woman who'd married a Highlander from the Black Isle. There were plenty who were clearly local, some telling me their families had been here for generations. There were farmers like Gus, but the majority worked in a variety of occupations in Dingwall or Inverness. No one seemed unwelcoming.

Several beers in, I found myself in a conversation with a middle-aged man. He looked like a stereotypical Scotsman, with swept-back ginger hair fading to grey and a full but neatly trimmed white beard. He was taller than I am, heavily built, and it occurred to me he was someone I wouldn't want to get on the wrong side of.

'I'm guessing you're not local?'

'Not difficult to spot,' I said. 'Moved up from Glasgow, but I'm a Mancunian originally.'

He nodded thoughtfully, his expression suggesting that this information might be useful to him. 'What brings you up to these parts?'

'It's a long story.'

'It usually is. Give me the condensed version.' From anyone else, the instruction might have seemed abrupt, even rude. But from him it simply sounded direct. I guessed he wasn't a man to waste time. I told him briefly what had led to my move north.

'Not thrown out of the force, then?' He sounded slightly sceptical.

'Entirely voluntary. Don't know if I've done the right thing, but it felt the right time.'

'Never be afraid to make a change.' The words sounded like the kind of inspirational motto you'd find on a decorative plaque in a garden centre, but not the way he said them. 'I imagine an encounter with Danny Royce would have been enough to make anyone consider their priorities.'

I hadn't mentioned Royce's name. 'You've heard of Royce?'

'I read about the shooting in the press. I guessed that's who you were talking about. I don't think any officers were named in the reports.'

At the time, both Critchley and I had been grateful our names hadn't leaked out. Royce had no doubt had some powerful friends. I don't imagine he was widely loved, but there'd been concerns about possible reprisals. 'You're right. That was definitely a factor.'

'So what about you? What do you do?' I'd asked the question only to make conversation, but almost immediately I felt as if I might have overstepped a mark. I almost expected to be upbraided for my impertinence.

Instead, he gave me a faint smile and a nod that might have indicated approval. 'I'm in business,' he said vaguely. 'Finance, mainly. This and that.' It was clear he wasn't going to tell me more. 'Do you have any plans?'

'Not really,' I admitted. 'I wanted to take some time out, but I need to make some decisions soon.'

He was looking thoughtful. 'I might be able to make use of a man with your background. If you're interested, give me a call and we can fix something up.'

'I don't know if I'm ready for a full-time job yet.' I still wasn't sure what to make of the man standing in front of me. I didn't want to offer any commitments until I knew more.

'Think about it,' he said. 'It doesn't have to be a full-time job. It could be freelance. But give me a call, Mr...?'

'Mellor,' I said. 'Jack Mellor.'

'Call me, Mr Mellor. You might find it's to your advantage.' He pulled an expensive-looking leather wallet from his jacket and extracted a business card.

I took it from him. It was a heavy gold-embossed item. As I'd already guessed, this was Cameron Fraser. The card was printed with his name and a mobile phone number, but no other information.

I looked up, intending to ask him where he was based, but he'd already turned away and was talking to someone else.

I looked back at the card. Then a voice behind me said, 'And now you've had your first encounter with Cameron Fraser, I'm guessing it won't be your last.'

CHAPTER FOUR

The woman was smiling at me indulgently, as if she'd caught me out in some minor misdemeanour. She was probably in her early thirties. I hadn't considered it till that moment, but we were probably the two youngest people in the room. She was tall, slim with dark hair cut short. Like me, she was casually dressed in jeans and jumper. Most of the other guests were dressed, at least by my standards, relatively formally.

She held a can of beer in each hand, and offered one to me. 'I thought you might need it.'

'Thanks. Do I look that desperate?'

'Not noticeably. But in my experience Cameron usually leaves people in need of refreshment.'

'I'm sorry...?'

She handed me the beer, then held out her hand for shaking. 'Lorna Jardine.'

'Good to meet you. Jack Mellor. I take it you know Mr Fraser?'

'Everyone round here knows Cameron Fraser.'

'You sound disapproving.'

'Not really. Or at least not entirely. I just accept that Cameron is Cameron. For good or ill.'

'I'm not sure I follow.'

'Cameron is, as they say, a law unto himself. He does what he wants, no matter who or what gets in his way.'

'That sounds more ill than good.'

'Just a force of nature.'

I had the feeling she was toying with me. 'What exactly does he do? He said he was in business.'

'Investment mainly, I think. Mainly in start-ups, especially locally. There are quite a few businesses round here wouldn't have got off the ground without him.'

'Quite the philanthropist.'

'I think you'd be looking at Cameron for a long time before the word "philanthropy" occurred to you. He's a businessman. He makes money. In fairness, he's good at it.'

'He gave me his card. Said I should contact him.'

She raises an eyebrow. 'Did he now?'

'I wasn't sure how seriously to take him.'

'You should always take Cameron seriously. I understand you're a former policeman, Mr Mellor?'

'My reputation precedes me, then?'

'I was chatting to Gus earlier. He told me you'd moved up from Glasgow. I hope you're not regretting it.'

'Not in the slightest. It's exactly what I needed.'

'Some people thrive up here and some don't. It's a matter of temperament.'

'What about yourself? I take it you're local.' To my untutored ear, her accent sounded like those of others I'd met in the area.

'It depends what you mean by local. I was born and brought up on Skye. Went to uni in Aberdeen. Somehow ended up living here.'

'What is it you do?'

'Nothing exciting. I'm an accountant. Started working for a firm in Inverness. Couple of years ago I set up on my own.'

'Is that how you came to know Cameron Fraser?'

She regarded me curiously, as if the question had taken her by surprise. 'Not really. I know Cameron mainly the same way everyone else does. Because he makes himself the centre of attention.'

At the far end of the room, the DJ had kicked off his set. I guessed Gus had picked him – or he'd selected his tracks – to suit the crowd, with a blend of sentimental country songs, Scottish dance music and the odd familiar pop hit. It seemed to be going down well.

'Not really my sort of thing,' Lorna said. 'Do you fancy chatting outside?'

'Shall I grab us a couple more beers?'

'You do that. I'll see you outside.'

I made my way through to the drinks table and found two more cans, then followed her through the doors of the outbuilding. The chill of the night air hit me immediately, but I was wearing a heavy sweater and the temperature was relatively mild for midwinter. Lorna had walked a few steps away into the darkness, and it took me a moment to spot her.

'No stars tonight,' she said, as I handed her the beer. 'Clouded over. Pity.'

'It's spectacular on a clear night,' I agreed. 'I don't think I'd seen the Milky Way properly till I moved up here. Assume you get the Northern Lights here too?'

'Sometimes. You'll be well placed to see them here. The landscape cuts out the worst of the light pollution.'

'You live locally?'

'Very. The cottage down the hill. Just off the main road.'

'That's pretty remote.'

'Not as remote as your place.' She laughed. 'Not that it's a competition.'

'Yes, but you're not running away from anything.' I'd spoken the words before I thought about them, and even I was surprised by what I'd said. I didn't know what had prompted me to say it, or even quite what I'd meant.

'And you are?'

'I don't know,' I said. 'Maybe.'

'Is this to do with your reasons for leaving the police?'

'Partly. But it's more complicated than that.' I'm not sure I'd ever managed to be this honest with myself before. It felt as if she was drawing the words out of me. 'I'm not sure I can explain.'

She'd moved closer and I could feel the warmth and beery scent of her breath. 'Don't try,' she said. 'Not till you're ready. But I'm happy to listen.'

That was the first moment when I felt there might be something between us. Not necessarily anything romantic or sexual but at least some kind of bond. 'I don't even know what I'm talking about.'

'Just give it time,' she said. 'It'll come if it's meant to.'

We chatted for a good while after that, mainly about the McBride development, though I can't remember much of what we said. Like everyone else I'd spoken to about the development, she was opposed to it. She told me there'd already been some forced eviction of tenants who'd been living on the land bought by McBride. Her own view seemed more fatalistic. Whatever the local opposition, eventually McBride would get his way.

At some point, we went back inside, standing as far as we could from the noise of the DJ. Gus had been right about the party growing more raucous as midnight approached. It was a genteel, middle-aged type of rowdiness but everyone was having a good time. There was dancing going on, but it had an ironic feel, no one taking it very seriously. Mostly, there was drinking.

Cameron Fraser was holding court in a corner of the room, surrounded by a group of other guests. Gus was rushing about replenishing the drinks, ensuring that everyone had a dram in hand to celebrate the New Year. Lorna and I watched, enjoying the spectacle.

Finally, the DJ led the crowd in counting down the seconds before playing a recording of the midnight bongs. There were cheers and shouts of 'Happy New Year!' and 'Happy Hogmanay!' before the inevitable playing of 'Auld Lang Syne'. Lorna and I were separated as we were dragged into the ragged joining of hands, everyone tunelessly singing along to Burns's words.

When the celebrations eventually quietened, I looked around for Lorna but there was no sign of her. I wondered if she'd gone outside, so I stepped back out into the darkness. As far as I could see the area outside was empty. I took one more look inside and waited a while for her to reappear, but she didn't.

Gus had told me that the party would go on into the small hours, and that I should slip away when I was ready. I'd offered to help clear up afterwards, but Gus had told me he never bothered till the following day. 'Even then,' he'd said, 'don't come round too early. I'll feed you some steak pie in the afternoon, and then we can get on with it.'

For my own part, I'd had more than enough to drink, and there seemed no reason to stay longer. I took one final look around the milling crowd and left, making my way back up the track to the cottage, using the light on my phone for illumination. As I approached the summit of the hill, I looked back down. The brightly lit outbuilding was visible to my right, the DJ's music reaching me faintly through the night. Lorna's cottage must be somewhere down to my left, though I couldn't recall if it was visible from this point. If it was, I could see no lights.

I continued on my way, realising that I felt more content, but also more thoughtful, than I had in years.

CHAPTER FIVE

New Year's Eve had fallen on a Friday, so there was no point in worrying about Cameron Fraser's invitation until the holidays were over. That gave me several days to mull it over, but I still failed to reach any conclusion about what I should do.

I'd spoken to Gus about Fraser, but he wasn't able to add much to what Lorna had already told me. 'He's got a bob or two, I know that. He's a local lad, a few years above me at the Academy. Father ran a shop in Dingwall, from what I remember. Cameron didn't have much interest in taking that over after his dad died, so sold up and headed off to Glasgow. Came back twenty years later seemingly loaded. Don't ask me how.'

'Lorna Jardine told me he's into investment these days.'

Gus smiled. 'Ah, you met Lorna too, did you? You made good use of the evening.'

'She seemed very pleasant.'

'She's that all right. Lovely lass. Had her share of problems, though.'

'I'm sorry to hear that.'

'I'm speaking out of turn. She'll no doubt tell you if she wants to. Why are you so interested in Cameron Fraser, anyway?'

'He gave me his card. Said I should contact him.'

'To do what?'

'It was all very vague. He said he could use someone with my talents, whatever that means.'

'Are you going to call him?'

'That's what I'm weighing up. I'm not sure how seriously to take him. I don't want to end up looking stupid if he was just shooting his mouth off.'

'I don't know the man that well,' Gus said, 'but everything I've heard about him suggests he's not one for doing that. He doesn't like having his own time wasted, and he's not going to waste anyone else's. I'd give him a call. You've nothing to lose.'

By the time Wednesday came around, I still hadn't made a decision. I was sitting at the kitchen table with Fraser's card in front of me. I'd done an internet search on Fraser's name but his online presence seemed minimal. I found references to his business on the Companies House website, but his entries told me little except that the company seemed to be in sound financial shape. Whatever business Fraser was involved in, he clearly worked very discreetly.

Eventually, I decided Gus was right. I'd nothing to lose by phoning. If I didn't like the sound of whatever Fraser might be offering, I could simply say no. If he seemed to have no idea what I was talking about, I'd apologise and say I must have misunderstood. Even so, something still made me hesitate. I had to force myself to dial the number.

I'd expected the call to go straight to voicemail. But it was the man himself who answered. 'Fraser.'

'Mr Fraser. I don't know if you recall—'

'Mr Mellor. I'm delighted you called. I'd hoped you'd be interested by my offer.'

'I'd like to find out more,' I said cautiously.

'Of course. It would be better to discuss this face to face. Are you available to visit me in the next day or two?'

'Whenever suits you.'

'Tomorrow, then? Two o'clock?'

'That's fine. Can you give me the address?'

'I work from home, Mr Mellor.' He gave me the address, the postcode indicating that it was relatively close by. 'It's not the easiest place to find. You can treat that as an initiative test.' I wasn't entirely sure if he was joking, but he added, 'If you have any difficulty finding me, give me a call. Tomorrow, then.'

I was about to offer some response, but Fraser had already cut the call. I stared down at his business card, wondering whether I'd done the right thing. I told myself I'd committed to nothing.

Even so, I had an odd sense that I was being drawn gradually into Fraser's net, and that there might come a moment when it was too late to step back.

CHAPTER SIX

I allowed plenty of time for my journey to Cameron Fraser's house. In the event, although the satnav proved of limited value, Fraser's house wasn't difficult to find. It was visible from at least a mile away on the hillside above the main road, an imposing stone-built edifice, which I guessed dated from the 1920s or 1930s. It had clearly been built to dominate the surrounding landscape.

It took me a little longer to find the track that led up to the house, a single-lane road identified only by a discreet sign tucked among the trees. I was twenty minutes early. I guessed Fraser might consider an early arrival almost as much a failure of initiative as turning up late. I drove on another few hundred yards and found a farm gate where I could park up and kill a few minutes. It occurred to me then that Fraser was already getting me to dance to his tune.

I eventually arrived outside Fraser's house a few minutes before 2pm. I pulled up next to a large Mercedes which I assumed belonged to Fraser himself. There were a couple of other cars parked further along the gravelled yard. Close up, the house was even more impressive.

I'd assumed that, living in a place like this, Fraser would have some domestic staff, but it was the man himself who opened the door. 'Mr Mellor.' He looked pointedly at his watch. 'You've passed the first test, I see. I appreciate punctuality. Come in. I'll organise us some coffee.'

As I stepped into the hallway, Fraser's reasons for choosing to live in a house this size became at least slightly clearer. I could see that the area to my left – which had presumably once been a drawing room or similar – had been converted into an office space. Fraser led me into the room, where two women were sitting working on computers. The original room had been divided into two, and what was presumably Fraser's own office was at the far end.

He waved his hand airily, the gesture taking in the whole room. 'This is the main nerve centre of the business. And Shona and Amanda here do the real work.' Both women looked up with a smile and a nod. They'd clearly heard this spiel many times before. 'Could you get us a couple of coffees, Shona? How do you take it, Mr Mellor?'

'Black. No sugar. Thank you.'

'Come through.'

Fraser's office was slightly larger than that allocated to the two women, accommodating both a desk and a large meeting table. A bay window offered a view through the trees to the valley below, He gestured for me to take a seat. 'I'm delighted you decided to follow up my invitation, Mr Mellor. Thank you for coming.'

'I decided there'd be no harm in at least finding out more,' I said. 'As I said the other evening, I'm not sure I'm necessarily ready to take up a full-time role just yet, but I'm interested to hear what you have to say.'

'Of course. Understood.' His accent was a slightly odd blend of the Highlands and Glasgow. It somehow managed to sound threatening and almost lyrical at the same time. 'As I told you, I'm prepared to offer you some flexibility. But, first, tell me a little more about your police career.'

The way he spoke suggested this might be another test. I wondered whether he'd done some of his own research and wanted to check the accuracy of my account. Not that I had anything to hide. My career in the force had been – at least until the end – successful but mostly unremarkable. I talked him briefly through the details from my early days as a PC through to my transfer into more specialist roles. He nodded occasionally with apparent approval, as if I was confirming information already in his possession.

'Would you say you were a good police officer?' he said, when I'd finished my account.

The question took me by surprise. I'd expected something more specific relating to what I'd been telling him. 'I did the job well enough. Sometimes more than that. I had a few moments of inspiration, let's say.' There was much more I could have said, but none of it was Fraser's business.

'But you didn't see it as a vocation?'

I hesitated, unsure how to respond. 'I never really thought of it in those terms. It was just something I fell into after university. I enjoyed a lot of aspects of the job. I liked others less. But I imagine that's true of everyone. I suppose there were a few officers who threw themselves more wholeheartedly into the job. Some who seemed to live for it. But I'm not sure that was healthy for either them or their work.' I wondered if I was being too honest, but there seemed no point in holding back. If Fraser was intending to offer me some kind of job, I wanted him to see me as I really was.

'Sounds a sane approach. Any skeletons I should be aware of?'

This time I hesitated. 'It depends what you mean by

skeletons. There's nothing I'm ashamed or embarrassed about, but I did make a few enemies.'

'Why was that?'

'Because I'm stubborn. Because I tend to say what I think. I was never evangelical about being in the police. But I was being paid to do a job, and I wanted to do it properly. I thought there were some basic standards we should be applying. Let's just say that not everyone thought the same way.'

'If I were paying you to do a job, I'd expect you to display the same attitude.'

'What kind of job might we be talking about?'

'From what you've told me, you've a solid track record in surveillance and investigation generally.'

'I'd like to think so.'

'Those are skills that I could potentially use.'

'In what way?' I was assuming he'd be offering me some kind of security role. I wasn't sure I was up for that. It's the standard fallback job for ex-coppers, including some of those who've left under a cloud.

'Research.'

'Research?'

'Of a kind. You're probably aware that I'm an investor?'

'So I've been told.'

'I've a range of interests. But part of my work is what I suppose you'd call venture capitalism.'

'Not really my area of expertise.' I couldn't see where this was going. If he wanted someone to analyse business accounts, I definitely wasn't the man.

'Of course not. But the point is that I mainly invest in businesses that have already been turned down by the more mainstream investors. That's sometimes because there's a lack of confidence in the business in question, or simply because the operation is too small to be attractive to the bigger players. I typically take a higher return, but it's generally an arrangement that works to everyone's advantage.'

I wondered how close this came to corporate loan-sharking, and how often Fraser's 'return' came from asset-stripping failing businesses. But it's not an area I'd even pretend to understand. 'I still don't really see where my skills would fit into that.'

'It's a high-risk business. That's the nature of what I do, but I control the risk as much as possible. That means I limit how much I'm prepared to commit. I do careful financial due diligence on any business I work with. But because these are generally very small businesses, I also consider the individuals running them. I like to know as much as possible about the people I'm dealing with. Some of that I can obtain from public domain sources. But not all of it.'

'This is the kind of research you're talking about?'

'I have a couple of people who do digging for me. They're not bad but they're Glasgow-based. These days, much of my business is here in the Highlands. It would be useful to have someone up here.'

'What kind of "digging" are we talking about?'

'Whatever we think is appropriate or necessary. Sometimes it's a question of talking discreetly to associates of the individuals in question – perhaps customers or suppliers. But it might also involve more clandestine research. That might involve surveillance. In extreme cases, I've even had people trawl through bins. I'm being honest with you here, Mr Mellor.'

'But why is this needed?'

'Because, sadly, not everyone is as honest as you or I. And sometimes the formal accounts don't give the full picture. In the past, I've discovered that potential clients are siphoning off profits to feed their own habits. I've had instances where they've cheated customers or suppliers, or where their lifestyle doesn't match the supposed income from the business. If there are problems, I'd rather know before I hand over any money than after.' He paused. 'Is this something that might be of interest to you?'

The honest answer was that I wasn't sure. I'd no objection to using my police skills in a civilian context, but I wasn't convinced about the ethics of Fraser's operation. 'Potentially. It's not exactly the kind of thing I had in mind, so I'd need time to think about it.'

'That's understood.' He smiled. 'I do have one other proposition.'

'Go on.' There was something in his tone that suggested what he'd been saying so far only constituted a preamble to his real business. I had the sense he'd been gently reeling me in for a more specific purpose.

'I'm sure you're aware of a US businessman called Gregor McBride.'

I looked up in surprise. Whatever I'd been expecting Fraser to say, it hadn't been that. 'Yes, of course. I mean, I've seen him on TV and I looked at the stall at the Hogmanay party. I don't know much else about him.'

'Loud-mouthed gangster with an inflated sense of his own abilities. That's probably all you really need to know. Inherited a fortune and hasn't quite managed to fritter it away despite a lifetime of poor business decisions. Even achieved the rare feat of losing money running casinos.' Fraser smiled. 'Quite impressive in its way, I suppose.'

'I don't understand what this has to do with me.'

'You'll be aware from Gus's campaign that Mr McBride has a number of business interests in Scotland. Claims Scottish ancestry, I believe, though I take that with a bucket of salt. Has a couple of large golf course and leisure resorts further south, and is looking to expand his interests up here. The McBride

Development. Bugger even has to have his name plastered across everything.'

I nodded. 'I know it's something Gus feels very strongly about. I understand you're involved in the campaign to stop it.'

'I was honoured to be asked. Though I fear that it'll take more than a petition to stop McBride in his tracks.'

I was intrigued by what had led a supposedly hard-bitten businessman like Cameron Fraser to sign up to the campaign. Was it just a nostalgia for his roots, or something more? 'I can understand why the local community's opposed to it. But couldn't there be potential benefits from the development. A boost to the local economy, for example?'

'That's the line McBride will be taking, I'm sure. The evidence from his other resorts suggests that won't actually be the outcome. He's a ruthless man, with seemingly enough power and influence to behave as he wants to. He did whatever it took to get the resorts built, regardless of the impact on the local community. The businesses are run as tax losses with profits siphoned off abroad so he pays minimal UK tax. The resorts are largely staffed by individuals working illegally at well below minimum wage. And he's taken every possible step to remove any possible local competition to the services he provides. So, no, I'm not at all sure that Mr McBride's presence will be beneficial either to the local economy or the community in general.'

'I don't really know enough to comment,' I said. I had no idea why Fraser was telling me all this.

'I used to have a business partner. A man called Archie Kinnear. In many ways, he's the person I'd call my mentor. He taught me everything I know about business. When I first moved down to Glasgow, nearly thirty years ago, Archie took me under his wing. I joined his company as a junior and worked my way up, eventually becoming his partner. We worked together for years. But we had a bad falling out. I won't go into the reasons, but they were both professional and personal. Let's just say that Archie Kinnear has much in common with Gregor McBride, so I'm unsurprised they've ended up as bedfellows.'

I still couldn't see what any of this had to do with me, even if it did give me some insight into how Fraser had accrued his wealth. 'Bedfellows?'

'McBride's a mediocre businessman, but he's not entirely stupid. When he first began to dabble in Scottish acquisitions, he realised very quickly that he needed good and reliable local contacts. People who understood the market, and who knew how the power structures and networks here actually worked. So he approached Archie to act as his agent. It was a smart decision. Archie's probably the only person in Scotland with the power, influence and contacts to deliver what McBride wants. Not to mention the ruthlessness.'

'I'm still not sure I understand.'

'I've no desire to see Gregor McBride damage this community the way he's damaged so many others. I may be a businessman, but I was born and brought up here. This is my home and these are my people.' The words seemed uncharacteristically sentimental but Fraser sounded sincere enough. 'If I can do anything to stop him, I'll try to do so. I've no leverage over Gregor McBride, so all I can do is find a way to put some pressure on Archie Kinnear.'

'How are you proposing to do that?'

'McBride probably doesn't realise it, but Archie's not the man he was. He's getting older. He makes mistakes. He's more reckless than he used to be. He's still a formidable figure, but there are chinks in his armour these days and I need to find them. One possible vulnerability is what passes for Archie's family. His wife walked out on him some years ago. I don't even know if she's still alive. He has little in the way of other close family. He had one daughter.'

'Had?'

'Does the name Kate Brodie mean anything to you?'

The name rang a vague bell, but I didn't know from where. 'Some news story?'

'It was briefly a moderately big story at the time, at least in the Scottish media. Kate is the daughter.'

It was coming back to me. 'She went missing. Somewhere up in these parts.'

'She was supposedly spending a weekend up here. Some friends of hers had rented a house in Cromarty for the weekend, and she was supposed to be driving up to join them. She never arrived. Her car was eventually found parked in a side street near the river in Inverness. The police checked out the bus and railway stations in the city. There were no sightings of her, either in person or on CCTV, and no evidence that she'd bought a train or coach ticket. If she did, she must have paid cash.'

'She was never found?' I hadn't been involved in the case, and I couldn't recall the full details. It had faded from media within a few weeks. I had no recollection of any follow up.

'She wasn't. At first, the police weren't inclined to take her disappearance too seriously. She was a fully grown adult in her early thirties. So it was a few days before the police took it seriously. Then they ran into a dead end. They found the car quickly enough – or at least some member of the public did. But then nothing. They had the usual claims of sightings from everywhere from Thurso to Bristol, but nothing that led anywhere. The unofficial conclusion was that she'd probably taken her own life, though I'm not sure if there was much evidence to support that. The body's never been found and, as far as I'm aware, the investigation is still open. Which brings me to my proposition. I'd like you to have another look at the case for me.'

'To what end?'

'I don't know what happened to Kate Brodie, but something about the investigation didn't smell right to me. I'd have expected the police to have bent over backwards in a case like that, especially with a high-profile figure like Archie involved.'

I found myself feeling unexpectedly defensive of my former colleagues. 'There's only so much the police can do, no matter who's involved.'

'I appreciate that, but Archie has plenty of friends in the force. I'd just like someone to have another look at the case. Try to get a sense of what really went on.'

'With respect, I don't think I'm likely to have any success where the combined resources of the police failed. And, to be honest, if you do want to commission some kind of private enquiry, there are people far better qualified than I am.'

'You may be correct on the latter point, Mr Mellor, but I prefer to keep this relatively low-key for the moment. And I'd like to get a sense of how you work. Perhaps think of it as another initiative test. On the former point, I really don't know. No disrespect to you or your former colleagues, but you perhaps have more confidence in the abilities of the police than I do.'

'I've varying views about my former colleagues,' I said, 'but I do know that they have substantial expertise at their disposal. One ex-copper can't begin to match that.'

'It may also be that some of Kate's associates – particularly the friends of her own age – might talk more openly to you than to a serving police officer. You have a very personable manner, Mr Mellor.'

I wasn't entirely sure what he meant by that. 'I still think I'd be wasting your time and money, Mr Fraser.'

'That's my business. I appreciate this is a long shot, and I'll attach no blame to you if you don't succeed. But I'd be interested to see how you tackle an assignment of this type. and it will give you a chance to see how I work. My suggestion is that we agree a timescale – say, a month initially and we can see what progress you're able to make – and I'll pay you a daily rate for that period. We can agree the precise fee, but I'll make it worth your while.'

I still couldn't fathom his reasons for making the offer. Fraser had first met me only a few days before and – though I wouldn't have been surprised to learn he'd done some research in the meantime – he'd no particular reason to trust either my honesty or my capability. There was something about the story that didn't ring true to me. 'Again, I'd need time to think about it.'

'Take your time. I appreciate there's a lot here for you to consider. But it's a serious offer, Mr Mellor, and it could well lead to a longer-term working relationship between us.'

'Give me a few days,' I said.

He nodded. 'If you have any questions in the meantime, please call me. Otherwise, I'll wait to hear from you.' He paused. 'One more thing, for the moment I'd like this to remain completely confidential between us. I don't want there to be any possibility of Archie finding out that I'm looking into this. Is that clear?'

As mud, I thought. But I nodded. 'Whatever you say.'

CHAPTER SEVEN

I drove the short distance back deep in thought. I hadn't had any idea what to expect from Cameron Fraser, but I'd anticipated something more conventional. His initial proposal – research into prospective clients – made reasonable sense, even if I knew little about the real nature of his business. But, although he hadn't said so explicitly, I'd been left with the impression that his initial offer was likely to be conditional on his second. If I declined to participate in the search for Kate Brodie, I suspected no further work would be forthcoming.

I parked up at the cottage, and decided I needed a walk to clear my head. It was still a fine clear day and the views from the hillside would be spectacular. I pulled on my walking boots, grabbed my waterproof jacket, and set off up the track, enjoying the chill of the wind on my skin.

I was a few hundred yards from the cottage when I heard a dog barking. It was unusual to run into anyone else up here. I turned, curious to see who was there. At first, I could see only the Labrador bounding enthusiastically towards me. Then a figure emerged over the brow of the hill.

I could see it was a woman, but she was wearing a woollen

hat and scarf that concealed her face. It was only as she drew closer that I realised it was Lorna Jardine. The dog had reached me, and was bouncing around seeking attention. I crouched down and stroked his head.

'I thought it was you,' Lorna said. 'I was about to call but Ziggy decided to do the job for me.'

'Ziggy?'

She grimaced. 'Not that there's anything wrong with it, but it wasn't my choice. I got him from a rescue centre. The previous owner seems to have been more interested in David Bowie than in caring for his dog.'

'Lovely dog, anyway. Not that I'm any kind of expert.'

'Good company during the long winter nights, especially when you live somewhere as isolated as this.'

That answered one question about Lorna Jardine. It didn't necessarily mean she wasn't in a relationship but it made it less likely. Just something to bear in mind, I thought.

I gave Ziggy a final stroke and stood up. 'Beautiful day.'

'I usually bring Ziggy up here for a walk if the weather's decent. It can be a bit exposed if it's raining, but on a day like this it's lovely.'

I was surprised I hadn't seen her up here before. 'You don't mind if I walk up with you?'

'Nice to have some company other than Ziggy.'

We walked on in silence for a few minutes, Ziggy racing ahead of us. At the summit of the hill, before the track began to descend into the next glen, we paused and looked back at the view. There was a stretch of open moorland, and beyond that the familiar tapestry of fields. In the distance, the sun glittered on the still surface of the firth. I took a breath, drinking in the freshness of the air.

Ziggy was racing around dementedly behind us, chasing something only he could see. He was in his element up here, and I was beginning to understand how he felt. Glasgow seemed not just a long way away but somewhere from another life. A life I wasn't sure I wanted to return to. But if I were to stay, I'd eventually have to find a way to make a living. 'I went to see Cameron Fraser this morning,' I said. 'A sort of job interview, I suppose. Though it didn't exactly feel like that.'

'How did it go?'

I told her about the meeting and about Fraser's propositions, including his comments about Gregor McBride, though leaving out the part about Kate Brodie.

She grimaced. 'He's right enough about McBride. If he succeeds in building this development, it'll be a disaster at every level. I don't know how many people are likely to be affected but it's a big area, and I'm told he has plans for other developments. And then there's the impact on the environment. His development in Perthshire destroyed several sites of special scientific interest. It's good that Cameron Fraser's involved, though I suspect this is beyond anything even he can influence.'

'He seemed sincere enough about wanting to protect the community.'

'He probably also sees McBride's involvement as a threat to his own business interests. But, yes, he's a local boy and that does seem to mean something to him. What are your thoughts on the job offer?'

'It wasn't what I expected. I'd assumed it would be some security role.'

'Are you interested?'

'I don't know. While I was talking to him, I thought I'd decided to say no, but as I've reflected on it I've become less sure. If I am going to stay here, I need to find something to do.'

'Do you want to stay here?'

'For a while, definitely. Probably for longer than I originally planned.'

'You seem to be surviving the winter okay. That's the first test.' She gestured down the track. 'Do you want to go on a little further?'

'If you're up for it.'

'Ziggy seems to be, anyway. So what about Cameron Fraser?'

'This research work sounds reasonably appealing. It plays to my strengths and experience. If I had reasonable guidance in what I'm supposed to be looking for, I could probably do it well enough. My main concern about that is that I wouldn't want to be involved in anything shady.' I thought back to our conversation on New Year's Eve. 'You said he was a law unto himself. What did you mean by that?'

'I'd had a few drinks. I don't really know much about the detail of Cameron's business. From what I've heard, he can be ruthless, but I don't know that he's involved in anything illegal. I'm not sure that's much help to you.'

'It's food for thought,' I said. 'And one of the thoughts it's feeding is: why me? Why is Fraser so keen to offer me a job? He only met me at Hogmanay. He knows nothing about me.'

'I wouldn't bet on the last point. Cameron makes it his business to know what he needs to. I wouldn't be surprised if he knew about you even before the party.'

'You think so?'

'Cameron does nothing casually. If he decided to offer you a job – even tentatively – he wouldn't have done it on the fly.'

'I'm not sure how to take that.'

'I'd take it as a compliment. I'm guessing he's serious. He wants you to work for him.'

'But why me? I'm nobody. I'm just a run-of-the-mill ex-cop.'

'I've no idea. I'm only telling you what I know about Cameron.'

We'd paused in our walk again, waiting for Ziggy to come

running back from wherever he'd disappeared to. It was only early afternoon but the sun was already low, throwing lengthening shadows across the open ground. The sun would be set by 4pm, though on a clear day like today the twilight would linger long after that.

'Maybe I need to do some digging of my own. Find out more about Cameron Fraser.'

'You do that. I'll be interested to hear what you decide.' She looked at her watch. 'I'm going to have to turn back now. Ziggy's had his run, and I've got work to do this afternoon.'

'I'll walk back with you. I only came out to clear my head after the meeting with Fraser. Chatting to you about it's really helped.'

We made our way back towards the cottage, chatting more generally about the area and our few shared neighbours. When we reached the cottage, I asked her if she wanted to come in for a coffee.

'I'd love to, but I'd better not. Too much to do this afternoon. But next time.' She paused. 'Or maybe you could come down for supper one evening. If you're not too wedded to the solitary life.'

'No, I'd like that. Or you could come up here.'

'Whichever. Or both. Look, I've got to run. But I'll drop by when I'm next walking Ziggy up here and we can fix something up.'

I watched her walk down the track, Ziggy bounding around her, before I finally turned to let myself back into the cottage. I think by then I'd already decided that, despite my initial reservations, I was going to accept Cameron Fraser's offer.

CHAPTER EIGHT

I spent the rest of that afternoon researching the Kate Brodie case. As Fraser had said, the story had received extensive coverage, particularly in the Scottish media. Even so, the news reports didn't add much to what Fraser had already told me, other than to give a flavour of how the story had been presented. Brodie was described as the daughter of the wealthy Glasgow businessman, Archie Kinnear. She'd enjoyed an education at an independent school in Glasgow before graduating from St Andrew's with a degree in History. At the time of her disappearance, she was in her early thirties, divorced, working in an executive role in some subsidiary of her father's business.

The coverage inevitably focused largely on Kinnear himself, partly because of his wealth and partly due to his declared opposition to the Independence movement and his bankrolling of various Unionist organisations. It took me a while to track down a reference to her ex-husband, Roy Brodie. He was described vaguely as a "businessman", now apparently living in London.

As Fraser had told me, Kate Brodie had been intending to drive up to Cromarty to join a group of former university friends for a long weekend in a holiday cottage owned by one of the group. There was some vague innuendo in the more lurid tabloids about the supposed nature of this "weekend of partying", but as far as I could see there was no evidence it was anything more than a bunch of old mates getting together. Either way, Kate had never arrived. At first, her friends thought she'd been delayed or had had to cancel for some reason, but became increasingly concerned when her mobile remained unanswered.

At the time she went missing, Kate had been living in a flat on the east side of the city. She'd left work some time around 4.30pm, a timing subsequently confirmed by several sightings on ANPR cameras on the A9.

Despite these camera sightings – and a confirmed stop for fuel at a petrol station in Perth – the police were unable to determine what had happened to the car as it approached Inverness. As Fraser had told me, it was found a day or two later parked on a side street on the edge of the city centre, close to the river. It wasn't clear whether it had been driven straight there on the Friday evening, or whether it had been taken elsewhere before being left in the city. The car was a relatively short walk from the main train and bus stations, but Kate hadn't pre-booked any ticket and there were no records of bank card payments on that or on the following days.

My impression was that the police hadn't covered themselves in glory in the early days of the investigation, even if their response was partly understandable. It was obvious that it had taken them some days to take Kate's disappearance seriously. That was reasonable enough. She was an adult. She was capable of making her own decisions. There was no evidence she'd come to any harm.

One of the newspapers had hinted that something might have happened to her at the holiday cottage itself, and that her friends had covered it up by denying her arrival and then driving her car into Inverness. This suggestion seemed to have appeared only once and hadn't been followed up by other sources, presumably because of fears of defamation. It wasn't clear whether the police had taken the suggestion seriously.

The car itself yielded no real clues. If the police had found any fingerprints or other forensic traces other than those from Kate herself, this information hadn't reached the media. Similarly, there were no reports of CCTV or other evidence indicating when the car had been left there. That didn't necessarily mean the police hadn't had that evidence, but if they had, they'd obviously chosen not to release it. I could only speculate on what the reasons for that might have been.

Beyond that, there was very little. There was some innuendo in the media about Kate's potential state of mind, with suggestions that she might have been depressed about some disagreement with her father. She'd apparently had some recent falling out with Kinnear on some business matter.

The story had stayed on the front pages of many of the Scottish newspapers for several weeks, but the accompanying stories were increasingly insubstantial and tenuous. There were pleas to the public from Kinnear, and interviews with some of those who'd stayed in the holiday cottage that weekend. There'd been supposed sightings of Kate both in Inverness and the Highlands, and in virtually every other part of the country, but clearly none had produced any breakthrough. Eventually, the news reports had become shorter and less prominent, and then they'd disappeared entirely.

By the time I'd finished scanning the innumerable websites, I felt I knew only a little more than I had before. I had more detail, more colour. I perhaps had a few ideas of where I might start if I were to take up Cameron Fraser's offer. But that was more or less it.

One question – and I wondered whether this had been in Fraser's mind – was whether I had any contacts within the force that I could call on to provide more background. I'd had no involvement in the case myself, and I didn't know any of the officers involved well enough to know who might be worth approaching. The starting point would be to put out a few feelers among those I knew I could trust.

I'd been engrossed in my search for much longer that I'd realised, and it was already late afternoon. I rose from the table and walked over to the front door of the cottage. I opened the door and gazed out into the thickening twilight, breathing in the chilly air.

I wanted to think about what I'd been reading. If I really was going to take on this job, I'd have to work out how to approach it. I'd need more background. I'd need to flesh out the narrative. I'd need to test the truth and accuracy of the reports I'd been reading. I'd had enough experience of reading media accounts of cases I'd been involved in – albeit at a relatively junior level – to know how unreliable they could be. Above all, though, I'd need to find out what hadn't been reported. The information that the police might have had that, for whatever reason, they'd chosen not to release to the public.

I could feel the first outline of a plan beginning to take shape in my head. Later in the evening, fortified by a dram, I'd have a shot at trying to develop my thoughts. I walked out of the cottage on to the track, and gazed down into the darkness of the valley. There was a scattering of lights down there, including those in Lorna Jardine's house. I'd wondered if she might bring Ziggy back up here this evening but there'd been no sign of her.

I stood there for a few moments longer, enjoying the freshness of the air, the sense of space, the darkening translucence of the sky. I was thinking not just about Kate Brodie, but also about Gregor McBride and about what Gus had said about the potential threat to this landscape, this community. If Cameron Fraser could do anything to prevent that, I wanted to support him even if I didn't fully understand what he was planning.

Then I turned and made my way back to the cottage, wondering what it was that I was committing myself to.

CHAPTER NINE

The following morning I phoned Cameron Fraser. As before, it was answered promptly, his tone suggesting almost that he'd been waiting for my call. An act, no doubt, but an effective one.

'Have you come to a decision, Mr Mellor? Or do you have more questions for me?'

'I've come to a decision,' I said. 'I'm happy to take up your offer.'

'I'm delighted to hear that. And that includes investigating the disappearance of Kate Brodie?'

'I'm assuming that's where I'd start.'

'That's where I'd like you to start. It'll give us a sense of what it's like to work with each other.'

'I want to be realistic,' I said. 'I'll do my level best and I'll draw on whatever resources I can, but I don't want to promise anything I might not be able to deliver.'

'That's understood, Mr Mellor. I've no unrealistic expectations of what you might be able to achieve. But I'm delighted to have you on board. The next step is for me to draw up a formal contract so that we're both clear how we're going to work together. I'm happy to pay you on a daily rate.' He quoted a rate higher than I'd been expecting. 'Does that sound satisfactory?'

'That sounds fine.'

'Shall we say for a month to begin with? And then we can review what progress you've made and decide whether it's worth continuing. If we decide it isn't – and assuming I'm content with the way you've been working – we can move on to the other research assignments we discussed. I'll get the contracts drawn up over the weekend. If you come over here on Monday, we can get everything signed and sealed. Shall we say 10am?'

'That's fine. I'll see you then.'

We ended the call and I sat for a moment reflecting on what I'd just committed myself to. I'd booted up my laptop, and my first inclination was to resume my research into Kate Brodie's disappearance. But I felt I'd already largely exhausted what I was likely to find in the public domain. Instead, on a whim, I searched Gregor McBride's name, wondering how much coverage there had been of his plans for this area. To my surprise, there was relatively little – if McBride was buying up substantial plots of land, he was clearly doing so very discreetly – although the campaign against the potential development was beginning to gain some traction in the local media. Beyond that, though, there was no shortage of material on McBride.

Most of it confirmed what Cameron Fraser had told me. Gregor's grandfather, one Arthur McBride, had emigrated to the US sometime in the nineteenth century, supposedly from Glasgow, although there were conflicting accounts of his origins. McBride's father, Malcolm McBride, had made his initial fortune running speakeasies during Prohibition, gradually moving into property development in Newark and elsewhere. He'd had a reputation as an exploitative landlord, with apparent links to the Mob and the Klan. Even so, his success and wealth had eventually enabled him to move into more salubrious circles, opening more upmarket housing estates and eventually a string of hotels and casinos.

Gregor McBride had inherited his father's wealth and business empire, along with his ruthlessness and apparent disdain for laws and regulations. It was less clear whether he'd also inherited his father's business acumen. There was certainly plenty of evidence to support Cameron Fraser's assessment of McBride's commercial skills, including a couple of failed casinos. McBride's primary talent seemed to be for self-promotion, and he was unquestionably very skilled in that direction. He'd somehow managed to combine his dubious mix of half-baked, often offensive opinions and overbearing, bullying manner into a distinctive personal brand. His original run for the Presidency had failed, but he'd attracted an unexpected level of public support, playing to the worst instincts of those who felt unrepresented by the supposed Washington elite.

I could see that the man possessed a certain charisma, even though it was obvious his only real interest was in himself. He'd surrounded himself with yes-men – and they were mostly men – who were immediately discarded if they showed any sign of challenging or questioning his judgement, and he'd trampled, ruthlessly and unhesitatingly, on anyone who'd tried to get in his way.

In the cold light of a winter's morning, I wasn't expecting to feel the same sense of malevolence I'd detected on watching the videos in the incongruous setting of Gus's Hogmanay bash. But it was still there, if anything stronger than before. McBride was a ludicrous figure, almost a caricature of a ruthless businessman, but there was something there that I found chilling. It was an almost inhuman quality, a sense that this was a man who didn't simply ignore conventional ethics or morality, but couldn't even comprehend them. A man who would corrupt everything he touched.

I was relieved when my gloomy musings were interrupted by a yapping outside. I opened the back door of the cottage and Ziggy came bounding round the corner of the house, heading towards me like an uncontrolled black ball of chaos. He crashed into me and licked furiously at my hand.

'Sorry. He's a bit manic today.'

Lorna Jardine was standing on the path, watching with apparent amusement.

'I'm still standing. More or less.'

'That's why I brought him up here. Thought it might help him get rid of some of the excess energy.' She watched Ziggy jumping around me. 'I'm not sure it's working, though.'

'Do you want to come in for a coffee?'

'Why not? I've a couple of online meetings this afternoon, but there's nothing spoiling this morning. Thanks.' She followed me into the kitchen. 'You okay with Ziggy coming in? I can tie him up outside if you prefer.'

'It's no bother to me. And Gus doesn't have any rules on animals. He keeps encouraging me to get a dog.'

'Maybe you should.'

'I might once I'm clearer what my plans are.'

She seated herself at the kitchen table while I filled the kettle. Ziggy took a look around then trotted through into the living room, clearly intent on exploring.

'You've not decided yet?'

'I've just been speaking to Cameron Fraser, as it happens.'

'And?'

'I'm going to give it a shot.'

'Really?'

'You don't think I should?'

'I don't have a view. It'll be interesting, I don't doubt. It's just that yesterday you seemed unsure.'

'I still am. But I might as well try. I can't see I've got much to lose.'

'That's true enough.'

I poured the water into the cafetière, then carried it over to the table along with two mugs from the cupboard. 'Milk?'

'No, thanks. And no sugar.'

'That may be as well. I'm not sure I've either in the house. I usually take it black too.'

She laughed. 'The perfect host.'

'I might have some biscuits somewhere, if they're not stale.'

'It's an enticing prospect, but don't worry. Speaking of hosts, I was thinking about inviting you round for dinner.'

'And you've decided firmly against it?'

'On the contrary, I was wondering whether tomorrow night might suit? I'd say tonight, but frankly I need to go out to buy some semi-respectable food and I won't get a chance today. Otherwise, it'll be stale biscuits from me as well.'

'No, that's fine. Are you sure, though? I don't want you to go to any trouble.'

'Don't be daft. It's ages since I had the chance to cook for anyone other than me and Ziggy. And he seems to prefer dog food. Though so might you once you've tried my cooking.'

'I doubt it. Anyway, thanks for the invite. It's kind of you.'

'We've a duty to make all incomers welcome. About seven suit you?'

'Sounds perfect.'

We spent another ten minutes chatting before she pushed aside her mug. 'I ought to be heading back. Need to get ready for these meetings. Though first I need to track down Ziggy.'

I followed her through into the living room. Ziggy was lying, seemingly comatose, in front of the wood-stove. 'You seem to be a good influence on him,' Lorna observed.

'He clearly needs a father figure.' I'd intended the words as a joke, but I regretted them instantly, feeling I'd said more than I'd intended.

'The last father figure he had wasn't exactly a positive influence,' she said. 'He'll need to do better next time.' She clipped the lead to Ziggy's collar, and then led him back out through the kitchen into the open air. 'Tomorrow, then. Seven o'clock.'

'I'll look forward to it.'

I watched her walking back down the hill, Ziggy pulling ahead of her. I still didn't know if I'd said something stupid, or quite what to make of her response. But at least I had tomorrow evening to look forward to.

CHAPTER TEN

That evening the weather turned. We'd enjoyed several weeks of decent weather around Christmas and the New Year, with clear skies and relatively mild temperatures. Now, on the off-chance any of us might have forgotten we were living in the northern Highlands, the skies filled with clouds and strong winds blew in from the west. The heavy rain started in the early evening and showed no sign of abating before I retired for the night.

I hadn't checked the weather forecast over the preceding days so the change took me by surprise. It was the first severe weather I'd encountered up here, though there'd been no shortage of rain in the autumn. The forecast threatened sleet and possibly snow overnight, especially on higher ground. My biggest concern was that the weather might scupper my chances of an enjoyable evening with Lorna the next day.

There wasn't much I could do about that. I stoked up the wood-stove, poured a whisky, and tried to lose myself in a book. If you had to be stuck up a hill in gale-force winds and pounding rain, this was definitely the way to do it.

As it turned out, the thriller I was reading was much more

putdownable than its blurb had suggested, and after a while, reinforced by occasional sips of the Scotch, I found I was drifting into a doze. I don't know if I actually fell asleep, but I was jolted back into full consciousness by the buzzing of my phone on the table. I picked it up, wondering who the hell was calling me at this time on a Friday night.

The number on the screen wasn't one I recognised and clearly wasn't in my address book. 'Hello?'

'Where *are* you?'

It was the voice of a petulant toddler in the middle of a game of hide-and-seek. Somehow, unbelievably, it took me a few moments to place it. 'Maddie?'

'Well spotted. Where are you?'

'What?'

'I've been to the flat. You're not there. You've let the bloody place out.'

As so often with Maddie, I was already on the back foot and I didn't even know why. 'It's my flat, Maddie. I can do what I like with it.' There'd been more than enough wrangling about our few joint assets during the split. Maddie had had no use for the flat by that stage, and she'd done well enough from the deal overall. I owed her nothing.

'That's not the point.'

'So what is the point?'

She obviously had no immediate answer to that. 'Where are you?' she asked again.

'It doesn't matter where I am.'

'I spoke to your tenants. They said you'd gone to the Highlands, but they wouldn't tell me anything more than that.'

I'd asked the tenants – a pleasant enough young couple working in financial services – not to give anyone my address without checking with me first. I'd been thinking more about potential associates of Danny Royce rather than Maddie, but the same principles applied. I wanted to keep away from trouble.

'Why do you want to know anyway?'

'I've walked out on Martin.'

I knew it would be that, or something like that. Maddie had walked out on me on numerous occasions. It's what Maddie did and it never lasted very long, at least not until that final time when, unknown to me, she'd already taken up with Martin Garfield. Her ostensible reasons for walking out on me were many and various, but had mostly been linked to any mild complaint I'd made about her unreasonable behaviour. I could imagine Garfield might have given her some more legitimate reasons. From the little I'd seen of him, he'd struck me as a nasty piece of work.

'I'm sorry to hear that,' I said as neutrally as I could.

'I mean it this time. He went too far.'

I didn't want to hear any of this. I thought Maddie was probably better off without Garfield and I wished her no ill will. I just didn't want to get sucked back into her particular whirlpool of neuroses and emotional manipulation. 'I don't know what I can say, Maddie. You have to do what you think's best.'

'I was wondering...'

I knew full well what was coming next. It was why she'd been round to my flat. 'It's not possible, Maddie.'

'You don't—'

'I do. You want somewhere to stay.'

'Only for a week or two, till I can sort something out.'

'It's not possible. It's not just that it's a terrible idea. It's literally not possible.'

I expected her to argue but instead she repeated her initial question. 'Where are you, anyway?'

'It doesn't matter.'

'But you can't be staying there. What about your job?'

'I've resigned.'

'Seriously?'

'Very seriously. I'm not planning to come back.'

'So what's prompted this?'

It was another discussion I'd no desire to get into. That was another thing about Maddie. If she wasn't getting what she wanted, she'd shift the conversation on to another topic. Then somehow you'd find yourself drawn back into whatever she'd been after in the first place. 'It's a long story.'

'It must be. It's not what I expected from you.'

'Well, there you go.'

'You're really not prepared to help me?'

'It's just not possible.'

'You're happy to see me out on the street?'

'You're not out on the street. You have plenty of places to go.' Including, I knew, her mother. She would always take Maddie back in but she also severely cramped Maddie's style.

'I don't want Martin to know where I am. That limits the options.'

'I can't help you, Maddie. It's as simple as that. I don't think it's helpful to continue this conversation.' I cut the call. It felt brutal, but Maddie would keep the dialogue going as long as she could, hoping to inveigle me into saying something I'd regret. I wasn't sure if she'd try to call back, so I turned off the phone.

It was nearly nine. I swallowed the last of my whisky, then stood up to pour another dram. After Maddie's call, I needed some more alcoholic fortification.

Hearing Maddie's voice had disturbed me more than I wanted to admit. My time with her was something I'd put firmly behind me. A dream which had gradually turned into a nightmare. I'd made a huge emotional investment in our relationship in the early days, and I'd been reluctant to admit it had gone so horribly wrong. I hadn't even dragged myself out of it. Maddie had made that decision for me. I'd felt distraught at the time, but that had just been my pride talking. I was much better off without her. The last thing I needed was her back in my life, however remotely or tangentially.

I walked over to the window and drew back the heavy curtain. The wind had been rising over the course of the evening, and heavy rain was crashing against the glass. The rain looked as if it might be turning to sleet, but as yet there was no sign of any settling snow. It felt like a good night to be indoors.

I sipped gently at my whisky, trying to calm my nerves. The call from Maddie had felt like an intrusion, as if she'd physically walked through the door. I'd come to see this place as a refuge. Other than Gus, the only visitor had been Lorna, just that morning. It somehow felt ominous that that welcome incursion should be so quickly followed by a much more unwanted intrusion.

It also made me wonder about Danny Royce. I'd asked a couple of my old mates in the force to keep their ears to the ground in case any of Royce's associates should show any interest in avenging his death. Of course, Critchley ought to be much more directly in the firing line than I was. Except that something about that whole set-up still didn't feel right to me. I'd never looked any further into it and had no real inclination to know more. I wanted to ensure my own backside was covered.

In practice, Royce's influence had pretty much melted away with his death. A man like Royce had no real friends, just hangers-on. Someone would have stepped into the breach as soon as he'd gone, but that person wouldn't have cared about Danny Royce's fate, other than to ensure they didn't go the same way. I guessed no one would be interested in travelling up here to deal with some low-level ex-cop.

Even so, I felt a little less secure, a little less confident that this refuge was as safe as I'd thought. For some reason I couldn't entirely explain, that made me think about Cameron Fraser, the unknown fate of Kate Brodie and the looming presence of Gregor McBride.

I finished my whisky and decided to call it a night. Outside, I could hear the wind growing even stronger. A storm was coming.

CHAPTER ELEVEN

I had no real idea how long it would take me to walk down to Lorna's cottage in weather like this. It was barely a quarter of a mile or so and it didn't seem worth taking the car, particularly as I knew I'd need a drink or two to calm my nerves.

I was taking a bottle of decent wine and a half bottle of a single malt, both of which I'd had in the house. I wondered whether I should have been out to get some flowers – after all, Lorna had taken the trouble to head out for the food – but I wasn't sure they'd have survived the journey down the hill.

The heavy-duty waterproof I'd bought at the start of the winter was barely enough to keep me dry. The wind had risen again and the cold rain was whipping horizontally as I made my way along the track. It was a wild night, and I wasn't looking forward to making the return trip later.

The track was slippy underfoot, a virtual stream of water running down its edge. My walking boots had a decent grip, but I had to take care, using my torch to pick up any unevenness in the surface. The walk became easier once I reached the bottom of the track and joined the single-track road that wound down the hill past Lorna's cottage.

I arrived a little after seven, which felt about right. As I entered the small front garden, I heard Ziggy barking frantically inside. The door was opened before I'd pressed the bell.

'Ziggy's the best watchdog,' Lorna said. 'Or at least he would be if he wasn't so friendly. I assumed it must be you.'

I paused on the doorstep. 'I'm a bit wet. Is there somewhere I can dump my coat and boots?'

'Hang your coat behind the door. The carpet's seen worse than a few drops of rain, believe me. I'll get some newspaper for you to put your boots on. I take it the weather's not improved.'

'Worse, if anything.' I handed over the wine and whisky in their plastic carrier bag. 'Small gesture of thanks for your hospitality.'

'I'd say you shouldn't have, but, well, it's booze.'

She fetched the newspaper while I divested myself of the waterproof and boots. The cottage was warm and welcoming, and I felt more relaxed already. I followed her through into the small living room.

'Anything I can do to help?' I said.

'You haven't seen my kitchen. It's barely large enough for me, let alone two. Not to mention Ziggy, who'd insist on joining us. You sit down and make yourself comfortable. I've done most of the prep anyway. Just needs to cook for a bit.'

'Smells good.'

'Venison casserole. And I was able to get some fresh langoustines so I thought we could have those as a starter.'

'Sounds terrific.'

'Edible, anyway. I hope. I'll get you a drink while I check how it's going. Beer? Wine?'

'Wine's great. Red, if possible, but I'll drink anything.'

I looked around me. Lorna's cottage was a small place, but thoughtfully furnished and decorated. One wall was filled with built-in bookshelves, holding an eclectic selection of volumes –

mainly classic or modern fiction. There were a few ornaments scattered about the shelves which looked like souvenirs from overseas trips. It felt as if Lorna's personality and background had been incorporated into the décor. A small dining table had been laid with a white tablecloth, cutlery, side plates and even candles.

She returned bearing two glasses of red wine, and sat on the sofa beside me. 'Casserole needs another hour. I thought if we kicked off with the langoustines in about half an hour, that should be about right. Unless you're starving?'

'I need to get my breath back after the walk down, to be honest,' I said.

'At least it isn't snow. Not yet, anyway.'

'Do you get much snow up here?'

'Seems to be less with every passing year. But it varies. Normally a day or two, but it doesn't usually last. I've never been snowed in for any length of time, though the road down can be a bit grim. The main problem today was flooding.' She sipped at her wine. 'I'm still intrigued by what brought you up here. When we spoke at Hogmanay you said something about running away. I wondered what you meant.'

'I'd had a few drinks. I'm not sure what I meant.'

She smiled. 'Okay, I can take a hint.'

'I didn't mean—'

'I know. But I shouldn't have asked. None of my business.'

'It's not that. But I don't really know what to tell you.'

'Okay, so tell me about your time as a police officer.'

'Not sure what there is to tell. Most of it was pretty dull.'

'I can't believe that. I'd heard you were a detective.'

'It sounds exciting, but the majority of the work's pretty routine.'

'You didn't enjoy it?'

I thought about that. Oddly, it wasn't really a question I'd ever asked myself. 'I don't know, really. I think I was pretty good at it but I'm not sure that's the same thing.'

'It's something,' Lorna pointed out. 'What made you good at it?'

'It's hard to explain. I mean, I was conscientious and rigorous. But it wasn't only that. There were a couple of things. I was a straight cop, which meant I was trusted by informants. I was able to get useful intelligence. But there was something else. A sort of instinct.' I paused, trying to think how best to describe what I'd experienced. 'I had an ability to step back from an issue, to look at it from outside. Make connections that others had missed.' I shrugged. 'Sorry. That sounds big-headed, and I don't even know if it makes any sense. But I got results.'

'That must have been valued.'

'You'd have thought, wouldn't you? It didn't quite work like that. I put too many noses out of joint. I was moved into roles that didn't really use the skills I had. I spent the last couple of years in covert surveillance.' I paused, unsure how much more I wanted to say. 'That was why I left in the end. Because of what happened in that role.'

She sensed my hesitation. 'I'm just making conversation. If you don't want to talk about it, that's understandable.'

'I think I do. I've not talked to anyone else about it. If I'd stayed on the force they'd have provided counselling. But I don't want to end up offloading my troubles on to you.'

'I'm a good listener. Say what you want. And nothing you don't want.'

It took me only a few minutes to recount and relive my experience with Danny Royce on that unforgettable night. 'If I really had been alone, I wouldn't be here now.'

'You must have been terrified.'

'I didn't have time to think about it. It was only later that it hit me. How close I must have come to being killed.'

'I'm glad you weren't.'

'Thanks.' I smiled. 'Me too.'

'You still don't know why this Critchley character was there?'

'No idea. He was a trained firearms officer, but he hadn't been allocated to that case. Not officially anyway.'

'Could he have been allocated to it unofficially?'

'Anything's possible. Sometimes they keep things covert even from the covert team. Especially if there's a risk of leaks. Somebody must have tipped off Royce that I was there.'

'You didn't try to find out?'

'I was on my way out. I reasoned that if anyone had wanted to tell me, they'd have done so. I wouldn't win any friends by delving further.'

'Was that why you resigned?'

'Part of it. But only a small part. The much bigger part was that I'd had enough. It wasn't even that I was worried about the risk. Most operations weren't that dangerous. Royce was a one-off. It was the whole thing. The game-playing. The politics. The whole culture. The endless administration. I needed a change.'

'You made a pretty dramatic one.'

'I took each day as it came. Waited to see what turned up. This is what turned up.'

'Are you pleased,' she asked, 'that you came up here?'

'Very, so far. I have to see what the future, and in particular, Cameron Fraser, has to offer, but so far it's working out well.'

'You haven't tried my food yet.'

'I'm expecting to be able to add that to the positives.'

'Speaking of which, I'd better check how things are doing. Don't want to serve you burnt offerings.' She gestured to my nearly empty glass. 'Top-up?'

'Thanks. Nice wine.'

I sat back, wondering about everything we'd been

discussing. The account I'd given Lorna had been accurate enough, but it hadn't been the whole truth. I hadn't mentioned Maddie, for example. Maddie hadn't directly contributed to my decision to resign – we'd already been separated for a couple of years by then – but she'd been part of what I wanted to get away from. There were other factors that had contributed too, but I hadn't yet disentangled all of those even in my own head.

'All on target.' Lorna had returned with the refilled wine glasses. 'I've put the water on to boil for the langoustines. Thought they'd be better if I cooked them fresh.'

'Sounds good to me.'

'So what about this Danny Royce character,' she said, 'do you think there really is any risk of a revenge attack?'

'I doubt it. Not on me, anyway. There's not much honour among thieves at any time, and Royce was feared rather than respected. My role in the whole thing was pretty minor.'

'Apart from nearly getting killed.'

'Apart from that bit.'

'What about Critchley?'

'Not sure. If I were in his shoes, I'd be watching my back. But, from what I knew of him, he was a chancer anyway. He can probably look after himself.'

'Sounds like it's a world you're well out of.'

'Too right. I just hope that dealing with Cameron Fraser isn't going to drag me back into anything similar.'

'You can always walk away.'

'I'll give it a go. But yes. I can always do that.'

'So you think you'll stay up here?'

'I think so. For the foreseeable. I genuinely like it here.'

'So do I, but it's not the most exciting place to be.'

'Excitement's the last thing I need.'

'Fair enough.' She glanced at her watch. 'I'd better get the langoustines in. I'll be a few minutes. Do you want some white wine with the shellfish or are you happy to stick with the red?'

'I'm happy with this. But I've always been uncouth.'

'Me too. Okay, back shortly.'

I was enjoying the evening even more than I'd hoped, though our conversation had barely got out of first gear. I felt at ease with Lorna in a way I rarely did with people, particularly women. It was partly a legacy of my time with Maddie. When I was with her, I'd always felt as if I were being judged and found wanting. It was unusual to feel I didn't need to prove anything.

The rest of the evening passed equally enjoyably. The langoustines were wonderful – still warm, perfectly cooked and served with home-made mayonnaise and freshly baked bread. The venison casserole was equally good, accompanied by a horseradish mash and vegetables. I was amazed by how much trouble she'd gone to.

'We do have a dessert,' she said, when we'd finished the venison. 'Cranachan. But you might want a break first.'

'I might need one. That was terrific.'

'Better than a stale biscuit?'

'Better than anything I could do. When I reciprocate, don't expect this standard.'

'I'm sure it'll be equally good.'

We chatted and drank more wine, and at some point Lorna brought out the cranachan, that distinctively Scottish mix of raspberries, cream, local Crowdie cheese, oatmeal and whisky. Lorna's version tasted perfect. After that, we moved back to the sofa and shifted from wine to the single malt. We hadn't drunk too much, but I was feeling pleasantly mellow. Lorna seemed in a similar relaxed mood.

It was perhaps the moment when one of us might have made a tentative move. But I'm not that kind of person. More than anything I didn't want to do anything to change the mood of the evening. Lorna had moved a little closer to me, but I didn't want to take anything for granted.

'You know,' she said, as if reading my thoughts, 'this has been one of the most enjoyable evenings I've had in a long time.'

'Me too. Thanks.' I was conscious we'd spent most of the evening either talking about my experiences in the force or about the local area and characters. 'You haven't said much about your own background.'

Almost immediately, I wondered if I'd said the wrong thing. I could feel her tense. It passed almost immediately and she relaxed, but I still felt as if I'd touched on something unwelcome.

'No, I haven't. Partly because there's not that much to tell. And partly because some of it's – well, not easy to talk about.'

'I'm sorry. I didn't realise. You don't need—'

'No, I do want to tell you about it. But not tonight. Tonight's been too good. I don't want to spoil it now.'

'Of course.'

'When I come up to yours,' she said. 'I'll tell you the story then. There's not a lot to it.'

'That's fine,' I said. 'But only if you want to.'

'I want to.' She reached out and, for the first time, took my hand. 'Look, Jack, I want to be honest with you.'

I was expecting that this might finally be the moment when she'd let me down gently. When she'd tell me that – I don't know – she wasn't ready for a relationship or that she wasn't interested in men or that there was someone else. But she didn't. To my relief, she said, 'I don't know how you feel, but I'd like to take this further. See how it goes between us.'

'I'd like that.'

She smiled. 'That's what I wanted you to say. I was scared you wouldn't. But I don't want to push this too quickly. You'll understand why when I tell you – well, what I've got to tell you.

I'm sorry if that sounds enigmatic. I want to tell it in the right way for me and for you. But I'm hoping that tonight's a beginning, not an end.'

'I hope so too,' I said. 'And of course, I'm ready to listen to whatever you've got to tell me.' We both fell silent and I was conscious of a slight awkwardness between us. It was as if, now she'd broached the subject, neither of us would be entirely comfortable until she'd been able to tell her story in the way she needed to.

It was approaching midnight anyway. 'You must be tired,' I said. 'I should be heading off soon. Can I help with the clearing up?'

'It's just stacking the dishwasher. I can do that in the morning.'

'If you're sure.'

'I'm sure.'

My boots and waterproof had dried out over the evening. Outside, the weather had improved. The rain had stopped, and there were stars visible between the scudding clouds. I paused on the doorstep. 'It's been a lovely evening. Thanks.'

'No, thank you. I really enjoyed it. So when are you going to return the favour?'

'When are you free?'

'Next Friday or Saturday? I mean, I could do it before then, but it's probably less fun on a school night.'

'What about Friday then?'

'Perfect. About seven?'

'Ideal. Can't promise the food will match yours, but it'll be more than stale biscuits.'

'It's the company I'm interested in.' She leaned forward and kissed me, initially softly on the lips, then with a greater intensity. The suddenness of the action was unexpected, but far from unwelcome. She drew her head back, looking mildly embarrassed. 'Sorry.'

'Perfect end to a perfect evening.'

'I can see you before Friday, you know. I'll call in with Ziggy.'

'That would be good.' We were both grinning like teenagers. 'You'd better get back inside,' I said. 'It's freezing out here.'

'Night, then.'

'Night.' There was a further, slightly more decorous kiss then I turned to make my way back up the hill. The walk back seemed much shorter than the walk down had been, partly because of the change in the weather but mostly because of my frame of mind. I'd wanted to reset my life – that was why I'd left my job and moved up here in the first place – but I'd had no real idea what that meant. I'd hoped something new and better would come along. Now it was beginning to look as if that might actually happen.

By the time I reached the cottage, the sky had cleared and was heavy with stars, the long pale streak of the Milky Way visible above me. Lights were still showing in the windows of Lorna's cottage, and I thought about her bustling about in there, preparing for bed.

I turned back, fumbling in my coat pocket for the keys. It took me a moment to find them, my hands numb from the cold. Then, as I walked towards the door, I saw that the key wasn't needed.

The front door of the cottage was standing open.

CHAPTER TWELVE

My torch was still switched on, but I slipped it into the pocket of my coat, not wanting to draw attention to my presence until I knew whether anyone was inside. The cottage was in darkness, and, as I stood straining my ears, I could detect no movement.

I stepped silently into the hallway and paused again, still listening. The small living room was on the left, the kitchen straight ahead, the stairs leading to the upper floor on my right. I switched off the torch, reached into the living-room doorway and turned on the light. Then I pushed back the door and stepped inside. The room seemed to be as I'd left it.

I continued on towards the kitchen. There was no point now in concealing my presence. I was still gripping the flashlight tightly. It was solid enough to use as a makeshift weapon if necessary. I switched on the kitchen light. The room was empty.

It took me another few minutes to check out the upper floor of the house and satisfy myself that there was no one inside. Then, reassured that there was no immediate threat, I made my way back downstairs. The front door was standing open as I'd left it. There was no obvious sign the lock had been forced or broken, but it was only a basic night latch that could easily be opened by anyone who knew what they were doing. I'd wondered whether I should approach Gus for some improved security but I hadn't got around to it.

I closed the door, relieved that there were a couple of sturdy bolts I could draw across. There were similar bolts on the rear door, so it would be difficult for anyone to break in overnight without alerting me to their presence.

The question was whether anyone had actually been in here. It was possible I'd simply failed to close the front door properly, and it had been blown open by the earlier winds. But it would be uncharacteristic of me. I'm normally one to double-check that the door's locked behind me. A legacy of my days living in Glasgow. I honestly couldn't remember whether or not I had on this occasion.

Why would anyone want to come in here, anyway? I had nothing worth stealing. My laptop was cheap and clapped out. There was a TV and radio belonging to the cottage, worth next to nothing. My phone, bank cards and any cash I had were in my pocket. There was nothing else here that would interest any housebreaker.

After carrying out a final check that the front and back doors were firmly bolted, I made my way upstairs. The bedroom felt cold – I was usually in bed well before this – and I wished I'd thought to turn on the small convector heater when I'd first returned home. But there wasn't much I could do about that now, other than not waste too much time getting into bed.

I pulled back the duvet. Like the living room and the kitchen, the bedroom had seemed undisturbed when I'd looked round it earlier. But there was something on the pillow that hadn't been there earlier. A small folded slip of paper.

I opened it. Just a couple of scribbled lines of handwriting.

Called but you were out. Sorry to miss you. Call me. Sean. The words were followed by a mobile number.

Sean. Who the hell was Sean? I didn't know anyone called Sean.

And then I realised I did. I knew only one person called Sean.

Sean Critchley.

CHAPTER THIRTEEN

'So what are you going to do?'

Lorna was sitting at my kitchen table, Ziggy at her feet apparently half asleep.

'What can I do? I'll get some better locks fitted, assuming Gus is happy with that.' I was standing waiting for the kettle to boil.

'That doesn't really deal with the issue, though, does it? I mean, it'll mean this Critchley can't get in without you knowing. But it doesn't stop him coming back.'

'I don't want him coming in here when I'm not around. But I'm not afraid of him.' I didn't really know Sean Critchley other than by reputation. But the reputation wasn't a good one. I'd never worked closely enough with him to witness anything first hand, but I'd heard more than enough stories. Even if I wasn't afraid of him, he was a man to be wary of.

'But why's he here? It's not exactly a place you pass through.'

'I've no idea. I can't think of anything that Sean Critchley would want from the likes of me.'

'He saved your life,' Lorna pointed out. 'Maybe he thinks you owe him one. Maybe he's in some kind of trouble himself.'

'If Critchley needs help, there must be people better positioned to provide it than I am.'

'Are you going to call him?'

'I don't know. He's not someone I want anywhere near my life now. But I don't want him to come back here either.' I poured the hot water into the cafetière and then carried it over to the table. I'd already set out a couple of mugs for the two of us.

'I bought you a present,' Lorna said. 'I was going to give it to you last night, but I thought it would be more appropriate to bring it this morning.' She fumbled in the small rucksack she'd brought with her. 'Here you are.'

I laughed. It was a box of upmarket chocolate biscuits. 'I'll try not to let them go stale.'

'I'm not going to give you the chance.'

I opened the box, pushing it towards her. 'Help yourself. Do you need a plate?'

'I'm not sure they'll last long enough to justify a plate. To repeat my question, what are you going to do about Critchley?'

'The first thing I'll do is put a few feelers out to ex-colleagues in the force. See if I can find out anything about what Critchley's up to. If I'm going to contact him, I'd rather have as much background as possible. I don't want to be going into anything blind if I can help it.'

'Sounds sensible. Then what?'

'Depending on what I hear, I'll call him, I guess. It's probably preferable to having him turn up on the doorstep again.'

I'd been hoping she might be able to stay longer, and that we could maybe have lunch together. But she said she still had some work to get done. I wasn't sure if she was telling the full truth or if she did simply want to avoid pushing things along too quickly. Either way, as she was leaving, she kissed me again, not quite with the urgent passion of the previous evening but with something more than politeness.

I watched as she headed back down the hill, Ziggy bounding around her. After the previous night's rain, it was a glorious midwinter day, the low sun throwing deep shadows across the hillside. In the distance, the mountains were white with snow, though there were no remnants left here on the lower hillsides. It was a spectacular landscape, I thought, and I was finally feeling at home here. I wasn't going to allow anyone – not Maddie, not Sean Critchley, and certainly not bloody Gregor McBride – to spoil that.

I made my way back into the cottage, closing the front door firmly behind me. Then, as if making some kind of symbolic gesture, I pulled across the two bolts.

CHAPTER FOURTEEN

'I trust you'll find everything satisfactory.'

Cameron Fraser slid the thin sheaf of papers across the table towards me. I skimmed down the first page. The contract wasn't couched in particularly legalistic language and it seemed reasonable to my inexpert eye.

'Take your time. If you want to take it away and pass it by your own legal advisor, that won't be a problem. I want you to be comfortable with what you're signing up to.'

I was amused by the idea I might have a legal advisor to consult. 'It all looks pretty straightforward. I'll read through it carefully in case I've any questions, but I'm sure it'll be fine.'

Fraser looked sceptical. I guessed he wasn't the type to sign anything without having his lawyers check it out first. 'You'll have noted the non-disclosure clause?'

I'd just reached that particular paragraph. As far as I could judge, the requirement was that I shouldn't disclose any information about my work for Fraser to any third party without his express agreement. I nodded. 'That presumably doesn't preclude me from talking to third parties in the course of carrying out that work? If I'm conducting an investigation, I'm probably going to have to explain why I want to speak to people.'

Fraser gave a slight nod, possibly of approval. 'With regard to your investigation into Kate Brodie's disappearance, I don't want my name mentioned. Beyond that, I'm content to leave matters to your discretion, Mr Mellor. But I would ask that, as a general principle, you say no more than you deem necessary. My main objective in including that clause – which is in the contracts of any staff I employ – is to ensure that you do not give any information to the media without my agreement.'

'I'd never talk to the media in any case.'

'Some of your former colleagues are not so scrupulous.'

'I've never been tempted to follow their example.'

I read through the contract again, more slowly this time, reassuring myself that Fraser hadn't included anything I might find problematic. Most of it was unexceptional stuff. There was no real description of my duties, and I was described only as a 'consultant'. The remainder of the document covered the day rate, arrangements for claiming expenses, submitting invoices, payment terms and the like. It all looked fine to me. I put the papers back down on the table. 'I'm very happy with that.'

'If you're sure.' He handed me an expensive-looking fountain pen. 'I've already signed both copies. If you add your signature to the line below mine, we can consider your employment confirmed.'

I did as he asked, then pushed one of the copies back to him. 'I look forward to working with you.'

'Likewise, Mr Mellor. I'm looking forward to seeing how you work. And I hope that you are able to shed a little more light on what has happened to Kate Brodie.'

'I hope so too.'

'Is there anything else you need from me at this stage?'

'It would be useful to have your thoughts on anyone I

should be speaking to. Any other friends or contacts of Kate you're aware of, for example.'

'I'm afraid I can't offer you much help in that direction. I can't claim to have been close to Kate. I know very little about her private life. Kate was a rather private individual.' He paused. 'The only contact I do have is Kate Brodie's ex-husband, Roy Brodie. I've had some business dealings with him. I can ask him to call you.'

'Wouldn't that risk getting back to Archie Kinnear?'

Fraser laughed. 'No chance. There's no love lost between Roy and Archie. If I ask him to be discreet about all this, he will be.'

'I'm sure it would be useful to speak to him. Thank you.'

'Can I suggest we meet again in two weeks for an update, if this time suits you? Obviously, if you need anything from me in the meantime, please don't hesitate to call.'

'That's fine. I hope I can make some progress for you.'

'So do I, Mr Mellor.' He gestured vaguely towards his computer. 'I'm afraid I have a stack of emails to go through. I assume you can find your way out?'

He said this with a smile, but his words were clearly intended to show me my place. I was an employee now, another of Cameron Fraser's minions. He might treat me well or badly but it was never going to be a relationship of equals.

On the drive back, my mind was focused mainly on Sean Critchley. I'd made a few calls on Sunday afternoon to ex-colleagues to see if I could find out any more about what Critchley might be up to. None of those I spoke to knew Critchley well, and no one was able to offer any concrete information. 'Haven't seen him around for a while, to be honest,' one had said. 'Not that that proves much. He's not someone whose company I'd actively seek out.'

I'd hoped Lorna might reappear in the afternoon, but

darkness fell with no sign of her. I couldn't help feeling disappointed. My other task for the afternoon had been to call Gus about changing the locks on the front door. I didn't want to tell Gus the reasons for my concerns, and I could hear the scepticism in his voice. 'Do you think it's really needed? I don't even bother to lock my doors half the time. Who's likely to break in up here?'

'I'm slightly paranoid. It's my background, Gus. I'm happy to cover the costs, but I didn't want to do it without consulting you.'

'No problem with me. I can put you in touch with a good local guy who won't rip you off. I'll text his number to you.'

I took another walk outside in the late afternoon. Outside it was already almost dark. The sky to the south-west was a deep mauve, translucent from the vanished sun. It was a clear night, likely to be very cold, the first stars already beginning to appear. I gazed down the valley and thought once again about Lorna going about her business a half mile or so away. I wanted to see her, but I knew – or I thought I knew – that she wouldn't want me turning up on her doorstep.

I told myself that I was just out here to enjoy the evening. But there was a part of me still thinking about Critchley's mysterious visit and what it might mean. For the first time since I'd arrived, I didn't feel entirely safe here. I stood, surveying the surrounding landscape, and it was another five minutes before I finally forced myself to make my way back into the relative warmth of the cottage.

CHAPTER FIFTEEN

I woke early the next morning and decided to make best use of the time and start working on the Kate Brodie case. I still had no clear idea of where to begin. I'd hoped that Cameron Fraser might be able to provide me with some initial leads, but there was clearly no hope of that.

All I had was a list of names I'd gleaned from the various news reports. The journalists involved had clearly struggled to find new angles to keep the story alive, and seemed to have worked their way through most of Kate's friends and associates. The list included some of those who had been staying in the cottage in Cromarty, other friends from university, colleagues at work, and her neighbours in Glasgow.

I spent the next few hours searching the names on the internet. My strike rate was surprisingly high. In some cases, I was able to find a website linked to the individual, particularly for those who were self-employed. In those instances, there were typically good contact details, both email and telephone. More commonly, I found individuals on various social media sites. There were generally no contact details but at least I had the option to send a direct mail.

I couldn't always be sure that the individual I'd found was the person named in the news report, but in most there was enough supporting evidence to indicate it was likely. By late morning, I'd assembled a decent list of names to be contacted.

The next question was how to present myself. My concern was that Kate's friends might assume I was some scandal-mongering tabloid journalist, raking over the details of the case in the hope of yet another story. In their shoes, I knew how I'd react to that kind of approach. I could simply tell the truth and say I'd been commissioned to reopen the investigation by someone who wished to remain anonymous. But that risked raising more questions than it answered, and might simply make Kate's friends even more suspicious.

In the end, I decided to take the fashionable line and claim I was conducting research for a true-crime podcast. I looked up the name and details of a respected US-based podcast specialising in unsolved mysteries. My story was that I'd been commissioned to research the feasibility of launching a British version and that Kate Brodie's disappearance was one of the cases we were looking to include. I hoped that those I contacted would either already be aware of the podcast or would look it up online, but I couldn't imagine anyone would take the trouble to check out my story any further.

Armed with this explanation, I began to work through the contacts, starting with the few where I had a telephone number. I had only limited success at first. Most of the business numbers took me to voicemail. One was unobtainable. I made an appropriate note beside each name, and left a message where I could. Only one of the numbers, belonging to a Sadie Wilson, one of the friends from the Cromarty weekend, apparently working as a therapist, was answered directly.

'More than happy to help if I can,' Wilson said in response to my prepared spiel. 'Anything that helps to keep the case alive.

It was a great shock to us all. I still want to believe she's out there somewhere safe and sound, though it doesn't seem likely after all this time. Ask me anything you like, but I don't know how much I'll be able to tell you.'

'How well did you know Kate?'

'Probably as well as anyone. She was very pleasant. Very likeable. But she wasn't the most open of individuals. I never felt I got close to her, not the way I have with other friends.'

'Standoffish?'

'She wasn't aloof, just rather private. Never talked about herself or what was going on in her life. Never talked about her work. Didn't throw herself into activities the way some people did. But I was very fond of her. She was very reliable, one of those people who'd never let you down. That was why we were so surprised when she didn't turn up in Cromarty. If she'd have been delayed, we'd have expected her to phone.'

'You met Kate at university?'

'We were both studying History, so we met at one of the freshers' get-togethers early on. There was a group of us who ended up as a fairly tight-knit bunch of friends. You know how it is at uni. You mill about a bit at first, then gradually you find the people you want to spend time with. We'd largely kept in touch after graduation, though obviously we were all doing different things.'

'So these were the people going to Cromarty that weekend?'

'Pretty much, along with a couple of partners.'

'What was the nature of the weekend? I mean, what were you planning to do?'

Wilson laughed. 'You've been reading the tabloid coverage, haven't you?'

'I've done some background research,' I acknowledged. 'There was some – well, let's say innuendo.'

'That's one word for it. In different circumstances, we'd

have found it hilarious. As it was, it was offensive. Utterly insensitive. The implication that we'd booked the cottage for a debauched orgy of sex, drugs and anything else you care to think of. It was just a quiet bunch of old mates getting together for a relaxing weekend. Sure, we'd have let our hair down a little. But it was a chance to relive old times, really. It would have involved a few beers and bottles of wine, nothing more.'

'What were you actually planning to do over the weekend?'

'Maybe a walk or two. There are a couple of pubs in Cromarty, so we'd have visited those. Maybe lunch out somewhere, though we were planning to cook for ourselves in the evenings. It was a long weekend – we were due to stay in the house through till Tuesday – but it would have flown by. We'd have spent the majority of it chatting about nothing much.'

'When did you first become concerned about Kate?'

'We'd been expecting her to turn up fairly late. Most of us had taken the Friday off or at least the afternoon. We were mainly driving up from the central belt, so a couple of us had shared cars, and we'd aimed to get there late afternoon. Other than Kate, we were all there by around six. Kate had had some work commitment on the Friday afternoon, so hadn't been able to get away early. We weren't expecting her till eight or nine at the earliest. We didn't really start to get concerned till after ten. We tried her mobile but it went to voicemail.'

'What happened after that?'

'There wasn't much else we could do that evening. We kept trying her number. Someone had contact details for one of her work colleagues, but she couldn't tell us anything except that, as far as she knew, Kate had been intending to join us and had brought a weekend bag into work that morning. We waited up till well after midnight in case Kate turned up, but that was about it. In the morning, when we'd heard nothing more, we really started to get concerned. There was still no answer on her phone, and no one had received a message or text from her. We debated whether we should call the police. We hesitated at first but when we'd still heard nothing by the afternoon, we called them. They didn't seem to take it very seriously at first.'

'What happened after that?'

'Not much at first. We continued with the weekend, partly in case Kate should turn up belatedly. I couldn't see how that was going to happen but it was almost a superstitious thing. If we'd packed up and headed home, that would have felt like admitting something was wrong. But our hearts weren't in it. We sat about speculating on what might have happened. I think we were all relieved when Tuesday came and we could all leave it behind.'

'When did the police start to take it more seriously?'

'I'm not sure exactly. Maybe someone finally twigged that Kate was Archie Kinnear's daughter. They didn't contact me or any of the others till a couple of days later. By that point, Kate's car had been found. That might be what prompted them to start treating it as a full missing persons case.'

'What did the police say to you?'

'They asked me various questions on the phone and then eventually came out to interview me. They spoke to all of us who'd been there over the weekend. They never said it in so many words but it was clear that one of their lines of enquiry was that Kate might actually have arrived at the house and something had happened to her there, whether by accident or foul play.'

'They thought you might be covering something up?'

'It wasn't an unreasonable line of enquiry from their point of view. It's the kind of thing that happens in crime novels, isn't it? Bunch of mates get together for the weekend, one of them gets killed, the rest try to cover it up. Not sure it ever happens in real life, or if it does I imagine it falls apart pretty quickly. The police were obviously looking for inconsistencies in our stories, but they didn't find any. It helped that we'd called Kate's colleague on the Friday evening. If something had happened to Kate at the cottage, it would either have to have happened as soon as she'd arrived and we'd been quick off the mark with our cover-up, or we'd pre-planned it and made that call as an alibi. I don't think even the police took that possibility seriously.'

'Did you have any further contact with the police after that?'

'No. They seemed to give up on that line of enquiry pretty quickly. We saw what was reported in the media, including stuff that we all knew was nonsense. But that was about it. My impression is that the police ran out of ideas early on.'

'What's your own view on what might have happened to Kate?'

'I don't have one. I don't know why she wouldn't have driven straight to the cottage. I don't see how anything could have happened to her on her journey if her car ended up in Inverness. If the car hadn't been found or if it had been found somewhere else, it might make more sense.'

'Is it possible she dumped the car and then took a train or coach somewhere else?'

'It's obviously possible. But why would she do that? Why leave the car?'

'Maybe to make it harder to track her down?' I was conscious that talking to Sadie Wilson was helping me to clarify, or at least explore, my own thinking. 'I don't know. I'm just trying to consider possibilities.'

'It doesn't feel like something Kate would do. She wasn't one for acting spontaneously. Even if she had, her bank account wasn't touched after her disappearance. What would she have been living on? I guess she could have had some kind of breakdown, but I'd expect her to have been found by now, one way or another. She wasn't the type who'd survive easily living on the streets. Too used to her creature comforts. There were suggestions she might have taken her own life, though I couldn't imagine what reason she'd have had. But who knows? My own feeling is that she must be dead, if only because so much time has passed, but I can't tell you any more than that.'

'Is there anything else you can tell me that might help me make progress? About the weekend or about Kate. Or about the people she knew. Is there anyone who might have wanted to harm her?'

'The police asked me that. Again, it sounds to me like something from a crime novel. Did she have any enemies, that kind of thing. The short answer's no. I'd have said Kate wasn't the sort to make enemies. Don't get me wrong. She wasn't a pushover. If she felt strongly about something, she'd let you know. But not in an aggressive way. She was generally easy-going and friendly with everyone.'

'What about her relationship with her father? I understand she worked in his business.'

'I don't know much about it. She had various bust-ups with him over the years, but always seemed to drift back into his orbit. That's what I meant about creature comforts. She had various administrative jobs after university, but when dear Archie offered her a well-paid bolt-hole, she wasn't going to turn it down.'

'You sound like you disapprove.'

'It wouldn't have been my choice. But I'm not her. It was her decision. It was something else she didn't talk much about.'

'Was she in a relationship? After her divorce, I mean.'

'Not as far as I'm aware. She was coming up to Cromarty by herself, and she hadn't mentioned anybody. To be honest, I don't think there's much more I can tell you. I was fond of Kate, but I hadn't seen much of her in recent years. I'm working in

Edinburgh, she was in Glasgow and we were both in busy jobs, so we hadn't really had a chance to get together. It was like that with most of our friends, which is why we'd organised the weekend. Things might well have happened in Kate's life that I wasn't aware of, but nobody's ever mentioned anything to me.'

'I understand that. It's why I'm keen to speak to as many people as I can. I imagine you'll all have your own perspectives on her.'

'Of course. I really hope you get somewhere with this, though I suspect you may be wasting your time.'

'All we can do is tell the story, find as many sources as we can. And hope that leads somewhere.' I felt slightly uncomfortable trotting out this fiction, but at least my own investigation was real enough.

We ended the call by discussing the contact list I'd come up with. Wilson was able to provide one or two more contact details and to add a couple more friends' names to the list. She promised to call me if she thought of any more or if anything else occurred to her, and we said a pleasant enough goodbye.

But that didn't mean I felt entirely comfortable with what I was doing. I didn't like lying to people, even in a good cause, and I didn't want to raise hopes that would probably never be realised. My only justification was that I hadn't initiated this. It had been Cameron Fraser's decision and I'd been completely honest with him about the likelihood of success.

I told myself I'd give it till my first catch-up with Fraser, and then I'd decide. Or maybe, if I was really getting nowhere, Fraser would make the decision for me.

I was about to take a break for a coffee, when my phone buzzed in my hand. I glanced at the screen to see who was calling. Steve Tanner. One of the former colleagues I'd contacted in trying to find out more about Sean Critchley. I hadn't really expected anyone would get back to me, though

Steve had been more of a genuine mate than some of the others. 'Steve?'

'Got a minute to talk, Jack?' Steve had always struck me as a decent, easy-going guy. He was one of those who seemed to let the rigours of policing wash over him. He never seemed unduly stressed or worried, and I couldn't easily imagine him being traumatised by anything he'd witnessed or experienced. Probably precisely the sort who'd eventually suffer from some serious psychological meltdown.

'I'm not in the job now, mate. Time on my hands.'

'Still can't believe you jacked it all in. Especially to move to the arse-end of nowhere.' Steve sounded genuinely baffled. He was a city boy like me, and he'd openly mocked my decision to head for the wilderness. It was probably one of the factors that had initially made me determined to stick it out.

'You should try leaving the city sometime.'

'Nah. You'll never catch me living in nowheresville.'

I laughed. 'Mate, you live in East Kilbride. So why are you calling?'

'You were asking about Sean Critchley the other day.'

'Didn't expect you to get back so quickly.' Or at all, I added silently to myself.

'Thought you might want a heads-up in the circumstances. It'll be all over the media later.'

'Go on.'

'Critchley's been found dead.'

CHAPTER SIXTEEN

It was the last thing I'd expected him to say. 'Critchley's dead?'

'Well and truly. And it looks like murder.'

'Christ. Where?'

'That's the thing. Up in your neck of the woods. Inverness.'

I felt a chill of unease in my stomach. 'Inverness?'

'He'd booked into a hotel for a couple of days over the weekend. Body was found Monday morning by one of the cleaners. They've released no real details but the word is that it looked like a pro job. Bullet in the heart at close range. No one heard anything but the hotel was largely empty at this time of year. No CCTV.'

'So why was he in Inverness?' I hadn't told any of my ex-colleagues about my near encounter with Critchley. I'd thought it better to keep quiet about that till I had a better idea what Critchley was up to. 'Not his usual stamping ground.'

'All a bit of a mystery. He was up there anonymously. Paid cash at the hotel and used an assumed name. If he was on an assignment up there, nobody seems prepared to admit it. Given your recent spark of interest in the guy, I thought you might have some ideas.'

'Not a clue. But Critchley's always swum in murky waters.'

We chatted a little longer, ending with the usual half-hearted commitment to meet up for a beer the next time I was in Glasgow. Frankly, at that moment, I couldn't think of any good reason why I should ever return to the city again, but that wasn't something you could say to Steve Tanner.

I spent the rest of the morning sending emails or direct messages to the remaining contacts on my list. I'd given some thought as to how I should word the message to encourage a positive reaction and I'd finally produced a draft which I hoped would do the trick, emphasising the US podcast's past successes in reopening investigations into unresolved cases. Even so, I was acutely conscious that there was little else I could do to guarantee a response.

Just before noon, my thoughts were interrupted by the sound of enthusiastic yapping outside, followed a minute or two later by the ringing of the doorbell. Relieved, I walked through to open the front door. Ziggy bounded past me, barking loudly, then stopped suddenly as if unsure why he'd entered the house in the first place. Lorna was on the doorstep, watching the dog with amusement. 'Make yourself at home, Ziggy, why don't you?'

'He's all right,' I said. 'Doesn't stand on ceremony. You'd better come inside too.' I looked past her. I'd been so caught up in my emails and phone calls that I hadn't really registered the weather. After a few days of bright sunshine, this looked like a typical Highland winter's day – grey, cold and with a persistent dampness in the air that never quite turned into rain.

'I wondered if you wanted to share some lunch,' Lorna said. 'I had to go down to the post office so I treated myself to a steak pie.' The post office in the nearest village at the bottom of the hill was part of a small convenience store that sold, among other delights, excellent pastries from a local bakery. 'Thought I'd get one for you, too.'

'You keep bringing gifts,' I said. 'I feel guilty.'

'You'll make up for it on Friday. I'm looking forward to a feast.'

'Now I'm even more worried. But I can make you coffee and heat up a pie for you.' We chatted while I put the pies in the oven and filled the kettle. 'I had some unexpected news this morning. Sean Critchley.'

'The guy who broke in here?'

'Apparently he's been found dead. Murdered.' I paused. 'In Inverness.'

'You're kidding.'

'Wouldn't be much of a laugh, would it? I had a call this morning. I told you I was contacting a few ex-colleagues to see what Critchley was currently up to. Nobody knew much, but one or two said they'd ask around. It turns out that what Critchley is mainly doing at the moment is being dead.'

'When was this?'

'He was staying in a hotel. The cleaner found the body on Monday morning, so most likely sometime on the Sunday.'

'The day after he came here.'

'And it looks as if it was a professional job. Someone who knew how to do it quickly, quietly and probably without leaving a trace.'

We both sat in silence for a few moments. I could see the concern in Lorna's eyes. 'I meant what I said on Saturday, you know. I want us to take this further. I want to get to know you properly.' She hesitated. 'But already I'd be devastated if anything happened to you.'

'Thank you,' I said finally. 'But I'm not planning to let anything happen to me.'

'We can work on that together, then.'

We ate our pies in a companionable silence, Lorna occasionally stopping to feed a titbit to Ziggy, who'd been lured from the warmth of the wood-stove by the scent of food. Afterwards, I joined her as she walked with Ziggy to the summit of the hill, and we stood watching the patterns of clouds, the ever-changing sequence of shade and occasional sunshine. I could see a band of rain heading in from the east. Up here with Lorna, I was probably feeling as contented as I had for years.

Conscious of the impending rain, we made our way back to the cottage. Lorna refused my offer of another coffee, saying she still had work to do. I watched as she walked down the hill, Ziggy bounding in circles around her. Even after she'd disappeared over the brow of the hill, I continued watching as if willing the moment to continue forever.

CHAPTER SEVENTEEN

The rest of the week passed in much the same uneventful manner. I had a few responses to my various messages, some keen to help, others less so. I spoke at length to another two of Kate Brodie's friends who had been at the cottage in Cromarty, but they added little to what Sadie Wilson had already told me. They were able to provide me with one or two more suggestions for potential contacts, but their contributions only increased the feeling that I was making little progress.

My telephone conversation with Kate's ex-husband had proved at least a little more interesting. He had a smooth, oddly reassuring voice which sounded as if it might have been better suited to a radio presenter than to whatever kind of businessman Roy Brodie really was. His accent suggested an upmarket Edinburgh drawl softened by a period in the United States. 'Mr Mellor. Roy Brodie. I understand from Cameron Fraser that you'd like to speak to me. I don't know how much I can help you. But I imagine everyone you've spoken to has said much the same. If I knew anything useful, I'd have told the police.'

'I appreciate that, Mr Brodie. At this stage, I'm really just trying to learn more about Kate. Gain an understanding of her personality, her state of mind.'

'I understand.' There was a sceptical note in his voice. 'You'll appreciate I wasn't in frequent contact with her after we split up. The divorce itself was acrimonious and for a long while we were barely on speaking terms. My guess is that dear Archie was also stirring the pot. But we did gradually rebuild some sort of relationship, at least to the point where we could talk like civilised human beings.'

'What sort of person was she?'

'When I first met her, she seemed a normal young woman. Pretty quiet and reserved, really, certainly compared with her father. But there was a steely core there. She had some strong opinions – and wasn't afraid to stand up to Archie when she had to – and she had a tendency to get what she wanted.'

'How did you meet?'

'It was at one of Archie's famous parties. He holds these periodic big bashes. More business than pleasure, of course, but that's Archie. A way of schmoozing his contacts. Always very impressive affairs. No shortage of booze, decent food, and I'm told more clandestine pleasures were available for the select few. Not that I ever made the inner circle, even when I was married to Kate. As I say, strictly business.'

'Clandestine pleasures?'

'Just what I've heard. I was company secretary of a firm that was doing business with Archie. I was a last-minute substitute because my boss couldn't make it. I was still young and wet behind the ears in those days, so I'd no idea what to expect. To be honest, it was all a bit livelier than I'd imagined. I mean, not exactly riotous but no shortage of booze flowing and some pretty indiscreet behaviour. I was a bit taken aback, particularly as some of these people were old enough to be my father. I can't say it was really my scene so I just hung about on the fringes, people watching. That was when I ran into Kate, who seemed to be in the same position. I didn't realise she was Archie's daughter at first. She was just someone relatively close to my own age – just a few years younger – who seemed as bemused by what she was watching as I was. But we got on well, and things developed from there.'

'How did Kinnear take your relationship?' I asked.

'He wasn't happy. It was partly the usual fatherly thing. "No man's good enough for my little girl". And it was partly that he suspected my motives. Thought I was just trying to marry my way into his money. But Archie suspects everyone's motives, probably because he's an untrustworthy bastard himself.' Brodie laughed. 'No, we never got on. Not that I cared much at first. I was in love with Kate and that seemed to be all that mattered. It wasn't, of course, particularly once our relationship ran onto the rocks.'

'Can I ask why you split?' I wasn't sure if my question was too close to the bone but Brodie seemed untroubled by it.

'There were a lot of reasons. In the end, it was probably just that we weren't right for each other. We were married for three years but I never felt I really got to know her. She never really opened up about her emotions or feelings, and there were parts of her life and her past she simply wouldn't talk about. That was exacerbated by Archie's constant presence. I don't mean that he was physically there – though I sometimes thought he might as well be – but I could always feel his influence over Kate. I knew what he said about me. I knew what he thought of me.'

'I'd understood Kate didn't get on with her father?'

'Depended on the day. Kate was never a soft touch. She could give as good as she got, to Archie and to anyone else. But she knew which side her bread was buttered. And in a way I don't think she ever stopped being Archie's little girl. He had a hold over her I could never quite fathom.' Brodie paused. 'In the end, the marriage just fell apart. There was no one incident that ended it. We became increasingly distant. When we did try to build some bridges, we ended up arguing acrimoniously. There was nothing there. In the end, I couldn't take it anymore and I walked out. Just literally like that.' He laughed. 'Christ knows what Archie said about me after that.'

'You don't seem to think much of Kinnear.'

'I don't. An upmarket spiv, in my view, with more than a touch of the gangster. A bully and a thug. I understand he's been associating with that American huckster, Gregor McBride. If you're familiar with McBride, that'll give you a sense of what Archie's like. Two cheeks of the same backside, though Archie's a lot smarter.'

'Sounds very different from his daughter.'

'Don't get me wrong. That's why I said upmarket. Archie had made his pile and hob-nobbed with the elite. He never quite shook off the accent, but he'd left his working-class origins way behind, and he made sure Kate went to the right schools and mixed with the right people. But he was still a thug.'

I decided to change tack. 'When did you first hear about Kate's disappearance?'

'One of her friends called me sometime on the Saturday after Kate failed to turn up at the holiday cottage. Partly just to let me know, I suppose, and partly just on the off-chance I might have heard something from Kate myself. They'd called the police but they'd proved worse than useless – as they continued to be, from what I saw.'

'You weren't impressed by the police's efforts?'

'That's one way of putting it. They made a show of taking action, no doubt because of Archie's profile in Scotland, but it felt half-hearted to me. They knew they'd screwed up by taking so long to get started, and they were more interested in the PR than in actually finding Kate.'

'They presumably spoke to you?'

'Several times, at length. They never said so explicitly but I imagine they must have considered me a potential suspect. They asked me what contact I'd had with Kate since the divorce, whether we were on good terms, that kind of thing. The truth was that I'd not seen Kate face to face since the day I'd walked out. Most of our contact had been through our lawyers, though we'd had a few more recent phone conversations, always just about practical issues. I had plenty of evidence that I'd been in London for the days preceding Kate's disappearance, and I could account for my movements for most of that time, so I assume they abandoned that line of enquiry pretty quickly.'

'Do you have your own theories about what's happened to Kate?'

'I haven't a clue. None of it makes sense to me. There are only two real possibilities. Either something happened to her on the journey or something happened after she'd reached Cromarty. We know she reached Inverness, so it's difficult to see how anything could have happened between there and Cromarty. Why wouldn't she go straight there? But I can't envisage that, if she somehow came to harm in Cromarty, her friends would have succeeded in covering it up.'

'Do you think she could be alive and well somewhere?'

'I suppose stranger things have happened. But, if you want an honest opinion, I think she's most likely dead.' There was a pause. 'Look, Kate and I had split up but once the dust had settled I didn't bear her any ill will. I'm glad Cameron wants someone to take another look at what happened, whatever his motives might be. I still think you're wasting your time, but I'm sure you know that. My impression was that the police investigation was inept. Whether it was a lack of resources, inexperienced officers, other priorities – well, who knows? I do know that if you do a thorough job, Mr Mellor, you've at least a chance of discovering something they didn't. You may not find Kate, but if you can find anything at all, good luck to you.'

After we'd finished the call, I sat mulling on what Brodie had said, particularly his closing words. It was a more encouraging response than I'd received from anyone else, but it also raised questions in my mind. Of course, the police could be inept. But Kate Brodie's disappearance would have been a high-profile investigation, and would have attracted whatever talents and resources were needed. Which made me wonder why it had made so little progress.

As the week wore on, I received a few more positive responses, including one from Kate's former neighbour, a young woman who'd lived in the flat below Kate's. That evening, I called the number she'd given me. The call was answered almost immediately by an enthusiastic-sounding woman. 'Hi, Heather speaking.'

I introduced myself. 'Is now a good time to speak?'

'Yeah, sure. Happy to help you if I can.' Heather Galloway worked as a solicitor in a commercial practice in the city. She had a vaguely upmarket Scottish accent, suggesting an affluent background and the right education. I imagine Kate Brodie would have sounded much the same. 'I still can't believe all this. Kate seemed such a lovely person.'

'Did you know her well?'

'Reasonably, at least as neighbours. She was a few years older than I am, but we had a lot in common. She'd invited me in for a drink a few times, and we'd had the odd meal out together. That sort of thing. But we used to run into each other on the stairs all the time, and just stop for a chat.'

'Did you see her in the days before she disappeared?'

'Yes, a few times. She just seemed her usual self. Chatty and cheery.'

'You didn't get any sense that she might have been worried or depressed.'

'The police kept asking me about that,' Galloway said. 'Whether she seemed in low spirits. I didn't see any real signs of that, with maybe one exception. She always seemed upbeat to me, and that last week was no different. In fact, the night before she disappeared she'd been chatting to me about the weekend she was spending with friends in the Highlands. She seemed excited about it.'

'So she was definitely expecting to go on the weekend? There was no sign she might change her mind?'

'Just the opposite from the way she spoke,' Galloway said. 'I ran into her again just as she was leaving for work that morning. She was carrying what looked like a weekend bag.'

'And she was expecting to go straight up there after work? She didn't mention going anywhere else first?'

'Not that I recall.'

'You said she seemed upbeat with one exception. What was that?'

'It was probably nothing. I was coming down the stairs to the front door one morning. This was just a few days before she disappeared. I was halfway down the stairs when I heard Kate talking in the hallway below. She'd obviously taken a phone call as she'd been about to leave the building. It sounded pretty intense and I didn't want to interrupt so I hesitated for a few moments on the stairs. I wasn't sure what to do and I was trying not to eavesdrop, but I couldn't help overhearing part of what she was saying. Something about whether there was any other way of handling things and that she was really pissed off that things had got to this point.'

'How did she sound? Emotionally, I mean.'

'Angry, mainly. But also worried, I thought. As if she was in some kind of trouble. I assumed it was some sort of work thing. I didn't know much about her job, except that it was some kind of executive role. To be honest, I was slightly stopped in my tracks because it didn't sound like the Kate I knew. She sounded more serious than she usually was. It was a side of her I hadn't seen. Even the language wasn't typical.'

'Did you hear anything else?'

'Not really. I needed to get off to work so in the end I just gave a loud cough to announce my presence and carried on down the stairs. By the time I reached the hall, she'd ended the call. She just smiled and wished me good morning, and she seemed like her usual self.'

'You told the police about this?'

'Yes. I mean, it wasn't much and it probably didn't mean anything, but they said to tell them anything that might have been significant. To be honest, they didn't seem too interested. I was conscious it didn't amount to much so I didn't push it very hard.'

We chatted for a little longer, but I sensed I wasn't going to get much more from her. She was keen to give me any support she could, and I promised I'd keep her informed of any developments.

It was already dark outside. I walked over to the front door. The rain had been falling sporadically all day and, as I stepped outside, I could taste the dampness in the air. I stood drinking in the taste of the cold night. There was a smell of woodsmoke, and somewhere in the distance I could hear a dog barking. Possibly Ziggy, but more likely one of Gus's farm dogs.

The next day was Thursday, and I was planning to spend part of it getting ready for my supper with Lorna. I had to decide what I wanted to cook and make a trip into Dingwall for the ingredients. I wanted to do this properly, and to make Lorna feel as comfortable and welcome as possible. I still wasn't entirely sure whether this yet constituted a date or just another friendly meal. It didn't matter too much. My plan was to go with the flow and not force the pace.

I couldn't hear the dog barking anymore, and I stood for another few moments enjoying the almost complete silence. The only sound I could hear now was the faint brush of the wind through the undergrowth. From the doorway, I couldn't see the lights from Gus's house, and any lights from further down the hill were lost in a rain-soaked haze. Maybe it was true that this land was less unspoiled than it seemed, but I felt then that I could have been alone at the end of the world. For the moment, after everything that had happened, I wasn't unhappy with that.

CHAPTER EIGHTEEN

I'd been planning to head into Dingwall on Thursday to buy the ingredients for the planned dinner with Lorna, so that I could use Friday to get everything ready. In the event, the morning turned out busier than I'd expected. First, my breakfast of toast and coffee was interrupted by the doorbell. It was only 8.30am, too early for the post delivery up here or for any other visitor I could imagine, so I assumed it must be Gus.

I was half right, as it turned out. It was Gus but accompanied by another older man with a mop of unkempt grey hair. He was dressed in a pair of well-worn grey overalls, and grinned at me as if I might be his new best friend. His manner reminded me slightly of Ziggy.

'Morning, Jack,' Gus said. 'Not that it's much of one.' He was right about that. The previous day had been a changeable mix of rain and sun. Today, the rain seemed set in for the duration. The sky was leaden and it looked as if the heavens might open at any moment. 'I mentioned to you I knew a chap who could help you with your locks.'

The man held out his hand. 'Grant McLeish. At your service.'

'Grant was up seeing me about a couple of joinery jobs so I thought I should introduce you.'

'You'd better come in,' I said.

'I've things to be getting on with,' Gus said. 'First, heading down to the village to see a nephew of mine and his girlfriend. Another couple who've been served a notice of eviction from a cottage now apparently owned by Gregor McBride. There's been a spate of them over the last month just as we bloody predicted, despite all their assurances up front. Not sure I can do much apart from offer moral support and direct them to the Citizens Advice Bureau, but there you go. Then I'm driving over to Dingwall to help with preparing for the protest.'

'Protest?'

'Ach, I forget you never listen to the news. Gregor McBride's over here at the moment, no doubt mainly to help schmooze the politicians. There's some sort of formal launch for The McBride Development, and he's honouring us with a walkabout in Dingwall. He thinks he's going to be surrounded by adoring fans. He's going to get a shock.'

I shook my head. 'He can't really believe he's going to be well-received?'

'The man's deluded. It was the same in Perthshire. He thinks he's coming as the great saviour. His minders surround him with a handful of paid "supporters" and try to keep the locals away.'

'I'm planning a trip to Dingwall myself later. I'll come and join you.'

'The more the merrier. Anyway, I'll leave Grant with you. He can find his own way down to my place once you're finished, can't you, Grant?'

'I should think so, given I've lived in this neck of the woods for over sixty years.'

I waved a goodbye to Gus and led Grant into the cottage. 'Nasty business, this McBride thing.'

'Aye. I don't think people realise quite how big a deal it is. How much he's managed to buy already. It's all been under the radar, buying it up piece by piece, offering prices the current landowners can't afford to turn down. Man's an utter bastard. We haven't seen anything yet, I reckon.'

I led him through into the kitchen. 'Can I get you a coffee?'

'Aye, why not. More than I'll ever get offered by that tight old bugger.' He jerked his thumb in a way that was presumably intended to indicate Gus. I had the impression that he and Gus had been engaging in this kind of exchange for decades.

'So what is it you want doing?' He was smiling cheerfully, as if he couldn't envisage anything more enjoyable than sitting in a stranger's kitchen discussing locksmithery.

I explained about my security concerns, telling him that I was looking at putting stronger locks on the front and back doors, as well as on the windows. Like Gus, his first reaction was amused scepticism. 'You're sure you want to spend your money on this. Nobody's going to break in up here.'

'I'd rather be safe than sorry.'

'Gus tells me you're an ex-copper. I can see how that would make you paranoid.'

'It's partly that. And it's partly that I've spent most of my life living in cities. I'm not used to trusting the neighbours.'

He looked at me pityingly. 'Aye, well. Don't envy you that. Mind you, it's not what it was up here now either. Even Gus has had farm equipment taken. Anyway, let's have a look at these doors.'

He spent the next fifteen minutes checking out the front and back doors, and then examining the windows. 'I can put decent deadlocks on them easily enough. If you really want the security to be as tight as possible, you'd probably want to replace the doors entirely. There's always going to be a vulnerability with what you've got currently. Even with the bolts, someone with a decent crowbar could force their way in. Depends how much you want to spend.'

My gut feeling was to do the job properly. Despite what I'd said to Gus and now to Grant, my main fear wasn't burglary. The chances of an opportunistic housebreaker making their way up here were small. My concern was someone with more professional skills. Even the highest levels of domestic security wouldn't keep out someone who knew what they were doing. But they might buy me a little more time. 'I'm not sure. What would be the difference?'

'I'll need to check out the price of the materials,' he said. 'Obviously, there'll be a bit more labour required if you replace the doors, but I'm not the expensive bit.' He grinned again. 'Let me check out the prices and I can get back to you with the respective quotes. Once you've decided what you want I can probably fit you in towards the back end of next week.'

'That's fine.' It was sooner than I'd expected, and I assumed he was doing this mainly as a favour for Gus. But it's how life seemed to work up here. Something else very different from Glasgow.

I was saying goodbye to Grant when my phone rang. Cameron Fraser. Grant waved farewell and set off down the road, while I took the call.

'Good morning, Jack. How's it all going?' It was the first time he'd called me by my forename. I didn't know if that was a positive sign or not. I couldn't yet quite envisage calling him Cameron, though I'd noticed that everyone else in these parts seemed to.

'It's going,' I said. 'Fairly slowly at the moment. But I'm gradually tracking people down.' I didn't want to sound too pessimistic – not until I'd really decided whether I wanted to continue – but I wanted to manage his expectations. 'I'm building up a picture of her. I've spoken to a number of her friends and her former housemates. There was one interesting titbit.' I told Fraser what Kate's neighbour had said about the overheard telephone conversation. 'They said they'd mentioned it to the police but they didn't know if it was followed up.'

'Interesting. Actually, that's why I was calling. I said I'd try to find you a more senior police contact who might give you some insights into the investigation. I had to tread a little warily. There's some sensitivity about the failure of the investigation.'

I imagined that all the senior officers would have had their backsides well and truly covered, but I wasn't about to say that to Fraser. 'I can understand that.'

'I spoke to a couple of people I could trust to be discreet. They put me in contact with a Detective Chief Inspector Morag Henderson. She's part of the major investigation team based out of Inverness.'

'I vaguely remember the name,' I said. 'I don't think I ever met her. She had a decent reputation.'

'I'm told she's happy to talk to you off the record. She wasn't directly involved in the original enquiry which was largely run from Glasgow, but she was called on at various points for her local knowledge. She has some concerns about aspects of the investigation which she's tried to raise informally without much success. I don't know how much she'll be prepared to say, but she should give you some insights.'

Fraser gave me a contact number which I scribbled down in my notebook. 'It'll be interesting to hear what she has to tell me.'

'I hope it'll prove useful. Good luck, Jack.'

The line was dead even before I could say goodbye. I decided there was no point in wasting time and dialled the number Fraser had given me. It was answered by a gruff voice. 'Henderson.'

I gave my name and explained why I was calling. 'I was told you'd be expecting a call from me.'

'Aye, I was.' The accent was relatively strong and local. 'Look, Mr Mellor, I want to be completely straight with you. I'm not entirely comfortable with this.'

'In your shoes I wouldn't be either.'

'I understand you're ex-job yourself.'

'Glasgow-based.'

'Big city boy.'

'Not anymore.'

'I remember. Danny Royce.'

Yet again, my reputation seemed to have preceded me. 'That was part of it. It's a long story.'

'And a twisty one. As long as I'm not talking to a bent cop.'

'You don't need to worry about that.'

'Probably against my better judgement, I'm willing to talk to you. You come with good references and I'm told I can trust you. For the avoidance of doubt, I wouldn't want to be in your shoes if that proves not to be true.'

'You can trust me.'

'It would be better for us to meet face to face. I don't trust phones. Even this call's making me nervous.'

'Just tell me where and when.'

'How about Monday evening?' She named a bar in the centre of Inverness. It wasn't somewhere I'd visited, though I'd noticed the place on one of my infrequent trips into the city. 'It's not somewhere the cops frequent, and it's generally quiet early on a weekday evening. We should be able to talk discreetly.'

'Fine by me.'

'Six thirty okay for you?'

'Perfect. I look forward to it.'

'I'll be interested to meet you, Mr Mellor.' Which wasn't quite the same thing as looking forward to it, I noted.

It was already nearly eleven, and I still needed to head into Dingwall to buy the provisions for the evening. I was feeling desperately unprepared for the supper with Lorna. Any half-decent host would have drawn up the menu, proper recipes, a full list of ingredients as a shopping list. All I had was a few vague ideas based on a perusal of various online recipes the previous evening, and a hope that the retailers of Dingwall would fill in the gaps.

Expressed in those terms, it felt very much the story of my life. I'd never really been one for planning. I preferred to take what life threw at me. Which was why I was here in the first place, and perhaps why I'd almost got myself killed back in Glasgow. Maybe it was time I started learning some lessons.

CHAPTER NINETEEN

In the end, my shopping expedition in Dingwall came together moderately successfully. The butcher had watched me in amusement as I gazed uncertainly at the array of meats before eventually taking pity and asking me what I was looking for.

'I'm cooking supper for someone. I'm keen not to mess it up.'

'Ah, like that, is it? So something foolproof?'

'Ideally. I don't want to be worrying about the timing.'

'Some sort of casserole? Or a curry?'

Lorna had cooked a venison casserole so I wanted to do something different. She had said she was happy with spicy foods, but it would be better to leave that until I had a better understanding of her tastes. 'Curry might be risky,' I said.

'What about a slow-cooked piece of meat? Lamb leg or shoulder, maybe. Stuff it with garlic, rosemary and thyme. Wrap in foil. Stick in on a low temperature. Long as you allow enough time, you can't go wrong. Serve it with a Greek salad and some lemon roast potatoes. Lovely. You can pretend you're on a Greek island rather than stuck up here in a bleak January.'

I bought the meat and the herbs there, along with a selection of local cheeses and some Orkney smoked salmon which would make a simple starter. I stowed those in the car, then headed to the supermarket for the rest of the ingredients. The only outstanding item was the dessert. I'm no baker and, despite the midwinter weather, I thought it would be better to prepare something light. Cranachan was out, again because that was what Lorna had prepared, and I couldn't immediately think of any other Scottish desserts that fitted the bill. In the end, I found some strawberries and some ready-made meringue to make a cheat's Eton mess. I didn't expect Lorna would mind that I wasn't cooking everything from scratch.

I was walking back across the supermarket car park when I heard the sound of shouting in the distance, a raucous set of voices chanting some kind of slogan. I presumed this was the protest against Gregor McBride. I dumped my shopping in the back of the car and hurried over the road towards the high street.

The small crowd was gathered at the far end of the street. From where I was standing, I could just see a line of people carrying banners. I hurried towards them, curious to get a glimpse of the infamous Gregor McBride. The chanting was growing louder, and somewhere I could hear a piper playing 'Scotland the Brave'. The crowd seemed to be largely good-natured but the contempt for McBride was more than evident in the wording of their posters.

I joined the back of the crowd and peered over the shoulders of the people in front of me. They were a mixed bunch. There were a few teenagers no doubt taking an opportunity to bunk off school, but most were older, some very much so. It didn't look like a crowd that could be dismissed simply as lefty troublemakers.

Finally, as I moved forward into the crowd, I spotted McBride himself. He was standing with his back to one of the shopfronts, his large ungainly frame unmistakeable. Next to him was a tall, imposing-looking elderly man I took to be Archie Kinnear. The two men were surrounded by a circle of muscular young men presumably acting as bodyguards.

I'd wondered whether McBride might have been intimidated by the protestors, but he simply appeared baffled, as if he couldn't understand what he'd done to provoke this kind of response. For his part, Kinnear – if that's who it was – looked furious, with the air of a man whose party had been crashed by a bunch of unruly interlopers. I wondered what other reaction he might have expected, but I suspected it didn't even occur to the likes of McBride or Kinnear to consider the impact of their actions on people like these.

So far, the protest had remained peaceful but, as I eased my way through the crowd, one of the teenagers threw something at McBride. It look me a moment to realise that it was nothing more harmful than an egg. It broke on McBride's coat, and he stared down at the mess in bemusement while the crowd cheered. Kinnear angrily gestured for one of the bodyguards to seize the young man responsible.

Almost immediately, a scuffle broke out as some of the protestors intervened to protect the teenager. McBride and Kinnear had moved back from the melee, and two of the bodyguards were dragging the teenager out of the crowd. An older man tried to intervene, thrusting himself in front of the bodyguards to allow the young man to slip back among his mates. It was only then that I realised that the man was Gus.

Deprived of their initial target, the two bodyguards turned their attention to Gus himself, pulling him out of the crowd into one of the side streets. I'd expected other members of the crowd to defend him but most seemed too shocked. These were people who'd come along to participate in a peaceful protest, not to involve themselves in a fight.

I forced my way through the crowd, incurring a few grumbled complaints, until I reached the corner of the side street. The two bodyguards had dragged Gus down the road and pushed him back against a wall. Gus was clearly doing his best to square up to them and look unintimidated. I knew from watching him about the farm that he had a wiry strength that shouldn't be underestimated, but he was anything but a violent man. I sensed that probably wasn't true of the two men facing him.

'Leave him alone.' I walked towards Gus and the two men.

'Fuck off, pal. This isn't your business.' It was a Glasgow accent, a would-be hard man.

'Leave him alone.'

'Or what, pal? What the fuck are you going to do about it?'

'I'll make you leave him alone.'

The man laughed. 'You and whose fucking army, pal?' Then he stopped and peered at me. 'I know you.'

It took me a moment to place him. Former PC Kenny Taylor. I'd come across him a few times during my early days in the force. I didn't know the details but I'd heard he'd been booted out following sexual harassment allegations. That hadn't surprised me. I'd disliked him from the start. He'd struck me as one of those who'd joined the police only as some kind of power trip. 'Afternoon, Kenny. This what you're reduced to, is it? Hired muscle for Archie Kinnear.'

'Jack Mellor,' he said. 'Mr Goody-Two-Shoes. I bet I earn more in a week than you do in a month.' He paused. 'Except I heard you'd left the force. Couldn't hack it, eh?'

'Least I wasn't booted out.' I wondered how he'd heard about me quitting. I couldn't imagine that Taylor would have much interest in the likes of me.

'That right, pal? Maybe only because you got out just in time. I heard you fucked up. No wonder you came skulking up here with your tail between your legs.' He seemed to have lost interest in Gus. The other bodyguard was just watching our exchange. I imagined they'd both get more satisfaction from beating me up rather than Gus.

Taylor walked slowly towards me until he was standing inches from me. He jabbed his finger into my chest. 'We know all about you, pal. We know what you're up to. We'll be keeping an eye on you.'

I'd assumed he was going to take a swing at me, and I braced myself accordingly. I probably wouldn't stand much chance against the two of them, but there wasn't anything I could do about that. If need be, I'd try to get myself back on to the main street, hope that the crowd would prevent me from taking a real beating. It wasn't much of a strategy but I couldn't immediately think of anything better.

Taylor pushed me hard back against the wall then smiled. 'You know what, Mellor? You're a lucky bastard. Me and my friend here aren't going to kick the living shite out of you. Not until we're ready, at least. But now we know the rumours are true, we'll be watching you fucking closely. If I were you, pal, I'd start getting my affairs in order. While you've still got time. Now fuck off and take your friend here with you.' He slammed me back once more against the wall, then, gesturing for the other man to follow, he made his way back towards the main road.

'You okay?' I asked Gus.

'I'm fine. Thanks to you. But I thought they were going to beat the hell out of you.'

'So did I.' I was still staring down the street after Taylor and the other man.

'So why didn't they?'

'I don't know.' I took a breath. My heart was still pounding. 'I've no idea what any of that was about.'

'Lucky escape, whatever the reasons.'

'Maybe.' I could feel my sense of unease growing. I didn't know why someone like Taylor would have any interest in me, but the reasons weren't likely to be good. 'Or maybe it was the exact opposite.'

CHAPTER TWENTY

I woke up the following morning still feeling uneasy about my unexpected encounter with Kenny Taylor. I wasn't entirely sure why I'd found it so disturbing. It was partly that Taylor hadn't seemed surprised to see me there – it felt as if my presence had simply confirmed something he'd already known. It was also partly that he'd known so much about my leaving the force. But it was also the stuff about knowing what I was up to and keeping an eye on me. No doubt that was just Taylor trying to sound intimidating, but it had felt as if there was something more behind it.

I tried to put thoughts of Kenny Taylor behind me and focus on the day ahead. At least on that front, I was feeling more relaxed. I had a plan for dinner that I was more or less capable of pulling off, and I felt more able to look forward to the evening. I'd bought more wine and another bottle of single malt, so if all else failed we'd be able to get enjoyably tipsy together.

By my own standards, I was feeling remarkably organised. I prepared the lamb and stuck it in the oven at a suitable low temperature. I parboiled the potatoes then tossed them in thyme, lemon and olive oil. My plan was to leave them in the fridge until I was ready to start roasting them. I prepared the elements for the Greek salad, again leaving them in the fridge until I was ready to assemble them later. Finally, I did the same with the strawberries, ready for the Eton mess.

I'd finished all that by mid-afternoon, and I was feeling unusually smug. It was still light outside, and I took the opportunity for another breath of air before the sun disappeared. I'd hoped Lorna might bring Ziggy up here during the afternoon but there'd been no sign of them.

I walked a short distance up the hill, enjoying the cool of the winter's afternoon after the heat of the kitchen. The day was clear and still, almost eerily silent, and the landscape was at its most spectacular, the peaks and valleys highlighted starkly by the low-lying sun. Below me, lights were coming on in the houses across the valley. From here, I could see Lorna's cottage. No lights were showing as yet, but there was smoke rising from the chimney.

After a few minutes, I turned back down towards the cottage. As I reached it, I heard a dog barking somewhere in the distance. This time, I thought it perhaps was Ziggy. It sounded too far away for one of Gus's dogs and it was yapping in the frenzied way I associated with the Labrador.

I spent the rest of the afternoon finishing off the preparations for the evening, periodically checking my emails to see if I'd had any further responses from my list of Kate Brodie's contacts. The only new email I'd received was from one of the friends present at the Cromarty weekend, saying that they didn't think they'd have anything useful to tell me and that they'd prefer not to be involved. Fair enough. There wasn't much I could do about that.

By 6.30, I had everything ready to go. The kitchen was filled with the scent of roasting herby lamb, the potatoes were cooking, the Eton mess was prepared and sitting in the fridge alongside the Greek salad and smoked salmon. I'd laid the table and tidied up the cottage so it looked moderately presentable.

I'd told Lorna I'd walk down to her house and accompany her back up here. She'd told me this wasn't necessary. It was no distance, and she was accustomed to walking around the area in the dark. In any case, she was intending to bring Ziggy up with her. Even so, I'd insisted on meeting her, partly because I wasn't entirely comfortable with her walking up here in the darkness – I wasn't entirely convinced by Ziggy's efficacy as a guard dog – but mainly because I wanted to spend as much time as possible in her company.

It was much easier going on the track down than it had been the previous Saturday. The path was dry, and I could keep my flashlight trained on the ground without having constantly to duck my head against the rain.

It was only when I turned off the track on to the road that I was able to see Lorna's cottage. To my slight surprise, no lights were showing. I assumed that Lorna must be in the kitchen at the rear. But as I drew closer I became less confident. From my recollection of the layout of the cottage, I couldn't believe no light at all would be visible.

For the first time, I felt uneasy. The sudden sound of Ziggy barking furiously provided some reassurance, but even that didn't feel quite right. He sounded even more frantic than usual and louder than I would have expected if he'd been in the house.

I walked up the short path and pressed the doorbell. I heard it ring inside, but there was no other sound other than Ziggy's incessant yapping. I pressed the bell again, holding it for longer this time, although I already sensed it wasn't going to be answered.

I walked around the cottage and opened the gate to the rear garden. Ziggy hurled himself at me, barking angrily. He calmed a little when he realised it was me and I bent to stroke him, but he continued barking frantically.

There were no lights at the rear of the house, and the back door was standing open. Ziggy bounded along beside me, still barking, but as I reached the cottage door, he drew back, cowering behind me. I shone my torch on the door. The lock was broken, as if the door had been prised open.

I peered through the doorway and cautiously shone my torch inside. At first I couldn't see anything. Then my torch beam fell on a shape in the far doorway, partially concealed from me by the kitchen table.

Lorna was curled up on the floor, as if trying to protect herself from some attacker. There was a dark pool beneath her which I took to be blood. Her face was turned away from me, her body twisted at an awkward angle.

In the darkness behind me, Ziggy began to howl.

CHAPTER TWENTY-ONE

'Are you sure you feel up to this, sir? We need a statement from you, but it can wait if you're not in a state to provide it.'

The voice was gentle, calming, sympathetic. Even so, I knew I had no reason to trust the speaker. I'd be considered a suspect, and they were unlikely to have anyone else on their list as yet.

'No, that's fine. I'm – well, I'm not okay, but I've no problem in providing a statement. Probably best to do it while it's fresh in my mind.'

'If you're sure, sir.'

'I'm sure.' I looked up at him. Detective Sergeant David McBain. The uniforms had turned up first at Lorna's cottage, and one of them had escorted me back up here. The air in here had still been rich with the scent of the roasting lamb. I'd turned off the oven, knowing now that the food was destined only for the bin, with a few titbits left over for Ziggy. I'd brought the dog back up here, and he was now lying in front of the wood-stove. I wondered how much he understood what had happened. Maybe more than I did.

DS McBain had turned up half an hour or so later. I assumed by now Lorna's cottage would have been sealed off and the examiners would be crawling all over it. It was the kind of scene I'd been involved in several times over the years, but not one I'd expected to be involved in again.

'Let's start with your full name, shall we?' McBain said.

'Jack Graham Mellor,' I said.

'Thank you, Mr Mellor. And this is where you live?'

'I rent it. From Gus who owns the farm down the hill.' I gave him the full address of the cottage.

'You're not local, I assume?'

'I moved up from Glasgow a few months back.'

'Quite a change. What brought you up to these parts? Work?' He was dutifully taking notes as we spoke, I knew that for the moment he was softening me up, relaxing me before he moved on to the more probing questions. It was another part of the process I was all too familiar with.

'In a manner of speaking. I'd left my previous job, and was deciding what to do next. I wanted to get away.'

He looked up at me, and I could see the spark of interest in his eyes. 'We've all dreamed of doing that, I guess. What was your previous line of work?'

There was no point in holding it back. 'The same as yours, funnily enough.'

He raised an eyebrow. 'Really?'

'Very similar. I was a DS. Mainly doing specialist surveillance work by the time I left, but I've been in your shoes, working cases like this.'

'Small world. What made you jack it in?' He asked the question casually, but I didn't doubt he'd be checking on anything I told him.

'It's a long story.' I gave him a condensed version of the Danny Royce incident.

I wasn't sure if he'd register the significance of the story immediately or not, but DS McBain was clearly not someone to underestimate. 'Sean Critchley? That would be the same Sean Critchley—?'

'Recently found murdered up here. So I understand. I only know what I saw in the media and what I've picked up on the grapevine.'

'Quite the coincidence, though.'

'I suppose so. But I've had no contact with Critchley since that night in Royce's garden. I was grateful to him for saving my life, obviously. But I hardly knew him otherwise.'

'He didn't contact you when he came up here?'

'No.' It was the first lie I'd told, and I don't know what instinct made me tell it. It was partly because I didn't want the investigation into Lorna's death to become deflected. There was no link between Lorna and Sean Critchley, except tangentially through me, and no reason why Critchley's killer should then have targeted her.

It wasn't clear if McBain believed me, and he'd no doubt be checking out my phone records in due course if I remained a suspect in Lorna's killing. 'Okay. So tell me how you came to know Ms Jardine?'

'We met at a Hogmanay party hosted by Gus. We were probably the youngest people there, and we got chatting. We got on well, and then I ran into her a couple of times when she was up here walking Ziggy.'

'Ziggy? Oh, the dog.'

'The dog,' I agreed.

'And she was coming for supper here?'

'That was the plan, yes.'

'This isn't an easy question in the circumstances, but I have to ask it. Was your relationship with Ms Jardine a romantic one?' The emphasis he placed on "romantic" made it clear he intended it as a euphemism.

'It wasn't a sexual relationship, if that's what you mean. I don't know whether it might have developed into something more but for now we were just friends. I went for a meal at her house last Saturday. She was due to come up here today. We'd had the occasional coffee when she'd came up here with Ziggy. Our relationship was nothing more than that.'

'I understand. I appreciate this must be very difficult for you.'

'It's been a huge shock.' I looked up at him. 'I don't even know how she died. I saw the body and the blood but I also knew not to compromise the scene. So once I'd checked she was really dead, I called you from outside.'

'We're still confirming the cause of death. I can't say any more at present. But let's go back to this evening. You were having supper here, but you went down to her cottage. Why was that?'

'She wanted to walk up to give Ziggy some exercise. I didn't like the idea of her coming up here by herself in the dark. She'd told me not to worry, but I wanted to make sure she was okay.' I gave a mirthless laugh. 'Ironic, isn't it?'

'Did you have any reason to be worried about her?'

'Only the usual concerns about a woman walking alone in the dark.'

'Even somewhere as remote as this?'

'I've spent my whole life living in cities. I behave as if I still do.'

'But you'd no particular reason to believe Ms Jardine was at any risk.'

'None at all. I can't imagine why this might have happened.'

'Talk me through your movements this evening. You walked down to meet her?'

'She was due to be here around seven, so I walked down there about six thirty. It's roughly a ten-minute walk each way. I had a torch with me as there's no lighting on the track down to the road. You can't see Lorna's cottage on the way down, so it was only when I turned onto the main road that I realised something wasn't right.'

'Which was?'

'There were no lights showing. I rang the doorbell a couple of times and then went to the back of the house. Ziggy came bounding out and jumped on me. Then I saw that the rear door had been forced open. I had a bad feeling about the whole thing, so I shone the torch in the doorway and I saw her.'

'And you went in?'

'Just briefly to check there were no signs of life. I tried not to touch anything. Then I went back outside, dialled 999 and waited till the response car turned up. That's all I can tell you.' I paused, thinking. 'No, there is one other thing. Earlier in the afternoon, I'd been for a short walk up the hill from here. It wasn't dark but the sun was low, and I could see some lights beginning to come on in the valley. You can see Lorna's cottage from up there and there were no lights showing then. That didn't surprise me, but what struck me was that I heard Ziggy barking frantically. I'm pretty sure it was him. It's a different bark from any of Gus's farm dogs and sounded more distant. He's an excitable old thing so I didn't think too much of it, but it was definitely noisier than usual.'

'What time would this have been?'

'I didn't notice exactly. Around two thirty? Something like that.'

He wrote the time in his notebook. 'Okay, we'll see how that ties in with what the pathologist thinks about time of death. Is there anything else you can tell me? Anything else you noticed at the scene?'

'I don't think so. I'm not sure I was really thinking straight.'

'Of course. Let's go back to Ms Jardine herself. You said you'd no reason to think she might be at risk. Can you think of any reason why anyone might want to harm her?'

'Not remotely. She was a small-town accountant, that's all. I can't imagine her being the type to make enemies. Isn't it more likely that this was some break-in that went horribly wrong?'

'I'm keeping an open mind on that at the moment. We don't get much of this kind of crime up here.' I could tell what he was thinking. Two brutal murders within a week, and I had connections with both of them. I'd have been thinking the same in his shoes. Police officers don't have much time for coincidences.

'I think that'll do for the moment,' he went on. 'I'm sorry to have had to put you through this. It must be an ordeal.' McBain pushed himself to his feet. I'd remained seated so he loomed over me. 'Thank you for your time, Mr Mellor. You're sure you're okay to be left on your own?'

'I think I need some time to myself. Just to take it all in.'

'In that case, I'll leave you to your thoughts. I can find my own way out. I take it you'll be around here for the next few days.' It wasn't a question.

'I wasn't planning to go anywhere.'

'We'll probably want to talk to you again.'

'I'll be here.'

'Thank you.'

I waited until I'd heard the front door close behind him, then followed him into the hall. I slid closed the two bolts on the front door, and then went through to check on the back door. I'd no idea who had killed Lorna or why, but I couldn't ignore the fact that there was a killer out there. Grant McLeish might well be right that these doors wouldn't keep out anyone who really wanted to get in – the damage to Lorna's door had demonstrated that – but it was the best I could do. For the same reason, I should let Gus know what had happened, assuming he hadn't received a visit from the police already.

I dug out my phone and dialled Gus's number. The call was answered almost immediately. 'Jack. My God, I've just heard. I was about to phone you.'

'I found her, Gus. I found her body. I found her dead.'

'Christ, I hadn't realised. I knew you two...' He stopped, clearly unsure how to finish the sentence.

'She was supposed to be coming up here for supper. I went down to meet her. The back door had been forced and she was there on the floor...'

'Look, Jack, do you want me to come up? Or you can stay here tonight if you like. You shouldn't be trying to deal with this on your own.'

'Thanks, Gus. I really appreciate it, but I think I need some time to myself. I'm trying to take it in.'

'Aye, of course. Okay if I pop up tomorrow?'

'I'll probably welcome it by then. Thanks.'

'I'm here if you need anything. Don't forget.'

The bottle of single malt was sitting on the kitchen table. I'd bought it to share with Lorna, and it seemed only right to pour a dram in tribute to her. I didn't want to end up losing myself in the bottle, but I needed something to kick-start my feelings, to dissipate the sense of numbness that had overwhelmed me since I'd discovered Lorna's body.

I poured a measure of whisky and returned to the living room. I'd thrown away the food I'd prepared, unable to face it, keeping only a few pieces of meat as a treat for Ziggy, who was sleeping calmly by the now cooling wood-stove. Even so, the smell of the roast lamb hung in the air, the ghost of the meal we'd never enjoyed.

Thinking about Ziggy made me realise how little I'd known

about Lorna. I'd only met her a couple of weeks ago. I didn't know if she had any surviving close family or other next of kin. I'd assumed she was intending to tell me some of that this evening, and I wondered now what it was she'd held back from saying the previous week.

I raised the glass to take a sip, and then stopped. It was the scent of the spirit, I thought. It was the same whisky we'd drunk after that previous supper, and somehow that seemed more evocative than anything else I'd experienced that evening. It was as if that aroma had finally brought it home to me. I'd expected that my reaction would be to sob uncontrollably, releasing all the emotion that had been building through the evening. But instead I simply felt nauseous, as if my stomach was full of bile.

I rose hurriedly and made my way to the front door, feeling as if I was actually about to throw up. I pulled back the bolts and opened the door, drinking in the cold night air. It was another few minutes before my stomach felt settled enough for me to sip the whisky. At the bottom of the track, I could see the silhouette of Lorna's cottage. Lights were burning in all the windows now, and I assumed the police examiners were still working. For a moment, the sense of nausea returned.

I took another sip of the Scotch, trying to calm my nerves and my stomach. It was beginning to hit me now, the sense of loss, the knowledge that my life, my world, my future were all diminished, and that nothing would ever put this right. I didn't even know that I'd ever had a future with Lorna. I only knew I didn't have one now.

With that knowledge came something else. The realisation that someone had done this, some person had committed this act. Until now I'd been too dazed to consider the implications of that. Someone had killed Lorna. Someone had forced their way into her house and killed her in cold blood. It didn't really matter whether it was some petty housebreaker or someone with an unfathomable grudge against Lorna. They'd taken her life.

I realised that the emotion I was feeling more than anything else – more than any sense of loss or bereavement – was anger. More than anger. Fury.

Fury at the bastard who'd done this.

CHAPTER TWENTY-TWO

I hadn't known how I'd get through that night, but somehow I managed it. I'd sat up for a while longer, working my way through a couple more drams of whisky. I'd felt tempted to finish the bottle, but I'd been clear-headed enough to recognise that would be a bad idea. In the end, I'd forced myself to go to bed. I'd tossed and turned for an hour or so, before finally falling into a fitful sleep. I remember vivid, oddly unnerving dreams. The details had melted away by morning, but the looming figure of Gregor McBride was in there somewhere, a threatening presence lurking on the edge of my consciousness. When I woke fully, it was still dark outside, but I dragged on some clothes and made my way downstairs.

It was later than I'd expected, nearly 8am. At this time, it wouldn't be fully daylight until after 9. I hadn't minded the short winter days previously, but now the darkness felt oppressive. Perhaps that was a message for me. Maybe, after what had happened, I should leave this behind, head back south.

Except I already knew I wasn't going to do that. Not yet anyway. In the course of my disturbed night, my resolution had hardened. I was going to find whoever was responsible for Lorna's death. Even putting aside my own emotions, I was conscious that DS McBain already had me firmly in the frame for Lorna's killing. He might not be able to cobble together enough evidence to charge me, but he'd have a good try before he turned his attention elsewhere.

That raised other questions. I'd been due to meet with Morag Henderson on Monday evening. She surely wouldn't speak to me as long as I remained a suspect in a murder enquiry. I wasn't even sure Cameron Fraser would want to continue employing me.

I made a coffee and carried it through to the living room. Ziggy had still been sleeping beside the wood-stove but as I entered the room he came across to me. He'd always seemed much calmer in here than outside, but this morning it was as if he'd been tranquillised. He nuzzled against me, rubbing his head against my leg, whining quietly. The previous evening I'd wondered how much he understood what had happened. Now, it was clear to me that he at least knew that something bad and life-changing had taken place.

I wondered what would happen to Ziggy. I'd be more than happy to keep him and I'd certainly look after him for as long as needed. But I supposed his eventual fate would depend on whether there was a next of kin and, if so, whether they were interested in taking Ziggy. I assumed I'd find out in due course.

Although the sun hadn't yet risen, it was growing lighter outside. I pulled on my heavy waterproof and led Ziggy out into the chilly morning. It looked as if it was set for another fine, clear day, the sky reddening to the south-east.

I wasn't accustomed to dealing with dogs, and I released Ziggy's lead with some trepidation, expecting him to go tearing down the hill towards Lorna's cottage. He seemed utterly subdued though, and trotted along beside me as I trudged uphill. I knew how he felt. I couldn't believe I'd never see Lorna again. That felt unreal, as if I was trapped in a nightmare and couldn't wake up.

Ziggy and I had reached the top of the hill. Up here, he regained a little of his former enthusiasm, and he bounded about me with some energy. Even so, I noticed he was reluctant to go more than a couple of yards from me.

From here, Lorna's cottage was fully visible. There were no lights showing, so either the examiners had finished their work last night or they were intending to resume it later. I knew from my own experiences how thorough they'd be in a case like this. If there was useful forensic evidence to be found, they'd find it.

I'd hoped that coming out here would help my state of mind, that the combination of the spectacular views and cold, clean air would provide some relief from the claustrophobia I'd been feeling in the cottage. But the sight of Lorna's house had simply intensified my sense of loss. I clipped Ziggy's lead back on and made my way back down the track.

I'd nearly reached the cottage when I saw the headlights of Gus's truck heading up the track towards me. By the time Ziggy and I had arrived at the door he was standing waiting. 'I wasn't going to bother you till later,' he said. 'But I saw you walking out with the dog so I thought I might as well see how you were.'

'Thanks, Gus. Come in and I'll make you a coffee. You've probably been up for hours.'

'I'm not one to sleep in. Especially not today. It's left me completely stunned. That poor wee lass.'

I busied myself filling the kettle and getting mugs out from the cupboard, conscious I wanted to keep moving, avoid Gus's eye. I had a feeling that if I allowed myself to stop the emotion would finally overwhelm me. It wasn't just the loss of Lorna – though obviously that lay at the heart of it – but also how much friendship, kindness and support Gus and others had shown me since I'd moved up here. I'd finally felt part of a community. Even beyond my own feelings for Lorna, this felt like a wider tragedy.

Gus shook his head. 'Who'd do something like that to a defenceless young woman like Lorna?'

'The one thing I learned for sure in the police is that there are some nasty bastards out there. But I can't imagine why anyone would have wanted to target her.'

'I'm not going to pretend everything's sweetness and light up here. There's more than enough petty crime, drugs, that kind of stuff. But we don't get this kind of crime. What did the police say to you?'

'Not much really. The DS wasn't giving much away. Just wanted me to recount exactly what had happened yesterday, how I'd found her, all that. But no detail. Not even how she died. I don't know anything except that she was lying in a pool of blood.'

'You didn't try to find out what had happened?'

'I went in long enough to be sure she wasn't still breathing, though I was already certain she couldn't be. Once I'd checked, I got out as quickly as possible. I didn't want to compromise the scene any more than I already had. And, frankly, I didn't want to stay in there.'

'Aye, I can understand that. Word I'm hearing is that she was shot.'

'Shot?' I didn't ask Gus how he'd come to hear this. I knew how the grapevine worked in these parts. Even between last night and this morning, Gus would have picked up on any gossip going. Probably indirectly from one of the uniformed officers who'd been at the scene.

Gus shrugged. 'Maybe bollocks. But it's what I've heard.'

'Burglars don't carry guns,' I said. 'Not the kind of burglars who break into Highland cottages anyway. If she really was shot, that suggests something more than petty theft.'

'I'm only telling you what I've heard. But, aye, I take your point.'

'The police asked me if I knew of any reason why anyone would want to harm Lorna. I told them I couldn't think of any. On the contrary. But I don't know much about her past.'

'She was a sweet lass. Not the sort given to making enemies, I'd have said.' His words sounded almost like a rebuke.

'You told me she'd had her share of problems.'

'Aye, I said that, didn't I? And I said she'd tell you about them if she wanted to.'

'She's not going to tell me now.'

He considered that. 'I feel uncomfortable about this. It was something she once said to me in confidence. She wanted someone to talk to about it, and she knew she could trust me. But I always thought it was up to her who else she shared it with. I probably said too much to you as it was.'

'If it helps,' I said, 'she'd told me she was planning to talk to me about some parts of her past last night. It was obviously something she felt uneasy talking about. She said she hadn't wanted to mention it during our first supper together because she didn't want to risk spoiling the evening.'

'I can see that. If things looked like they might have been getting serious between the two of you, she wouldn't have wanted to put that at risk. But she would have wanted you to know.'

'You can't leave that hanging, Gus. I think I deserve to know whatever she was going to tell me.'

'Aye. You do. But none of this is a reflection on Lorna. She was just a – what's the term they use nowadays? – a survivor. Sadly, I'm not even sure it's a particularly unusual tale. I only know the bare outline. Lorna didn't want to go into the details. I guess she found it all too painful.' He stopped for a moment, seemingly lost in thought, then looked up at me. 'How did Lorna strike you? As a personality, I mean.'

The question had taken me by surprise, and I had no ready answer. 'I don't know. Self-assured, I guess. Self-confident.'

'That's how I'd have seen her, but I wonder if it wasn't a bit of an act.'

'How do you mean?'

'I think it was – I don't know, a kind of mask to cover what she was really feeling. I sometimes felt I never saw the real Lorna.'

'Most of us are faking it most of the time.'

'That's true enough. It's not my place to judge. I have a sense Lorna was more vulnerable, more fragile than she seemed.'

I wondered for a moment if Gus was building up to a suggestion that Lorna might have taken her own life. But there'd been no hint of that from DS McBain, and it certainly hadn't been an idea that had occurred to me when I'd found her body.

Gus shook his head. 'Christ, I'm telling this really badly, aren't I? The point is that I'm not sure that what I'm telling you is the full story. I suspect there were other things that Lorna didn't tell me. What she did tell me went back to her first job after university. She was a trainee accountant in Glasgow. She reckoned she was very naive, quite shy and reserved, wanted to keep her head down and do a good job. She had an aptitude for the work and she enjoyed it. She was focused on getting qualified and building a career for herself.'

'So what happened?'

'A client happened. A very senior, very wealthy client. He took a shine to Lorna. Wanted to treat her as a kind of protégé. Said that once she qualified he'd offer her a job in one of his businesses. Pestered her repeatedly. Kept asking to take her out for dinner.'

'I'm assuming she didn't fall for that.'

'She was naive, but she wasn't stupid. This guy was apparently forty or more years older than her. Still good-looking and imposing, she said, but she knew the score. Unfortunately, her employer didn't.'

'Usual story, then.'

'Exactly. Important client. Didn't want to risk losing his business. A couple of the partners told Lorna there'd be no harm in humouring the old man. She should go for lunch with him, at least. Lorna felt she had no choice. So she agreed to go for lunch with him at some fancy place. The lunch was as boring and grisly as she'd expected, but there was no hint of the kind of try-on she'd feared. She went back to the office feeling relieved, assuming that would be the end of it. Of course, it wasn't.'

'Why am I not surprised?'

'The client started pestering her about going out for dinner, and yet again the partners backed him up. Lorna tried to dig her heels in and say no, but this time it became nastier. They implied that if she was going to be difficult about it, there wouldn't be a job for her.'

'Jesus.'

'Aye. So in the end she agreed to it. At that point, her main concern was that she had to spend a boring evening with a man she didn't like. She hadn't thought there was any personal risk, particularly as he'd shown no signs of inappropriate behaviour at the lunch. To Lorna's embarrassment, the client insisted on sending a car to collect her from her shared flat. She assumed the car would take her directly to the restaurant, but instead she was driven to some upmarket apartment. He had a house out in the Borders somewhere, but this was a bolt-hole he used in the city. All Lorna's instincts were telling her to get the hell out of there, but she couldn't see any way to do it. The client took her into a very smart living room, complete with cocktail cabinet. Said they could have a relaxed drink before proceeding to the restaurant.' Gus was watching my expression. 'You're ahead of me, aren't you? Aye, well, Lorna felt trapped. She sat down and accepted a drink. Her plan was to have one and then insist they went on to eat. But the drink had been spiked. She must have been unconscious for several hours. When she woke, feeling awful, she was lying, apparently still fully clothed, on a bed somewhere in the flat.' Gus stopped, as if having to force himself to continue. 'She didn't have any doubt she'd been raped.'

'What did she do?'

'After a few minutes the client came into the room, seemingly solicitous, asking how she was. He comes up with some tale about how she fainted and he and one of his staff had brought her in here to recover. She knew he was talking shite but was too scared to challenge him. She wanted to go home. He insisted on getting his driver to take her.'

'So what happened after that?'

'Nothing. That's almost the worst part. Lorna considered going to the police, but was scared they wouldn't believe her, particularly given the client's wealth and influence. She knew she'd get no support from within her own company. In the end, she jacked in the job and found herself another traineeship here in Inverness.'

'So the bastard got away with it?'

'Aye. Makes you sick, doesn't it?'

'Do you know who the client was?'

'She wouldn't say. I don't know if she was still scared of him. I suspect she was mainly afraid I'd go round and beat the bastard to a pulp. Or, more likely, get myself beaten to a pulp by his security.'

'She might have been right.'

'Aye, well, I'd have been sorely tempted if I'd thought it would do any good. But Lorna wanted to put it behind her.' He paused, as if considering how best to frame what he said next. 'It left her badly affected. From what she said, she hadn't felt able to enter into any relationship since then. It's one reason why she'd hidden herself away in this remote corner of the world.'

'Are the police aware of this?'

'I can't imagine so. As I said, she didn't approach them at the time, rightly or wrongly. As far as I'm aware, she'd never told anyone other than me. Do you think they ought to know? I'm uncomfortable about betraying her confidence.'

'It's what you said about her still being scared of this guy. It strikes me as an avenue the police ought to be at least exploring.'

'But this all happened years ago. Why should anyone take action now?'

'I've no idea. But can you think of anyone else who might have reason to harm Lorna?'

'Not remotely. She was the last person to make enemies, I'd have thought.'

'So this is the only person we're aware of who might have a motivation for silencing her. It's a very long shot and they might decide not to pursue it, but we ought at least to tell them.'

Gus was silent for a long time. Finally, he said, 'I suppose you're right. Should I approach them?'

'My guess is they'll want to interview you anyway. There aren't many other potential witnesses in this neck of the woods. Look, Gus, in other circumstances, I'd be prepared to tell a white lie and say Lorna had told me the story herself. If I could keep you out of this, I would. But it's never smart to lie to the police in a major enquiry. However honourable my motives, if the police discover I've not told them the truth about anything, I'll be even more firmly in the frame as a suspect—'

'They see you as a suspect?' The idea had clearly not even occurred to him.

'They're bound to, aren't they? I found the body. If you're right that she was shot, then I'm an ex-cop trained in using firearms. And there's something else.' I told him about Sean Critchley.

'I saw the story on the news,' Gus said. 'This is the guy who saved your life?'

'The very same. So from the police perspective, I'm the only link between two very recent violent murders in an area that – well, isn't known for its violent murders. Detectives aren't keen on coincidences.'

'It can't be anything else, surely?'

'I honestly don't see how. I hadn't seen Critchley since that night in Danny Royce's garden, and I've no idea what brought him up to Inverness. I can't see any meaningful link between him and Lorna. But it's the kind of thing that will give the police food for thought.'

I could see from his expression that what I'd said had also set Gus thinking. After a moment he said, 'You didn't, did you?'

I knew exactly what he meant, but I also wanted to make him ask the question directly. 'Didn't what?'

'Kill her. Kill Lorna. I just want you to tell me you didn't.'

Part of me wanted to be outraged at Gus's sudden lack of trust, but I couldn't blame him. He'd known me only for a few months. We liked each other and got on well, but he knew nothing about my background other than what I'd chosen to share. I'd just given him all the reasons why the police might want to treat me as their main suspect. In the circumstances, it was a fair question.

'I didn't kill her, Gus. On my life. I'm devastated by what's happened.'

He looked as if he'd been holding his breath waiting for my answer. 'Aye, I know. I shouldn't have asked that.'

'You had every right to ask it. You loved Lorna. You had to be sure.'

He had no reason to believe me even now, but he seemed in no doubt I was telling the truth. I felt an enormous relief. It would have been too much if I'd lost Gus's trust as well as losing Lorna.

He swallowed the last of his coffee. 'I'd best get on. Things don't stop even at a time like this. Will you be okay?'

'I'll manage. Just need time to process things.'

'If there's anything I can do, let me know.'

'Thanks, Gus. Appreciated. I'll see how I'm feeling.'

'Don't hesitate. If you need anything at all, even if only to talk, I'm there for you.'

I nodded, unable to respond. I was still feeling the previous night's fury, though it had lessened to a more controlled anger. Anger of course at whoever had done this, but also anger at myself for allowing it to happen.

Or even, I added to myself, for somehow *causing* it to happen.

CHAPTER TWENTY-THREE

Later in the morning I took Ziggy out again, once more heading uphill away from Lorna's cottage. He still seemed subdued, but he seemed to have accepted that, for the moment at least, he was staying with me. He trotted obediently beside me, and when I unfastened his lead he ran only a yard or two ahead.

At the summit, I looked back down. There were two white vans parked on the road beside Lorna's cottage along with a marked police car. The examiners continuing their work.

This time I carried on walking down towards the next valley. I needed the exercise and some time to pursue my thoughts. But I'd only walked a few hundred yards further when my mobile phone rang in my pocket.

I was surprised there was even a signal up here. I looked at the caller details on the screen. A name I'd entered into my address book very recently. DCI Morag Henderson. 'I assume you're phoning to cancel our meeting?'

'On the contrary, Mr Mellor. I'm phoning to see if you're at home. I'd like to speak to you.'

'Are you sure that's wise?'

'It's not only wise. It's necessary. I've been appointed SIO of the investigation into Lorna Jardine's killing. My condolences. I understand you were a friend of Ms Jardine's. This must have been a dreadful shock.'

'You might say that. You're presumably aware I've already spoken to DS McBain.'

'Of course. But in the circumstances I thought it would be best if I spoke to you myself.'

'I'm out walking the dog, but I can be back at the cottage in fifteen minutes or so.'

'Perfect. I'm down at Ms Jardine's cottage. I'll see you shortly.'

She was already there waiting when I arrived back at the cottage. I hadn't known what to expect of DSI Morag Henderson. In my experience, female police officers didn't make their way up the ranks unless they were capable of holding their own in what remained a largely male-dominated environment. That meant they tended to be women with imposing personalities and a steely determination not to take any crap. From the way she'd sounded on the phone, I didn't imagine Henderson would be much different.

'Mr Mellor, I presume?' She was probably a little older than I was, with short dark hair and a seemingly easy-going demeanour. She smiled in a manner that I imagined was intended to put me at ease.

'That's me. Come on in.' I unlocked the front door and led her inside. 'Coffee?'

'Why not. It's been a long morning already.'

I'd been half-expecting a more intimidating approach, prefaced by a warning that she was here only to discuss Lorna's killing and wouldn't be diverted into talking about Kate Brodie. I felt mildly disconcerted by her casual approach. Perhaps she was hoping if I relaxed I might somehow trip myself up.

I left her in the living room while I made the coffees. When I returned, she was standing by the bookshelf, examining my small selection of paperbacks, mostly crime thrillers of one sort or another. 'You like police procedurals?'

'More now I've left the job,' I said. 'Previously they were too much of a busman's holiday.'

'Tell me about it.' She took the coffee from me with a nod of thanks. 'First, as I said on the phone, my condolences. I'm very sorry.'

'I haven't really come to terms with it yet.'

'For what it's worth, it'll probably take longer than you imagine.' She sounded as if she was speaking from experience. 'But you will get there.'

'It doesn't quite feel that way at the moment. I hope you're right.'

'I've been there, for what it's worth. Your experience won't be the same as mine. But I don't think it'll be that different.'

'I'm grateful for the sympathy. But I assume I'm still top of your suspect list.'

'I'm not sure you're on it at all.'

'I don't understand why not. It's an unlikely killing in a remote location. I found the body and was the only person on the scene. My fingerprints and DNA must be in the house because I spent a recent evening there. If I were investigating this, I'd be on my list of suspects.'

'Did you know Ms Jardine had security cameras?'

'No, I didn't.'

'Quite a high-spec kit, actually. Well concealed and good definition. She had a decent alarm system as well, though it wouldn't have been turned on during the day if she was in the house. In general the house is pretty secure, though sadly not enough to keep out her killer.'

'Why would she have needed all that?'

'Maybe just because she was a woman living alone in a remote location.'

'My landlord tells me no one even bothers to lock their doors in these parts.'

'Things have changed even up here. Ms Jardine did have a few possessions that might have been attractive to thieves. Jewellery. Some items that look as if they might be family heirlooms.'

'So what does all this mean for me?'

'The security cameras did their job. They captured you turning up at the house at the time you said, dealing with this chap.' She gestured to Ziggy in his usual spot by the wood-stove. 'And then you finding the broken door and peering into the kitchen. Your shock's pretty obvious. The pathologist is certain that death occurred a good few hours before that. Probably around the time you heard the dog barking, in fact.'

'There's no reason I couldn't have been there earlier in the day.'

'You seem very keen to be considered a suspect, Mr Mellor.'

'I want to understand your thinking.'

'The camera did its job earlier too. There was another visitor, again at around the time you heard the dog barking. He's not caught on the camera at the front of the house so it seems he went immediately round to the rear. Even at the rear, he largely moves in a way that avoids the camera, but there's no way to access the rear door without being captured at least briefly.'

'Do you see his face?'

'Unfortunately, no. He's made sure of that. He's wearing a baseball cap and scarf round the lower part of his face, and he keeps his head turned away from the camera.'

'So how do you know it wasn't me?'

'Because this man's a good six inches taller than you, and much more heavily built. It isn't you.'

'So this was the killer?'

'He doesn't waste any time. He checks the door is locked and pulls out a crowbar from inside his coat and forces his way in. Again, he looks as if he knows what he's doing. He presumably made some noise, but he's inside so quickly it probably made no difference.'

'Do you catch him coming out?'

'Briefly. Only a few minutes later. He's gone straight in, done what he wanted to do, and come straight out. We only see him momentarily before he slips out of range.'

'You're saying he went in there specifically to kill Lorna. He wasn't a burglar.'

'Obviously other scenarios are available. But this man wasn't some smackhead housebreaker. This was someone who knew what he was doing. The way he killed her suggests that too.'

My coffee had grown cold but I swallowed it anyway. 'How do you mean?'

'Are you sure you want to hear the details?'

'I think so.'

'She was shot. Twice. In the head. She was killed coolly and cold-bloodedly. The pathologist thought she was shot once as she entered the kitchen, and then once more on the ground, presumably to ensure she was dead. The timing of the killer's entrance and exit suggests that was all he did.'

'Christ.'

'I'm sorry.'

'So I'm no longer a suspect?'

'Don't get ahead of yourself,' she said. 'I know you didn't kill Ms Jardine. What I'm less sure about is whether in some way you might have been involved in her death.'

This was the twist I'd been half-expecting. 'In what way?'

'There's a lot we don't yet know about Ms Jardine and yourself.'

'I'll happily tell you anything I can.'

'As far as we know, Ms Jardine was a sole trader accountant with a mainly rural practice. Most of her clients were local farmers and the like. Not the sort of person we'd expect to become the victim of a professional killer. So that raises questions.'

'Now you're going to ask me if there's any link with the murder of a police officer called Sean Critchley.'

'I understand Dave McBain raised this with you.'

'Not exactly. I was the one who first mentioned Critchley. I was telling DS McBain my reasons for leaving the force. He recognised Critchley's name.'

'We don't get many murders here. The ones we do get aren't normally professional killings.' Henderson picked up her coffee mug and gazed at the no doubt stone-cold contents. 'As Dave McBain noted, you have a link to both.'

I gestured to the mug. 'Would you like another coffee?'

I expected her to press on with her questions about Critchley. Instead, she said, 'Thanks.'

She followed me into the kitchen, sitting herself at the kitchen table as I prepared the coffees. 'Tell me about Sean Critchley.'

'I'm not sure I can tell you much more than I said to DS McBain. I didn't know him well. We were colleagues, but we never worked closely together.'

'Except when he saved your life?'

'Even then. I wasn't expecting him to be there, and I still don't know why he was. I was very grateful for his intervention. But – well, let's say it was a surprise.'

'We've checked out your account of why you left the police.'

'I'd expect nothing less. I take it you confirmed that my account was accurate.'

'We confirmed your account of that night in Danny Royce's garden, certainly. A routine surveillance operation which somehow went wrong.'

'Somehow.'

Her face was expressionless. 'What was most interesting was that when we enquired about Critchley's role in that operation, the water suddenly became very muddy.'

'What did they tell you?'

'Not much. We were told Critchley was – what was the phrase? – "a detached member of the team who used his own initiative when it became clear there was a problem".'

'Critchley wasn't a member of the team, detached or otherwise,' I said. 'Or, if he was, no one told me.'

'Which brings us back to why the operation went wrong in the first place. What do you think about that?'

I carried the refilled mugs over to the table. 'You can imagine I've given a lot of thought to that. The exercise was well-planned, or at least we thought it was.'

'What was the purpose of the operation?'

'We'd had intelligence that Royce had organised a meeting that night with a number of associates. There'd been something of a turf war going on around Royce's empire. Royce was an old-school gangster increasingly moving into more legitimate business activities. He'd been building new alliances. That strategy had opened up a vacuum behind him, with plenty of dubious characters looking to fill the gap. That evening was intended as some kind of summit to decide what to do about that. We were keen at least to know who might be there. We had authority to carry out appropriate intrusive surveillance, but there were no listening devices in Royce's house. Given his track record, the risks of trying to install them were too great. The aim was to get as much intelligence as we could. It was a fairly low-key operation. We were working with the NCA but the immediate team was small and comprised only of police officers.'

'So what went wrong?'

'I don't know. Maybe we were unlucky and Royce stumbled across me by accident. Stuff happens. Perhaps I didn't do my job as well as I could have done. I could have spotted I was in danger sooner. It's all a blur now.' I paused, thinking back to that night. 'But, if you want my view, I'd say Royce knew I was there.'

'That's a serious claim.'

'I know. And I've no evidence for it. I'm just telling you what I think.'

'Even more fortunate that Critchley was there then.'

'Wasn't it?'

'You told Dave McBain you'd had no further contact with Critchley. Is that right?'

'I've not seen or spoken to him since that night. I was interviewed as part of the follow-up enquiry but I didn't come across Critchley again before I left.'

She nodded, giving no indication whether she'd noticed I hadn't entirely answered her question. 'That was why you left the police? Because of what happened that night?'

'That was part of it. Maybe a bigger part than I realised at the time. But not the whole story. I wanted a change, really.'

'You've certainly made a pretty clean break. Are you planning to stay up here?'

'I'd intended to. But now's not the time for me to be making any decisions.'

'Going back to Critchley, you've no idea why he might have been up here?'

'None at all.'

'The word is that he was up here on some kind of private business, but nobody has any idea what that might have been. Or if they have, they're not sharing it with us. You can't think of any possible link between Critchley and Ms Jardine?'

'Other than me, you mean. Not remotely. I'd told her about my reasons for leaving the police. I probably even mentioned Critchley by name. If she'd come across him somewhere, she'd have said so, surely.'

'So that brings us back to you.'

'If I'm the link, I've no idea how or why. I don't want to believe I was somehow the cause of Lorna's death, even inadvertently.'

'Shall we move on to Cameron Fraser?'

'I didn't know if you'd want to discuss that in the circumstances.'

'I was wary of meeting you. I'm even more so now. You do seem to be at the centre of a rather baffling spider's web.'

'If I am, I'm not the spider. I'm just another fly. I'm as confused by all this as you are.'

'How did you come across Fraser?'

I told her how I'd met Fraser. 'He made some comment about having some work he might put in my direction. I didn't take him seriously at first, but he gave me his number and asked me to call. I decided I'd nothing to lose. He offered me the Kate Brodie assignment, with the promise of some further investigatory work to help check out potential investments.'

'Why you?'

'I don't know. Sure, I'm an ex-detective and surveillance specialist, but I've no real experience in this kind of work. I was honest with him about that. It didn't seem to trouble him. Maybe he's someone who goes with his gut instinct. You'd have to ask him.'

I expected her to ask more about Fraser but she was gazing past my head through the kitchen window. After a moment, she said, 'It's a decent day out there. Do you fancy going for a walk?'

CHAPTER TWENTY-FOUR

Her suggestion that we should take a walk took me by surprise. But then most of this interview had been unexpected. 'If you want to.'

'I could do with a breath of air. And I imagine that dog's getting restless.'

Ziggy was showing no obvious signs of it. When I re-entered the living room, he was curled up by the stove, although he jumped up eagerly as I approached. I clipped on his lead and returned to the hallway to pull on my coat and boots. Henderson was waiting by the front door. 'I'll grab my coat from the car,' she said.

She was right that it was still a fine day. The wind had dropped and the temperature was warm for the time of year. Henderson had put on a heavy waterproof and was striding along beside me, Ziggy bounding ahead as usual. 'Are you going to keep the dog?' Henderson asked.

'I don't know. I don't even know if Lorna had any next of kin.'

'We've not identified anyone so far. Her parents had both died and she was an only child. We've not tracked down anyone beyond that and we don't know if she had a will. But it's early days.'

'I'm happy to keep Ziggy if no one else wants him. Though he might bring me some painful memories.'

'And some positive ones. It cuts both ways.'

We walked to the top of the hill in silence. When we reached the summit, Henderson turned and surveyed the view. 'Pretty spectacular. I can see the attractions of living up here.'

'It has its compensations. Gus is worried about development ruining the area.'

'Is this the Gregor McBride thing? It's a concern, definitely. We've already got too many examples of overseas billionaires buying up large stretches of land in the Highlands. Building gated communities and leisure resorts for the super-rich. They just see the place as their playground. Not that the existing landowners are necessarily much better, but McBride's about as bad as they come.'

I wondered how much Cameron Fraser had told her about his own interest in the matter and about Archie Kinnear's association with McBride. I considered mentioning my encounter with McBride's bodyguard, Kenny Taylor, but I couldn't see how it could be relevant to our discussion. Henderson was still gazing out at the landscape as if that had been her sole purpose in coming. After a moment she said, 'What have you learned about the Kate Brodie case so far?'

'Not a huge amount beyond what's in the public domain. There was one point I'd not seen reported in the media but I've no idea if it's significant or if the police had reasons for not making it public.'

'What is it?'

'The possibility that she might have been troubled about something in the days before her death. Maybe a work issue.' I told Henderson what Heather Galloway had said about overhearing the telephone conversation. 'It might be nothing, or the neighbour might have misunderstood, but I wondered if the police had followed up that lead. The neighbour said she'd mentioned it to the officer who took her statement.'

Henderson was looking thoughtful and offered no immediate response. Finally, she said, 'I'm going to be as honest as I can be with you. I'm taking a risk even talking to you about any of this. But I've taken a few soundings from your former colleagues. Everyone reckoned that, as a copper, you were as straight as they came. Some of them suggested that might have been why you left. Is there any truth in that?'

'It was a factor. I'd seen too much bad behaviour. I'd had one or two run-ins when I'd tried to challenge it. Nothing major, but let's say I didn't feel supported by the hierarchy.'

'I'm prepared to trust you, up to a point at least. If I find there are reasons why you don't merit that trust, I'll make sure you get exactly what you deserve.'

'Understood.'

'For what it's worth, I'm pretty sure what you've told me wasn't investigated by the team working on the Kate Brodie case. There could have been legitimate reasons for that. From what you've said, it might well have been something and nothing. But there were so few leads I'm surprised it wasn't at least looked into.' She paused. 'I shouldn't be saying this, but this is why I'm prepared to talk to you. That investigation stank to high heaven.'

'In what way?'

'The first question was why it was run out of Glasgow. I mean, it wasn't entirely inexplicable. Kate Brodie was from Glasgow and they've got the resources. But the local team were frozen out. They made no use of our knowledge or intelligence. I eventually had some limited involvement because it was becoming painfully obvious that they lacked any local contacts. But I was never part of the team.'

'So what's the point of having Major Investigations people up here in the first place?'

'Quite. But it was more than that. From what I saw of the investigation they were doing little more than going through the motions. And there seemed to be some no-go areas, particularly where Archie Kinnear was concerned.'

'They must have talked to Kinnear, though?'

'Of course. But given that Kinnear's a man who's made more than a few enemies over his career, I'd have thought he might have merited more attention.'

'You think there was some kind of cover-up?'

'I don't think anything. I'm just telling you what I saw. The investigation team briefed the media very selectively. They gave the impression they were being much more proactive and making more progress than they really were. You've been there. You know how hard people work on a major investigation. It always has its ups and downs, but people bust a gut to get that breakthrough. Not in this case.'

'But why would they do that? Especially when someone as influential as Archie Kinnear was involved.'

'That's what I was left wondering. Kinnear's a man with a lot of influence, even if some of it's questionable. I wouldn't necessarily expect anyone senior in the force to jump just because he told them to – with a few exceptions – but I'd have expected them to pull out all the stops to find his missing daughter. But what I saw was people treading very carefully, perhaps afraid of what they might uncover if they turned over too many stones.'

Ziggy had ceased running around and had come to rub himself against my legs. I took that as a sign that he was keen to return to the cottage. I gestured back towards it. 'Shall we head back down?' We hadn't actually walked all that far, but I was hoping she'd take the hint.

'Yes, sure. I didn't want to talk about any of this inside.'

'You seriously think there might be some sort of surveillance device in the cottage?'

'I think it's highly unlikely. But when I raised some of these questions internally – well, things happened that made me mildly paranoid. I'm going out on a limb talking to you about this and I don't want to take any unnecessary chances.'

'That's what I don't understand,' I said. 'Why are you talking to me?'

'I trust my instincts. And I checked you out and I know you're straight. That's two reasons. And there's a third.'

'Which is?'

'That I can't trust anybody else.'

CHAPTER TWENTY-FIVE

'There must be other people you could talk to about this?'
We were making our way back down the track towards the cottage, but I could tell Henderson was walking slowly, making the most of our time outside.

'You'd think, wouldn't you?'

'You're saying there isn't a straight copper in the whole force?'

'Of course not. I'm sure the vast majority are as honest as the day is long. Okay, maybe not the best analogy at this time of the year, but you know what I mean. The straight ones I know aren't in a position to do anything, and I don't know who else to trust.'

'Even so, I don't really see what I can do.'

'You've been commissioned by Cameron Fraser to look again into Kate's disappearance. I don't entirely understand why Fraser's so interested, but I'm happy to take advantage of the opportunity. There may be the potential to identify evidence not uncovered by the original investigation. Which might give us an excuse to get it reopened.'

'Even if someone's not keen for that to happen, for whatever reason?'

'If the evidence hits the media first, we might have no choice. We've got a relatively new chief who's keen to make an impression. If he can demonstrate that mistakes were made on his predecessor's watch, I'm guessing he wouldn't be too sorry about that.'

'Even if the original enquiry was as flawed as you say, I don't know how much chance there is of me making any more progress. I might be honest, but I'm one guy. One guy without much experience of doing this kind of thing by myself.'

'You've already found a piece of information that, as far as I'm aware, was either not discovered or not taken seriously in the original investigation.'

'There's another issue.'

'Go on.'

'If I'm still suspected of possible involvement in Lorna's killing I don't know that Fraser will want to continue employing me. If I were in his shoes, I'm not sure I'd want to risk being associated with a possible murderer.'

'From what I've heard about Fraser, that wouldn't trouble him too much. But that's another reason I'm talking to you about this. For my own part, I'm pretty sure you're not a killer and that you're not personally involved in Ms Jardine's death. But I am intrigued by the possible link between this and Sean Critchley's killing. I'm wondering if it's a coincidence that those killings should have happened shortly after you began looking into Kate Brodie's disappearance.'

'None of us had anything to do with Kate Brodie.'

'As far as you know.'

'I don't see what connection there could be.'

'Neither do I, as yet. It's a potential line of enquiry anyway. Just so you know. And, for the avoidance of doubt as the lawyers say, I'm not going to risk compromising myself further by sharing any other information with you about the ongoing investigation into Ms Jardine's death. I'm trusting you to be discreet about what I have told you, though most of it should be in the public domain soon anyway.'

'What if I want more information on the Kate Brodie case?'

'Feel free to ask. I can't promise I'll always be able to answer. But I'll help if I can.'

We'd reached the cottage, and she unlocked her car. 'I won't take up any more of your time at the moment, Mr Mellor. We may well want to speak to you again, but next time it'll be one of my colleagues. If you need to speak to me, call me on the number Cameron Fraser gave you. Preferably outside work hours, though Christ knows what those are going to be in the coming weeks. It's a personal phone. I change it from time to time, but if I do I'll make sure you have the new number.'

'You're a cop with a burner phone?'

'I'm a cop who's learned to watch her back.'

I watched as she drove the car back down the steep uneven track to the bottom of the hill. I wasn't sure what to make of DCI Morag Henderson. She was clearly nobody's idea of a fool, but she'd been much more open with me than I'd expected. On the other hand, I wondered how much she'd really told me. She'd revealed the nature of Lorna's death, but I guessed that would be released to the media shortly anyway. She'd told me her views of the Kate Brodie investigation, but that was nothing more than personal opinion. She'd given me enough to make me trust her, without necessarily revealing anything substantive. Maybe she was cannier than I'd thought.

I let myself back into the cottage, and watched as Ziggy lolloped across to the wood-stove. He had a quiet and slightly baffled air, but he didn't seem disturbed or unhappy.

It was only early afternoon, though my early start made it

feel much later. I still wasn't hungry but I forced myself to eat a sandwich, munching my way dutifully through the cheese and pickle. I was carrying the empty plate back through to the kitchen when my phone rang again. I seemed popular today. That was probably a positive for my mental health, I supposed, though there was a part of me that never wanted to speak to anyone ever again.

I looked at the screen. Cameron Fraser. He opened without any preliminaries. 'I've just heard the news about your neighbour, Ms Jardine. An awful business.'

I wondered how he'd found out so quickly about Lorna's death. 'It's dreadful,' I said.

'I've heard it was you who found her. I'm sorry. That must have been a terrible shock.'

'The whole thing's been a shock. I can't begin to imagine why anyone would do something like that to Lorna.'

'The poor wee lass. You were friends, I believe.'

'I met her at Gus's Hogmanay party, after I'd been talking to you. We got on well, yes.' I wasn't going to tell Cameron Fraser any more than that.

'The reason I've called, Jack, as well as to offer you my sincere condolences, is to ascertain whether, in the light of this dreadful news, you're happy to continue the assignment I've given you.'

'Is there any reason why I shouldn't?' If Fraser was intending to sack me, I wanted him to so say explicitly.

'Not that I'm aware. I was thinking more of your own psychological and emotional state. I wouldn't want you to continue working if you didn't feel up to it.'

'To be honest, at the moment the last thing I'd want to do is to stop working. I'd prefer to have something I can focus on, if you don't have a problem with that.'

'I don't have a problem at all.'

I thought it was time to move the discussion on, and maybe to probe a little more into how much Fraser actually knew. 'On that topic, I've been talking to DCI Henderson. She's leading the enquiry into Lorna's murder.'

'So I understand. Did you find the conversation illuminating?'

There seemed to be little that Fraser didn't know. 'Up to a point. Her view is that the investigation into Kate Brodie's disappearance was poorly handled. Or perhaps worse than that. It was run from Glasgow, with the local team largely frozen out.'

'I'd heard rumours to that effect. You might be one man, but you may be more likely to make progress than a team which is trying its best not to achieve anything.'

'We'll see,' I said. 'I'll do what I can.'

'I'm sure you will. And I'm pleased to hear you still feel up to the job.'

'If that changes, I'll let you know.'

'Keep me informed, Jack. That's all I ask. And, once again, my commiserations.'

After we'd ended the call, I sat reflecting on what I'd said. I knew that what I really ought to do was take a few days out, wait to see what impact Lorna's death would have on me, take my time to reflect on what I wanted to do next. Any decisions I made in the immediate aftermath of her killing were bound to be clouded by unresolved emotion, the heady cocktail of grief and fury I'd felt the previous evening. For all I knew, I might even be in a state of shock. The last thing I needed was to throw myself straight back into the fray.

But I knew it was the only thing I could do.

CHAPTER TWENTY-SIX

I dragged myself through the rest of that bleak Saturday. Other than the leftover lamb, I had no food for Ziggy. I had vague memories of the type of dog food I'd noticed in Lorna's cottage, so I made a trip over to the supermarket in Dingwall to buy provisions for myself and for Ziggy.

I had to turn my head away as I drove past Lorna's cottage, unable to look directly at the site of her death. A white van was pulled into the side of the road, so I assumed the examiners were still working in there.

They say you shouldn't go food shopping if you're hungry. By the same token, it's a mistake to shop for food if you've no appetite. I had to force myself to put items in my trolley, trying to pick food I might at some point actually feel up to eating. It was a discipline I had to maintain. It took me a while to track down what I thought was Ziggy's preferred dog food. I'd felt bad leaving him behind at the house, and I could hear him whining behind the front door as I'd locked it.

I completed the shopping as quickly as I could and headed back to the cottage. The white van was no longer outside Lorna's cottage, so presumably the examiners had either finished or packed up for the day. There was no crime-scene tape or other evidence that the police had been there, but that was unsurprising. Even if the police hadn't finished, there was no point in drawing attention to the place.

As I opened the front door, Ziggy came bounding out of the living room, yapping furiously. The poor mutt had probably assumed he'd been abandoned completely. I'd bought a couple of food bowls for Ziggy in the supermarket, and I put out some food and water for him in the hallway. I really had no idea how to look after a dog. I'd need to seek advice from Gus.

I spent the rest of that day doing not much. I was feeling frustrated, full of pent-up emotion I didn't know how to dissipate. There was grief, of course, but there was little I could do about that. I hoped that over time it would deal with itself but I didn't know what I'd have to go through before that happened.

Beyond that, though, there was the fury that had overwhelmed me the previous evening. That hadn't lessened. If anything, it had been intensified by my conversation with Morag Henderson. I knew now we weren't dealing with some random smackhead or housebreaker. The person who had murdered Lorna was a cold-blooded professional killer who'd visited her house with that single express purpose. Whoever that bastard was, and whatever his motives might have been, I wanted to deal with him.

That was where my determination ran into the sand. I had no idea where to begin. If my efforts to investigate Kate Brodie's disappearance had felt a potential waste of time, this seemed an even more vain quest. I had no access to any information or evidence other than the little that Henderson had chosen to share with me. I had no idea who the potential suspects might be. In short, I had nothing.

The sensible course of action would be to accept this and

leave the task to the police. It wasn't as if they were likely to thank me for trying to interfere in their investigation. I should focus my efforts on Kate Brodie, where I might at least expect tacit support from Morag Henderson. But I knew I wasn't going to do that. I just didn't yet know what I was going to do instead.

I forced myself to cook and eat a frozen pizza for supper, though my appetite hadn't returned. I'd bought a new bottle of single malt at the supermarket, because I knew I'd need it to get through the evening. But I had to be careful. I've never been a heavy drinker but in my current state of mind the attractions of getting lost in alcohol could easily change that.

I limited myself to a couple of glasses and decided to get an early night. I was physically and mentally exhausted by my early start and by the emotional stresses of the day, although I had no idea how easy it would be to find sleep.

I lay awake for a while. The weather had changed again over the evening, and the heavy rain against the window felt oddly comforting in the darkness. I wasn't really aware of falling asleep, and when I woke it felt as if I'd nodded off only for a few minutes. I'd woken suddenly and at first I couldn't work out what had disturbed me. Then my phone buzzed loudly on the bedside table. Simultaneously, the doorbell rang downstairs, someone holding the button down insistently. A moment later, there was a banging on the front door.

I was only half awake and for a few seconds I had no idea what was going on. I rolled over on the bed and grabbed the phone. I'd hardly slept at all, and it was still only around 10pm. I answered the call without bothering to look at the screen. 'Yes?'

'For fuck's sake, are you in there?'

'What?'

'Are you in there?'

It took me another half-second. 'Maddie?'

'No, it's the Archbishop of sodding Canterbury. Of course it's me.'

'You do know what time it is?'

'I've spent most of the last four hours driving. Of course I know what time it is.'

'Where the hell are you?'

'Where the hell do you think I am? I'm standing outside your fucking cottage. I hope to Christ you're in there.'

'What? What do you mean?'

'It's not complicated, Jack. Even for someone as dumb as you. I'm outside your cottage. If you're in there, come and open the door.'

'Are you on your own?'

'No, I've got the Band of the fucking Coldstream Guards with me. Of course I'm on my own. Now will you let me in? Apart from anything else, it's pissing down out here, and I'm cowering under this poxy little porch of yours.'

'Hang on. I'm coming down.'

'About sodding time.' It was characteristic of Maddie that, even when she'd turned up unexpectedly on my doorstep late at night, she felt no need to ingratiate herself.

I dragged on my dressing gown and stumbled down the stairs. To add to the pandemonium, Ziggy was barking furiously in the living room. I hurried down the hall and unbolted and opened the front door. Maddie was on the doorstep, managing to look furious and miserable at the same time. 'About fucking time.' She stamped past me into the hall. 'Where do I go?'

'Left into the living room. I take it you'll want coffee?'

She shrugged off her damp raincoat, tossed it in my direction, then threw herself down on to the sofa. 'Coffee, and any other sustenance you can offer. I'm bloody starving.'

I'd forgotten quite how imperious her manner could be. 'I can offer you a ready-meal chilli, if that's good enough.' I'd bought a selection of ready meals to get me through the coming days, knowing I wouldn't have the inclination to cook. I'd learned from experience there was no point in trying to drag any explanation out of Maddie while she was hungry.

'If that's the best you can do,' she responded grumpily.

'It's the best offer you're likely to get round here at this time of night,' I pointed out. Before she could respond, I left the room, hung up her coat in the hall, and made my way through to the kitchen. I filled the kettle then dug the ready meal out of the freezer, setting it to heat in the microwave.

'You let out the flat so you could move to this place?' Maddie had already grown restless, and was standing in the kitchen doorway.

'Don't you like it?'

'Not exactly spacious, is it?'

I spooned coffee into the cafetière, trying to ignore Maddie's efforts at provocation. Anyone else might have offered some kind of apology for disturbing me and maybe expressed some gratitude for the food and coffee. But that wasn't Maddie's style. 'It's spacious enough for me.'

'And you've a dog. I thought you weren't keen on dogs.'

I wasn't aware I'd ever expressed any opinion about dogs. 'It's a long story. And on that note, I don't know why you're here, Maddie, but this really isn't a good time.'

'If I could have got here earlier, I would have.

'That's not what I mean—' I stopped. Obviously, she'd known that wasn't what I meant. Conversation with Maddie was always verbal jousting. 'Why are you here, anyway?'

She sat down at the kitchen table. 'Let me get some food down and I'll tell you.'

I pushed the mug of coffee across the table towards her. I still had no milk or sugar but Maddie had always taken it black. She took a mouthful, swallowed and said, 'I needed that.'

It was another few minutes before the chilli was ready, but clearly Maddie had no intention of saying any more until she'd eaten. Fair enough. The silence was probably easier for both of us.

When I finally put the plate of food down on the table in front of her, she smiled for the first time since she'd arrived. 'I hadn't realised how hungry I was. This actually looks okay.' It was as much thanks as I was likely to get.

I sat down opposite her and sipped at my coffee, watching her eat. When the plate was empty, she looked up and said, 'Thanks for that. Any chance of another coffee?'

There was no point in trying to force this. Maddie did everything at her own pace. I'd wasted a lot of time and energy in the past trying to change that. Instead, I made another jug of coffee and brought it back over to the table. I suspected that I was going to need the caffeine as much as Maddie did. 'Okay,' I said, patiently, 'so why are you here?'

'You know I said I'd left Martin?'

'I remember. In my view, you're better off out of that relationship, but you don't want to hear that from me.'

'I don't want to hear it from anyone. It was my choice.'

None of this surprised me. I'd disliked Martin intensely. That hadn't been because he'd taken Maddie from me – after the initial shock I'd actually been grateful to him for that – but because I'd thought he was a genuinely nasty piece of work. I never bothered to check whether he had a police record, but I suspect he did. He was one of those vague business-types with his fingers in countless pies, at least some of which were dodgy. I'd never discovered how Maddie had initially met him, or how long she'd been having an affair with him. I'd had direct contact with him only on the occasions he'd come to help move Maddie's stuff out of the flat, and nothing in his manner or behaviour had endeared him to me. After that, I had done everything I could to distance myself from Maddie and him, for both personal and professional reasons. 'So what made you walk out?' I asked.

'It doesn't matter. But I have.'

That was probably as much as I was likely to get, at least until Maddie decided she wanted to tell me more. 'But you're not going back?' I remembered how many times she'd made a big deal of leaving me, only to return a few days later with no acknowledgement of what had happened.

'Not this time. I've given him more than enough chances. I waited till he was at work, packed my stuff and left. Stayed with a friend for a few nights. That was when I called you.'

'And I made it abundantly clear I didn't want to see you.'

'Yes, you didn't leave me in much doubt about that.'

'And yet here you are. Look, Maddie, I don't know how you tracked me down, but my position hasn't changed. Nothing's changed.'

'Yes, it has. That's why I'm here.'

I was at risk of being drawn back into Maddie's unique form of personal drama. 'So what's changed?'

'Someone's tried to kill me.'

'Is this a joke, Maddie? If so, it's a sick one even by your standards.'

'What are you talking about? Of course it's not a joke. Someone tried to kill me.'

'Is that why you're here? Because someone told you what's happened to me, and you thought it would be a good opportunity to have a laugh?'

'I've no idea what you mean. Do you really think I'd have spent the best part of four hours on the road to have some fun at your expense? I've told you, the reason I'm here is because someone tried to kill me.'

She seemed deadly serious. And in fairness Maddie didn't

have a sufficient sense of humour, sick or otherwise, to make this kind of joke. 'Okay, then, I'll buy it. Someone tried to kill you. Are we talking about Martin?'

'Martin can be a bastard, but he has no reason to try to kill me.'

'You walked out on him.' I pointed out. 'For someone like Martin, that might be enough.'

'The point is that I don't know who it was. I just know it happened. Twice.'

'Twice?'

'The first time could have been an accident. I was using the subway, standing on a crowded platform waiting for a train. As the train was coming in, I felt someone push me. Not hard, not much more than a nudge. But I was standing close to the edge and I could easily have fallen. Luckily, someone next to me realised I was toppling forward and they grabbed my arm and pulled me back. It took me a few seconds to recover from the shock. By the time I turned round there was no one immediately behind me, and no way of knowing whether any of the people standing there beside me had been responsible.'

'You said yourself it could have been an accident.'

'That was what I assumed at first. But then there was a second attempt. Much more serious. I'd moved out of the friend's place and moved back to my mum's.' She grimaced. 'Not ideal, but I didn't have a lot of choice.' From what I recalled of Maddie's mother, the main problem was that the two of them were too alike. The original irresistible force and immovable object.

'I wasn't keen to spend any more time in her company than I could help,' Maddie went on. 'So I'd been for a drink and a bite to eat with a couple of people from work. We'd been to a place in the west end so I decided to walk up to the station to get the train back.' Maddie's mother lived somewhere around

Milngavie, I recalled, north of the city. 'It wasn't particularly late. Around ten. But you know how it is. You step into a back street and suddenly feel as if you're the last person in the world. I was already feeling nervous and I was hurrying. Then I realised someone was following me. I could hear footsteps, growing closer. Eventually I looked over my shoulder. There was a man behind me. He had one of those hoodie things on and a scarf round his face so I couldn't see any features except his eyes.'

'What happened?'

'He grabbed me and threw me against the wall of the building behind me, his hand across my throat. Then I saw he was holding a knife.'

'Christ.' Up to this point, I'd been wondering whether all this was nothing more than another example of Maddie's usual performative victimhood.

'At first, I thought it was a mugging. Not that that wouldn't have been bad enough, but I was prepared to hand over anything he wanted in return for getting out of there alive. But he didn't ask for anything or show any signs of wanting to take my bag or anything else. He showed me the knife blade and then raised his arm to use it.' She stopped and swallowed, and I realised how much it was costing her to recount this. 'Is there any more coffee?'

'I'll make some.'

'I hadn't realised how knackered I'm feeling.'

I rose to fill the kettle again. 'So what happened then?'

'To be honest, I panicked. I kicked out at him and started screaming. I was lucky. A group of young men had turned into the far end of the street. I don't know if they even knew what was happening, but they obviously realised it was nothing good so they shouted and ran towards us. The guy who'd grabbed me made one lunge with the knife, but I dodged and it just caught my hand.' She held up her left hand to show me a bandaged finger. 'He obviously didn't want to risk tangling with any of the young guys, so he legged it down the street.'

'I assume you went to the police.'

'Yeah. The young guys made some effort to chase after the guy, but there wasn't much chance of catching him and they were more concerned about my welfare. They wanted to take me to A&E, but the cut wasn't really bad enough. I'd got a few plasters in my bag, enough to get me back to my mum's. I just wanted to get away. But I called the police the next day and reported it.'

'And?'

'You were a police officer, Jack. What do you think?'

'I'm guessing you didn't get much joy.'

She brought her hands together in mock applause. 'Star prize. First, they were convinced it was a mugging. Second, they thought – though they didn't quite put it in so many words – that there was bugger all chance of identifying the guy.'

'They were probably right on the second part. They might have been right about the first.'

'He wasn't interested in robbing me. He wanted to kill me.'

'Okay. But do you think he was actively targeting you in particular? Isn't it more likely he was just some lunatic, and you were in the wrong place at the wrong time.'

'I don't think so. That's why I'm here. That wasn't the end of it.'

'I saw him again. The next day. I was heading straight back up to my mum's after work. I hadn't wanted to risk another late journey. I was walking back to my mum's from the bus stop. I heard someone behind me, and there he was.'

'The same guy?'

She shrugged. 'I can't be absolutely certain. I hadn't really registered what he was wearing the previous night, other than the black hoodie. This guy was wearing a waterproof with the hood pulled up, but also had a scarf round his face. His build was about the same as the man who attacked me.'

'Did he do anything?'

'He couldn't, really. There were other people on the street. But that was luck. It's not a busy road. Another night there might have been no one. At the very least, it felt as if he was trying to intimidate me. Maybe also find out where I was living.'

'But why would anyone want to kill you?' As I asked the question, it occurred to me that there were a few people who might, but probably not enough to make them actually do it.

'That's what I can't understand. I guess he could have fixated on me for reasons of his own.'

That wasn't impossible, I supposed. Maddie was an attractive and striking woman. Some obsessive might be drawn to her for that reason alone. 'Okay. I can understand why you're worried. But how come you've ended up here? And how did you track me down?'

She did at least have the grace to look mildly embarrassed. 'I was terrified by the thought that this guy knew where I was living. I knew I'd never rest if I stayed there. I wanted to get away.'

'There must be places nearer than this.'

'Fewer than you might think. I'm not short of friends, but there aren't many who'd be prepared or even able to put me up for more than a few nights. Also, I wanted to get as far away from the city as possible.'

'You've managed that all right. But I thought I'd made it clear I wasn't prepared or able to put you up.'

'I knew you didn't really mean it. I knew you wouldn't let me down if I really needed help.'

I wanted to tell her she'd got that completely wrong, but

there didn't seem much point in getting back into that argument. 'You still haven't told me how you tracked me down.'

'I lied. I worked through the list of all our former joint friends and picked out the ones you might have trusted with your new address. I spun them a whole load of nonsense about why I urgently needed to get in touch with you. And eventually someone gave me the address.'

I didn't ask her which of my friends had given her the information. It wouldn't have been their fault. I knew how persuasive Maddie could be. 'And then you drove up here?'

'As soon as I got the address. I was scared. Probably not thinking clearly. I made some excuse to my mum, and then set off.'

'This isn't the easiest place to find, especially in the dark.'

'Tell me about it. I spent half an hour searching these back roads looking for it. It was only luck that I saw the name of the cottage. Otherwise, I'd have had to sleep in the car till morning and find someone to ask.'

'You really are insane at times, Maddie.'

'That was why you loved me.'

'Very much in the past tense. Look, obviously I'm not going to throw you out now, but you being here is a really bad idea. And this isn't a good time.'

'Would any time be a good time?'

'No. But it wouldn't be as bad as now.'

'What do you mean?'

'It's another long story, Maddie.'

'Is there someone else? Up here, I mean.'

I swallowed hard. 'It wouldn't be any of your business if there was. But there isn't. Not now. Look, you're exhausted. You need to get some sleep. You can use my room upstairs. I'll sleep on the sofa.'

'I really am grateful, Jack. I'm probably being an idiot, but I needed to get away. Give me a few days.'

I wasn't sure how we'd manage this even for a few days, or what would change for Maddie in that time. But that was an argument for another day. 'What about your job?'

'I've got loads of leave owing, I'll call them on Monday and say some family issue's come up. It'll be fine.' She looked at me and offered a smile. 'Just like old times, isn't it?'

It occurred to me that if she'd come here seeking safety and security, she might be in for a shock, given everything that had happened. For the moment, though, I just shook my head. 'I hope not, Maddie. I really hope not.'

CHAPTER TWENTY-SEVEN

I slept uncomfortably on the sofa, while Maddie disappeared into the bedroom upstairs. When I woke, it was getting on for 7.30am, and Ziggy was awake, pestering me to take him out. The rain had lessened, though there was a fine drizzle as we took our usual route up the hill. It was still dark, although the sky was lightening to a bruised purple in the south-east. Ziggy ran ahead of me, yapping in his usual style, clearly delighted to be out of the house.

There were lights showing in Gus's house, but that was unsurprising. Gus kept a farmer's hours. He'd have been up and about long ago. I wondered if he'd seen Maddie arrive. Her car was parked immediately in front of the cottage, a Mini in a startling shade of yellow. I couldn't really imagine Maddie driving anything understated or simply functional. She wanted a touch of drama in every aspect of her life.

That might extend to her belief that her life was under threat. I didn't think she was lying – I'm sure she believed every word she told me – but Maddie would turn up the dramatic volume wherever she could. I was struggling to accept her narrative because the coincidence seemed too extraordinary. I was already the only apparent link between two actual murders. If I were also connected, however indirectly, to a third attempted killing, the fates really must be playing some kind of sick joke at my expense.

We were at the top of the hill, Ziggy racing down the far side into the next glen. I didn't feel in the mood to walk much further, and I didn't want to miss my footing in the darkness in unfamiliar territory. I paused at the summit, waiting for Ziggy to return. The drizzle had stopped and the earlier cloud cover had lifted, the sky clearing and brightening, a patchwork of light and dark behind me. With the sunrise approaching and my eyes growing accustomed to the gloom, I could make out Lorna's cottage, a black unlit shape against the paler sky.

I'm not sure I'd have spotted the car if it had remained stationary. It must have been parked somewhere close to Lorna's cottage. It was the unexpected movement that caught my eye, a shift of darkness against darkness. I peered down, trying to work out what I was seeing. It took me a moment to identify a slowly moving car, no lights showing, apparently turning round in the narrow lane. From this point, I couldn't hear the sound of the car engine and if I'd glanced down a moment earlier or later I probably wouldn't even have registered its presence. As I watched, the driver succeeded in negotiating the constrained space and pulled away, still showing no lights.

I'd rarely seen any unfamiliar vehicles up here. The only visitors were generally the post van and an occasional delivery courier. I couldn't imagine why anyone would be here at this time of day, let alone someone so keen not to be detected that they were prepared to negotiate a narrow winding lane without lights. Had they been visiting Lorna's house? If so, why? It seemed unlikely the police would have left anything of significance to be found in there.

Ziggy came bounding back to me, and I reclipped his lead

back on. I walked back down the hill, lost in thought. I increasingly felt as if I was caught up in some incomprehensible nightmare, the kind of dream where all the elements seem realistic but meld into each other in a way that defies logic.

Back at the cottage, I made another coffee and a couple of slices of toast, and returned to the living room. I assumed Maddie was still sleeping. I wasn't expecting her to surface for some time, which was fine by me.

Chewing on my toast, I booted up my laptop and searched against Lorna's name. I'd no idea what I was looking for, other than thinking that it might be useful to learn something more about her and her background. As far as I could see, her online presence was limited. I found various Highland-based Lorna Jardines on social media platforms, but none seemed to match the Lorna I'd known. There was a website for her accountancy practice, but, other than a very brief professional biography, it told me nothing new.

There wasn't much else I could find. I looked up her company on the Companies House website, but that didn't tell me much more. She was the sole director, and her accounts had unsurprisingly been filed on time. The accounts suggested that the business had been doing well, if not spectacularly so. As far as I could judge, Lorna had been exactly what she appeared to be.

It was nearly noon before Maddie appeared. She hadn't yet dressed and had borrowed an old dressing gown of mine. I had to confess that it suited her, reminding me of how beautiful I'd found her in the early days of our relationship. She hadn't become any the less physically attractive after that, but I'd found it increasingly difficult to separate that from the more toxic aspects of her personality.

'Thought I'd grab a shower, if that's okay?' she said.

'Help yourself. Have you had enough sleep?'

'Who knows? Less than I'd have liked, but more than I'd expected. Thought maybe my head was too buzzing with the drive and the caffeine, but my exhaustion was more than a match for it.'

'Do you want a coffee now?'

'Sounds good. I'll grab that shower while you're making it. I'll need to get my case out of the car. Didn't think about it earlier.'

'I'll get it,' I said. 'Don't want you scandalising the neighbours flouncing around in my dressing gown.'

'You haven't got any neighbours to scandalise.'

'Even so.' I didn't want to take any risk that Gus might see her, especially dressed only in my dressing gown. I didn't want him to jump to the wrong conclusion so soon after Lorna's death.

Once I'd retrieved the case from her car, she disappeared back upstairs. I noticed that she'd brought a relatively sizeable piece of luggage. More than an overnight bag. I guessed that told me something about her intentions, or at least her hopes.

I made another jug of coffee and took it through to the living room. I was conscious that this was my umpteenth of the morning, and I was already feeling the effects of the caffeine. Or perhaps simply the effects of Maddie's presence. Both had the potential to make me feel tense and slightly nauseous.

When Maddie returned, she was wearing a complete change of clothes. Even if she'd left in a panic, Maddie was never one to risk being underdressed. She slumped down on the sofa while I poured her a mug of coffee. 'I feel a lot better for the shower,' she said. 'I'll feel even better for the coffee.'

'Are you hungry?'

'Not at the moment.' She took a sip of the coffee. 'But I am beginning to feel more human now.' She looked around her at the small living room. 'I have to say, I feel quite secure here. Is that one of the attractions of the place for you?'

'It used to feel like a sanctuary,' I said. 'But people keep turning up.'

'Very funny.'

'I'm not joking, Maddie. Why do you think I came up here? I wanted to get away from everything. I didn't expect it to come following me.'

She gazed at me thoughtfully. 'Is this just about me? Because if it is, I've got the message, even if I don't know what to do with it yet. But I get the impression there might be something else.'

That was one of the things about Maddie. She could be utterly obtuse when it suited her, but she could also be unexpectedly perspicacious. 'There are a lot of other things. That's why it's the worst time for you to be here. Not that there'd ever be a good one.'

'So tell me about it.'

I didn't really want to. My instincts were telling me that this was just another of her ruses to inveigle me back into her orbit. I'd fallen for it before. At the same time, I did need to talk to someone about this. The only other candidate was Gus, and I didn't want to impose all my grief on him. If I offloaded some of my emotion onto Maddie, I could at least reassure myself she wouldn't seriously care about my feelings and that she'd soon be out of my life again.

I told her the whole story. About Danny Royce and Sean Critchley. About why I'd left my job, and how I'd come to move up here. About meeting Cameron Fraser and being offered work by him. And finally, about meeting and getting to know Lorna Jardine. And what had happened after that.

Maddie listened to all this in uncharacteristic silence. When I finished, she still didn't respond, as if she were trying to process everything I'd told her. After a few moments, she said, 'And you came up here for a quiet life?'

'Something like that.'

'Christ, Jack. I'm sorry. I know I can be a self-centred bitch, but that's awful. If I'd known you were living with all this, I wouldn't have spent all of yesterday evening boring on about my troubles.'

I noted that she hadn't said that she wouldn't have come, but it was a more empathetic response than I'd received from her for a long while. 'You were scared. I didn't mind. I wouldn't have been in a mood to talk about this last night anyway.'

'I'm sorry,' she said again. 'It sounds as if you might have had a future together.'

'I'll never know, will I?' I was conscious of a note of bitterness in my tone, but I made no attempt to conceal it. 'But, yes, I think we might have.'

'Why would someone want to kill her?'

'I've no idea. The police reckon it was a professional job. Not some tooled-up housebreaker.'

'It's a weird coincidence, isn't it? I mean, given the attempts on my life.'

'It's not the only one, funnily enough.' I'd told her about Sean Critchley's actions in Royce's garden, but hadn't told her about what had happened to him subsequently. 'Sean Critchley was killed too. Up here, a few days ago. In a hotel room in Inverness. Another pro job.' I smiled. 'Maybe I'm just not safe to be around.'

'Coincidences happen, I guess.'

'One of the first things you learn as a detective is not to trust them.' I was silent for a moment. I'd been too shocked by Lorna's death to acknowledge this point fully until now, even though DS McBain had made the point explicitly when he'd interviewed me. The idea had been nagging at the fringes of my consciousness, but I'd dismissed it as a product of my grief, a self-flagellating way of trying to take some responsibility for her death.

But now, sitting here talking to Maddie, I realised I couldn't dismiss the idea, either emotionally or rationally. Sure, coincidences happen, but this felt as if it was stretching the concept well beyond its usual limits. I was left with too many questions. Why was Critchley up in this part of the world in the first place? What had he wanted to speak to me about? Why and how had he come to visit my house, and why hadn't he waited for my return? Why would someone want to kill him? Most of all, why would anyone want to kill Lorna in what sounded to have been a very similar manner?

Then there was Maddie. At any other time, I'd have dismissed her account as a fairly typical instance of her constant desire to over-dramatise her life. But I knew Maddie wasn't easily spooked. One of her abiding qualities, for good or ill, was that she didn't take any shit from anyone. It was always difficult to be sure of Maddie's motives for doing anything, but my instinct was that if she'd been scared enough to flee up here she must have genuinely believed she was at risk.

I was conscious I'd been silent for too long and Maddie was watching me with curiosity. 'Penny for them.'

'Not worth even that,' I said. 'I was reflecting on the nature of coincidence.'

'Very profound.'

I nodded. 'That's me.' I paused, my head full of unresolved thoughts. 'Let's talk about something else. Tell me more about Martin.'

CHAPTER TWENTY-EIGHT

To be honest, the only thing I really knew about Martin Garfield was that I disliked him. I hadn't had any particular justification for that antipathy, at least not initially. He'd taken Maddie from me, of course, but that had come to feel almost like a blessing. I'd almost felt sorry for him.

But then I'd finally met him – he'd come to the flat to take away some stuff of Maddie's – and I'd taken an instant dislike to him. He was clearly an intelligent man – if maybe not quite as intelligent as he assumed – but that was where the positives ended. He struck me as arrogant, rude and generally obnoxious. He'd no particular reason to be pleasant to me, I suppose, other than the normal human politeness you might expect from someone visiting your house in potentially awkward circumstances. But he'd been pushy and dismissive, and when I'd questioned his right to some of the items he wanted to take he'd more or less threatened me with physical violence.

At the time, I'd felt that, in their different ways, he and Maddie deserved each other. It wasn't as if I was likely to cross paths again with Martin, except perhaps professionally. He struck me as the type of man who might well have had dealings with the police, though I never bothered to check out his record. Maddie had told me, rather vaguely, that he was some sort of businessman with various ranges of interests, which hadn't made me any less inclined to be suspicious of him.

'What about him?' she said now.

'Anything. What's the nature of his business for a start?'

'Why are you asking about this?'

'I don't know,' I said. 'But we have a series of coincidences. I'm trying to see if there's anything that might connect them other than my loose involvement.'

'But what's Martin got to do with any of this?'

'Almost certainly nothing. But he's one part of this story I know nothing about.'

'I don't know what to tell you. I honestly don't know much about his businesses. He never shared that with me much.'

'I bet he didn't. What did he tell you?'

'Just that it was some sort of import-export stuff. Whatever it was, he seemed to make a decent living out of it, which was what I mostly cared about.'

'What was the company called?'

'Companies, plural. He had various interests.' She gave me a couple of names. 'There were others, but I can't remember all of them.'

My laptop was sitting on the coffee table between us. I picked it up and searched on the names she'd given me. Neither company had a website, and the only mentions I could find were on the Companies House site. I checked out the accounts. Both companies seemed to be doing well with substantial turnover and profits. I followed that with a search on Garfield's name. He was a director of nine different active companies, as well as several which had been wound up. In some cases, Garfield was the sole named director. In others, he was one of several. In each case, the published accounts indicated that the company was in sound financial health, perhaps surprisingly so for businesses which seemed to have no other online visibility.

The related question was why anyone should need to be involved in so many companies. There could well be legitimate reasons, but I wasn't inclined to give a man like Garfield any benefit of the doubt. The most likely motive for establishing a network of companies would be to facilitate tax avoidance or some form of criminality. Or, in Garfield's case, quite possibly both.

'Anything useful?' Maddie asked.

'Only that he has a lot of companies.'

'He was always talking about the benefits of spreading risk,' Maddie said. 'I don't really know any more than that.'

'What about his business associates? Did you ever meet anyone he worked with?'

'Not often. He liked to keep his business and domestic lives very separate. A few times he took me for dinner with a client or asked me to attend some formal event with him. But it didn't happen often. I used to worry about that, and I did wonder for a while if he was afraid I might embarrass him or say something inappropriate. But I think I'm pretty presentable and I know how to talk to people in that kind of set-up.'

'I suspect it was because he didn't want you to know too much about his businesses or about the people he was dealing with.'

'Yeah, that was the conclusion I came to as well. Which was fine by me. I can't say I exactly warmed to the ones I did meet.'

'You warmed to Martin,' I pointed out.

'I warmed to his money. And to the fact that he was prepared to pay me some attention at a time when my relationship with you was falling apart. I think I knew it wouldn't last.'

That was another of Maddie's qualities, I thought. She was as honest with herself as she tended to be with everyone else. 'What were they like, Martin's business associates?'

'Pretty much like Martin, really. Overbearing, a bit too sure of themselves, mainly only interested in money. Not too bothered about how they chose to acquire it.'

I shook my head. 'Why did you stick it out so long, Maddie?'

She smiled. 'Because I'm mainly interested in money, too. And I'm not too bothered about how people acquire it. That's what you think, isn't it?'

'Not for me to judge. Do you think any of Martin's businesses were actively criminal?'

'If I'm honest, I imagine they probably were. I was happy to turn a blind eye to it.'

'Did he do any business in this part of the world?' I wasn't even sure why I was asking the question, except that I was fumbling around trying to find something that might link the apparent coincidences.

Maddie frowned. 'Not up here, or at least not as far as I know. Most of his business was in the central belt, with a few interests in England. Mostly around Glasgow. But I couldn't really tell you what kind of deals he was involved in.' She'd poured herself another coffee and was staring into the black liquid as if hoping to see her future in there. After a moment, she looked up at me. 'What was the name of the guy who nearly killed you?'

'Danny Royce. As in Rolls. Why?'

'I thought that was what you said, but I didn't take it in when you were describing what happened. I'm sure the name rings a bell from somewhere.'

'His death was reported in the media, so you might be remembering that. The comms team did their best to keep it low-key at the time. The last thing we wanted was anyone trying to use Royce – a scumbag of the highest order – as yet another stick to beat the police with. At least that was the thinking at the time. Might have been different if anyone had given a bugger about Royce's fate, but he had no family and no real friends.'

'No, it's not that. It's closer to home.' She was silent for a moment. 'I think I might have met him.'

'Through Martin?' It certainly wouldn't have surprised me if Royce and Garfield had moved in the same circles.

'Yes. In the early days of our relationship, when Martin was still making some effort to impress me. Or, more likely, making some effort to impress his associates by parading me alongside him. It was a drinks do in some upmarket bar in the West End. Can't even remember what it was for now. Some dodgy business type trying to schmooze other dodgy business-types, I imagine. But I remember Royce because he kept trying to make a pass at me. Whenever Martin's attention was elsewhere, he was pawing at me. Implying I could do better than Martin – which was no doubt true, but not with Royce.'

'Did Martin actually work with Royce at all?'

'I don't know. I doubt it. The two of them seemed to loathe each other. I suspect that's why Royce was paying so much attention to me that night. I don't know if he was even really interested in me. He was probably just doing it to piss off Martin. I actually thought that Martin might be slightly scared of him. He wouldn't have put up with some of the things Royce said to him that night if they'd come from anyone else. Martin was never as tough as he liked to think.'

'A lot of people were scared of Royce. A genuinely nasty

piece of work. In a different league even from someone like Martin. Psychopathic.'

'When was it that Royce was killed?'

'Last October.'

'Now I think about it, I might have overheard Martin talking about that. I only overheard part of a phone call, but Martin seemed to be gloating about someone's death. I didn't hear a name, just that Martin said the death was going to open up some opportunities. "All coming together at the right time", he said. Something like that. Actually seemed in a good mood for once.'

'I imagine that's how a lot of people were feeling. Royce wasn't exactly well-liked. So that gives us another link. Between Martin and Danny Royce. Which I suppose then links to me, you and Sean Critchley. Not that that gets us much further.'

'Maybe we're seeing patterns that don't really exist. It's that degrees of separation thing, isn't it? If you make enough connections, you can find links between any two people.'

I couldn't really argue with that. Each supposed connection we found only made the picture more confusing. There were probably more urgent questions for me to think about. Like what the hell I was going to do about Maddie.

I was about to broach that subject when my phone buzzed on the table between us. I picked it up and looked at the screen. A number I didn't immediately recognise. 'Yes?'

'Mr Mellor? It's Heather Galloway. We spoke the other day about Kate Brodie.'

'Yes, of course. What can I do for you?'

'I hope you don't mind me calling. You said to get back to you if anything else occurred to me. It's just that I've been thinking over my conversations with Kate. Just in case there was anything else that might help you.'

'No, that's fine. Have you thought of something?'

'I'm not sure. Again, it may be nothing. It's something else that I think I did mention to the police, but they didn't seem very interested.'

I gestured to Maddie to finish off the coffee, then rose to take the phone into the kitchen, closing the door firmly behind me. I hoped that even Maddie would be prepared to take the hint for once. I might be stuck with Maddie for the moment, but I didn't have to share every aspect of my life with her. 'Go on.'

'It was when you asked if she was intending to drive straight up to Cromarty that Friday evening. From the way she'd spoken about it, I'd assumed that was her intention but that was only my impression. If she'd had other plans, there's no particular reason she'd have shared them with me. But then I remembered a conversation I'd had with her a few weeks earlier. My boyfriend had suggested we might try a trip round the North Coast 500 route next summer. I wasn't keen on the idea and asked Kate if she knew anyone who'd done the journey. She didn't, but said she'd spent some time in the Highlands and knew a couple of people up there so could ask around. It was just a passing comment, and she never said anything else about it.' She stopped, sounding mildly embarrassed. 'I'm sorry. That's all it is. It's not much, I'm afraid.'

It wasn't much in itself, but it was the first time anyone had suggested that Kate Brodie might have had friends or contacts actually in the Highlands, or indeed that she'd spent any time there herself. 'You told the police about this conversation?'

'Yes. The officer who interviewed me noted it down, but didn't seem very interested.'

'Kate didn't give you any idea why she'd spent time in the Highlands or who her contacts might have been?'

'She just said what I've told you. I'm sorry.'

'Don't be sorry. It's information I didn't have before. No one else has mentioned Kate knowing anyone in the Highlands.'

'Maybe I misunderstood, but I don't think so.'

'It's another avenue we could explore in the podcast, anyway. All grist to the mill.'

'I hope it helps shed some light on what happened to Kate. Good luck with it.'

There was no question that what I'd just heard constituted a potentially useful lead. If Kate did know other people in the Highlands, that opened up new possibilities as to what might have happened on that Friday evening. The next step, I supposed, was for me to check this out with Morag Henderson. Try to find out whether the investigation had done anything with this information at the time or if it was another piece of intelligence that had been ignored. Had the police made any attempts to identify any sightings of Kate's car other than on the routes from Inverness to Cromarty, for example?

I was still thinking when there was a soft tap on the kitchen door and Maddie's head appeared. 'You finished then? I heard you go quiet.'

That presumably meant that Maddie had been listening at the door. 'Just.'

'Private call?'

'Work stuff. You know.'

'I thought you were unemployed.'

'It's the research stuff for Cameron Fraser. Sorting out the fine details.'

Maddie was already looking bored. But that was often how she looked when the subject was something other than herself.

'You might have been safer in the big city.'

'That's what I'm beginning to wonder,' I said. 'There are moments when it feels as if everything I thought I'd left behind has followed me up here.'

She smiled. 'Literally, in some cases.'

'Well, exactly. But maybe that's the point.'

'What is?'

'I don't know. What if my involvement in all this isn't coincidental? What if I really am somehow at the heart of all this?' It was the same thought I'd finally managed to articulate to myself earlier, although I still couldn't make any real sense of it.

'Maybe that's the answer,' I said now. 'Maybe something really has followed me up here.'

CHAPTER TWENTY-NINE

My Saturday supermarket purchases had been intended to get me through what I'd expected to be a bleak few days – a selection of ready meals, some bottles of wine, a bottle of single malt. I'd also bought some bacon, sausages and eggs on the basis that I might be consoled by the idea of a comforting fry-up. In retrospect that idea had been singularly optimistic, but at least it meant I had something to offer Maddie.

She responded enthusiastically to the idea. 'Just what I need after last night's drive.'

I was reluctant to admit it, but – against all my expectations and better instincts – I was almost beginning to welcome Maddie's presence. I'd thought I'd prefer to be alone, but I'm not sure that wouldn't have dragged me further down into inertia and despair. Maddie's demanding presence was at least forcing me to continue living in the present, rather than dwelling on the past or some half-imagined future. It wouldn't last, of course. There'd come a time, probably sooner rather than later, when I'd find her as infuriating as I had when we were together. I couldn't allow her to stay for more than a day or two. Apart from anything else, I'd need to work out the practicalities of where we were going to sleep. In practice, I assumed that meant I'd be spending more nights on the sofa.

For the moment, though, I busied myself frying sausages, bacon and eggs for Maddie's brunch. She was sitting at the kitchen table, drinking yet more coffee. The atmosphere wasn't exactly strained, but felt slightly awkward. Normally, I imagined Maddie would have been chatting amiably, if overbearingly, about nothing in particular. It had always been one of her gifts, assuming it wasn't a curse. She'd always had the capacity to fill the air with inconsequential small talk. I'd initially found it a huge asset, particularly as it was a talent I demonstrably lacked. By the time our relationship was falling apart, it had become little more than an irritation, but I'd have welcomed it today.

As it was, either she was too shaken by her recent experiences and her panicked drive up here, or she simply felt it would be inappropriate to blether on in the face of my recent bereavement. So she was sitting largely in silence, uttering only monosyllabic responses to my questions about the food. When I finally put the plate in front of her, she smiled gratefully. I suspected the gratitude was less for the food than for the chance to occupy herself with an activity. I hadn't felt up to the full fry-up, but I'd made myself a bacon sandwich which I chewed unenthusiastically.

'This is genuinely strange,' I said. 'I never imagined we'd be in the same room again. I still don't really know why you came here. There was really nowhere else you could go?'

'I couldn't think of anywhere. At least, nowhere I'd feel safe. You need to understand, Jack. I'm not joking. I really do think someone tried to kill me.'

'I understand that. I don't know if you're right, but I understand why you'd think it. And given everything that's happened, I'm not dismissing the possibility. You realise you can't stay here, though?'

'For a day or two, Jack. That's all I ask.

'Then what?'

She was silent for a moment, eating her food. I suspected she had no answer to my question. 'I need to work it out, Jack. Work out what to do next. Work out what's going on. I'm just asking for a few days to do that.'

I registered that the time frame had already expanded from "a day or two" to "a few days". I knew that Maddie was more than capable of continuing to expand it for as long as she was allowed. 'I'm not going to throw you out now, Maddie. But it can't be for more than a day or two.'

'Yeah, sure. I get it.' She sounded like a child who'd been given a five-minute warning to stop playing.

There was no point in pressing the point for the moment, but I knew I couldn't let it slide. 'I'm not going to change my mind, Maddie. A couple of days, then you need to find some other solution.' I pushed myself to my feet. 'You finish your food, I'm going to make a phone call.'

'Who to?'

'My business, Maddie. You don't need to know.'

I called Morag Henderson from the living room. The phone rang a few times before she answered.

'Mr Mellor. And on a Sunday. What can I do for you?'

'I've just been having another chat with Heather Galloway, Kate Brodie's neighbour. She'd remembered something she hadn't mentioned when we first spoke.'

'Go on.'

'Kate had told her she'd spent some time in the Highlands and knew people up there.'

'You're sure about that?'

'It had only been a passing comment, but Galloway was sure that's what Kate had said.'

There was a silence, suggesting that Henderson was thinking through the implications of what I'd told her. Finally, she said, 'That's news to me. All the friends we identified were from Edinburgh or Glasgow.'

'Another thing that Kate kept close to her chest.'

'Did Galloway give this information to the police?'

'She says she did. They didn't seem very interested.'

'I've no recollection of it being mentioned at the time. It would have changed the direction of the investigation. She didn't give Galloway any other information?'

'Unfortunately not.'

'As far as I recall, the whole investigation was predicated on the basis that Kate Brodie knew no one in the Highlands. We managed to track her vehicle sporadically with the ANPR cameras up the A9, and the timings suggest she didn't make any stops, other than one for petrol in Perth, prior to passing Inverness. We've no sightings of her beyond that, so if she did make some kind of detour on that Friday night it must have been somewhere between Inverness and Cromarty.'

'Sadie Wilson reckoned Kate had told the others in Cromarty she was likely to be arriving late, but she hadn't given either them or Wilson any idea she was likely to be substantially delayed. If she was planning a detour, it would have to have been relatively short.'

'Which implies that we're talking about somewhere within easy striking distance of the route from Inverness to Cromarty. If we'd had this information at the time, it would have given us a whole new avenue to explore. We must have checked for sightings of her car in the roads off that route, but I don't know how much effort was put into it. Not a great deal, I'm guessing.

The real question is who she might have planned to see. Who did she know up here?'

It was my turn to pause before answering. 'I've been thinking about that. I mean, it might be anyone. She could have friends from university who've ended up in this part of the world, I guess.'

'We didn't identify any during the investigation as far as I'm aware. But then I don't know if we were looking for them.'

'There's only one other person I can think of. Cameron Fraser.'

'Fraser? Would Kate have known him?'

'I don't know, but it's possible. He and Kinnear were business partners for a long time. She worked for Kinnear. She must have met Fraser, I imagine, even if she didn't know him well. Was he ever interviewed during the investigation?'

'Not to my knowledge. But if Fraser had been expecting to see her that weekend surely he'd have come forward to tell us?'

'You'd have thought so, unless she was planning on turning up unannounced. But why would she do that? In any case, I can't really imagine what reasons she might have had to see Fraser, given that he and Kinnear weren't on speaking terms. It was just a thought.'

'And, as you said, she could have known anyone up there. As far as I'm aware, no one ever came forward, though. The original investigation doesn't exactly seem to have covered itself in glory.' She paused. 'How are you feeling now, anyway?'

'Better than I feared. I've a friend staying for a day or two, so that's helping.' I wasn't sure I'd ever described Maddie in that way before, not even in the early days of our relationship. But I'd thought it best to say something about her in case the police made a return visit, and I'd no desire to explain my real relationship with Maddie.

'That's good to hear. Don't push yourself too hard.'

'I'll try not to.'

We ended the call and I sat for a moment, enjoying the brief period of solitude before I had to interact with Maddie again. I'd desperately wanted to ask Henderson what progress they were making in investigating Lorna's killing, but I'd assumed she wouldn't be willing to say anything. Any effort I might put into the Kate Brodie case was nothing more than displacement. The mystery I really wanted to solve was that of Lorna's death.

Yet I had the growing sense that, in some way I couldn't yet begin to fathom, the two might not be unconnected. I was increasingly feeling that there was a picture there, as yet nothing more than an unconnected swirl of half-glimpsed images, but slowly, very slowly, coalescing into something I might eventually begin to understand.

CHAPTER THIRTY

Maddie and I spent the evening working steadily through the bottle of whisky. Supper had been a chicken casserole I'd dug out of the freezer, the last of a batch I'd cooked a few weeks before. Halfway through defrosting it, I realised that when I'd cooked it I'd only recently met Lorna. That thought took away my appetite, but I forced myself to eat anyway. On the other side of the table, Maddie actually seemed approving of my efforts.

'I'd forgotten,' she said. 'You're not a bad cook.'

'That wasn't what you said when I was cooking for you regularly.'

'Maybe you've improved.'

'Maybe you're having to be less picky.'

After that, we'd repaired to the living room and the Scotch. I sipped at it cautiously, recognising the risk of drinking too much. Which wouldn't be a good idea for countless reasons, particularly in Maddie's presence.

For a few moments we sat drinking in silence. Maddie hadn't said much over the supper, other than the odd bout of verbal sparring. Her usual chatty ebullience seemed to have deserted her.

Eventually, she looked up from her glass – she'd already knocked back the first dram – and said, 'Why did you really leave the police?'

'I told you. I'd had enough. The thing with Danny Royce was the last straw. I wanted a change.'

She looked sceptical. 'Is that true, though? I mean, I know you, Jack. Maybe better than you think I do. You don't walk away from things. You didn't even walk away from our bloody relationship though we both knew it was beyond help.'

'This time I did, okay? I realised there was more to life than getting shot at and filling in endless forms.'

'But you enjoyed the work. You said so.'

'I did for a long while. But things changed.'

'What changed?'

None of this was what I wanted to be talking about. Probably, at that moment, there was nothing I wanted to be talking about. Finally I said, 'I got on the wrong side of some people. I made complaints about the behaviour of some of my colleagues.' I laughed. 'It's funny. All the stuff I complained about has started to emerge now. The misogyny, the homophobia, the casual racism. Maybe if someone had listened to us – it wasn't just me, there were a number of us raising concerns – something could have been done long before now. But nobody did. We were pissing in the wind.'

'You never told me about any of this.'

'It was mostly after you'd left. To be honest, I didn't think it was a big deal. I complained about a few people who were behaving in ways that were clearly unacceptable. I expected they'd be reprimanded, maybe disciplined, and we'd all move on. But it never happened.' I took another sip of the whisky, tempted now to down the rest of the glass. 'No one took a blind bit of notice. And I became, among some of my colleagues, persona non bloody grata.'

Maddie had picked up the bottle and poured herself another larger dram. She waved the bottle vaguely in my direction, but I shook my head. 'That's pretty shitty,' she said.

'I should have expected it. I was bloody naive in retrospect.'

'You always were.' Maddie spoke almost with affection. 'That doesn't make you wrong, though.'

'I thought I could ride it out. And mostly I did. I mean, don't get me wrong. There were plenty of decent coppers who were well and truly on my side, even if not all of them were prepared to stick their heads above the parapet. Mostly it was okay. But it was stressful. That's the thing about policing. You need to be able to trust your colleagues. You don't want to find yourself in a position of danger and discover you've been shafted.'

'I can see why the Royce incident got to you.'

'That's the point. Sean Critchley saved my life. I don't know the whys or the hows of that. Critchley wasn't exactly on the side of the angels where this stuff was concerned. But he saved my life. On another day, if it had been another officer, they might not have bothered.'

'That was what drove you out?'

'It wasn't only that. It was a stack of stuff. But that was a big part of it. I didn't feel it was sustainable. It can be a tough job at the best of times, and those were far from the best of times.'

'I suppose that makes sense. Do you regret it now? Calling out your colleagues, I mean.'

'Not remotely. Not now. I can't pretend there weren't moments when I wondered if I should have kept my mouth shut. But not anymore. I know I did the right thing, and I can live with myself.'

Maddie smiled. 'You always were the quixotic type, Jack.'

'That's probably all I was doing, though. Tilting at

windmills. I'm not sure my intervention achieved anything.' I sipped gently at the whisky. 'You know, this is the first time I've talked to anyone about this.' I'd told Lorna about my past, but not this part of it. I suppose it had been something I didn't want to think too much about. Maddie was right. I wasn't the type to walk away. But that's exactly what I'd done in the end. I didn't exactly feel ashamed or embarrassed about it – I knew my original actions had taken some courage – but I hadn't quite had the nerve to stick it out.

'I don't imagine you ever thought I'd be the one you shared it with.'

'Not in a million years.'

'Life's full of surprises, I guess.'

'That's what I'm learning. And some shocks.'

'Shit, Jack. I'm sorry. I didn't mean—'

'No, I know. And you're right. I came up here because I was looking for – I don't know, some kind of stability, I suppose. Somewhere where one day would follow the next, and I could get my head in order.' I laughed, though without much humour. 'It's not exactly worked out like that.'

Maddie was pouring herself another dram. One thing I'd almost forgotten was her ability to consume substantial amounts of alcohol without any obvious ill effects. She held out the bottle to me, and this time I splashed a small amount into my glass. 'What about you?' I said. 'What are you going to do now?'

'Is this another hint, Jack?'

'It's a genuine question. Though I will say it again. You can't stay here for more than a day or two.'

'I know. I realise there isn't the space.'

'It's not just that. Even if I had the room, it would be a genuinely bad idea. You know that.'

'Yeah, I guess I do. I'm grateful to you for giving me refuge when you did.'

That was the first time I could remember her expressing real gratitude for anything I'd done. I wasn't entirely sure if the sentiment was sincere or if it was another attempt to soften me up, but I decided I might as well take it at face value. 'That's okay. But to come back to my question, what are you going to do next?'

'I've been trying to think about that, but I don't honestly know. I don't want to go back to Glasgow, not until I know what's going on.'

'You really think someone's trying to kill you?'

'It looked that way to me. I could be wrong, but it's not a risk I'm keen to take.'

'You can't hide away forever.'

'I know. But I don't have any idea what else to do. Unless you've got some smart suggestions.'

The truth was that I had nothing to suggest. In normal circumstances, I wouldn't even be taking Maddie's concerns seriously. But after what had happened to Lorna, I didn't feel I could dismiss them. 'Let's sleep on it. Maybe we need to get the police to take it more seriously.'

'From what you've just told me, you may not be the ideal person to exert influence on the police.'

'I don't know. But there are good people in there who might be prepared to listen to me.'

'May be worth a try, I suppose.' Maddie didn't sound convinced. I'm not sure I would have been in her position.

We spent the rest of the evening chatting amiably enough. Maddie occasionally displayed her spikier side, but for the most part kept it under control. We finished the bottle, though my contribution to that was relatively limited. Eventually, as the clock reached ten, Maddie yawned. 'I need to get some sleep. Still feeling the effects of last night.'

'You take the bedroom again. I'll manage on the sofa.'

'If you're sure.'

'I'm sure. I can make myself comfortable enough.'

That wasn't entirely true, but I'd cope. The sofa was big enough to accommodate me and I had a spare duvet and some pillows. For one or two nights, I'd be fine, though I wasn't intending to make that too obvious to Maddie.

After she'd retired upstairs, I sat thinking over our conversation. I was pleased I'd finally managed to speak to someone about my experiences before leaving the force even if Maddie wouldn't have been my chosen audience. It was one of the conversations I'd been hoping I'd eventually have with Lorna.

But even talking to Maddie about it had felt cathartic. It was something that had been lurking in the back of my brain for far too long, a pressure I couldn't find any way to relieve. I wasn't sure I'd fully succeeded even now, but I did feel there was more chance I could eventually come to grips with how difficult that period had been. I don't think I'd even realised it myself at the time. I'd simply pressed on and made the best of things. It was only after I'd walked out of the door on that last Friday that it all finally hit me. After that, I'd felt a kind of survivor's guilt, aware there were still people in the force undergoing the same pressures I'd faced. As Maddie had implied, that had led to a further pressure. The knowledge that, when the going had got tough, I'd walked away.

I put out some food for Ziggy, who was snoozing quietly by the now cooling wood-stove, as he had been for most of the evening. I pulled the duvet over the sofa, turned off the lights and lay down, more or less fully dressed, to get some sleep. After the disruption of Maddie's arrival, I'd slept restlessly the previous night and I quickly drifted into sleep.

I woke suddenly what felt like minutes later. I'd been in the middle of a dream – I was left only with the dissolving shreds of a discomforting scene yet again involving Gregor McBride – and at first I was simply confused. I didn't know what had disturbed me. Then I heard a low growling from the far end of the room. Ziggy was restless, also disturbed by something. I reached to turn on the table light, but some instinct made me pause. I'd never heard Ziggy behave this way before.

Moving as silently as I could, I sat up and strained my ears for any sound beyond Ziggy's growling. There was something. A scraping I couldn't immediately identify but which seemed to be coming from the hallway. Then another, slightly louder crack.

Someone was trying to break into the house. I fumbled in the darkness for something I could use as a weapon and my hand closed on the empty whisky bottle. It was a heavy enough object, better than anything else that was likely to be around.

The cracking continued. Whoever was trying to break in wasn't making any effort to be subtle, presumably reasoning that the noise would be insufficient to disturb my sleep upstairs. Or perhaps simply not caring.

Grasping the neck of the bottle, I moved silently across the room until I was by the door, hoping I'd at least have the element of surprise. I heard a louder cracking and then felt a blast of cold air. The front door was open. I tensed, gripping the bottle more tightly, my ears strained to hear any movement from the intruder.

Suddenly, Ziggy went wild, barking furiously as he raced into the hallway. He'd never seemed the most effective of guard dogs – sadly for Lorna – but now there was a genuine savagery in his behaviour. There was a cry of surprise from the intruder, then more angry barking from Ziggy.

I stepped into the hall. Against the open doorway, I could see the silhouette of a figure trying to fend off Ziggy. The man was desperately trying to raise his arm but Ziggy kept furiously biting at his hand. Trying to avoid getting entangled with the dog, I stepped forward and smashed the bottle hard against the intruder's head.

The bottle remained intact, but the impact drove the figure back against the side of the door. Until that moment, the intruder hadn't registered my presence. I took advantage of his surprise by striking him again with the bottle. This time, he caught his head on the door-frame and staggered back, stunned by the double blow. I followed him out of the door, smashing the bottle on the exterior brickwork as I stepped forward.

I held out the broken bottle threateningly. I saw now that the intruder was holding a pistol, and it occurred to me that if he chose to shoot I'd managed to make myself a perfect standing target. Ziggy was behind me, growling threateningly. I tensed, waiting to see what would happen next.

To my relief, the man – out here, I could clearly see that the figure was male, though his face was largely concealed by a scarf – turned away. He'd obviously decided to cut his losses. There was a car on the track behind him, facing down the hill. The car was empty, but the engine was running and the driver's door wide open. Not looking back, he jumped into the car, then, without lights, drove back down the hill at full speed. It was only as the car reached the bottom of the track and turned onto the road that the headlights were turned on.

I took a breath, then turned to Ziggy, growling in the doorway. 'Good boy. Well done.' I walked back into the hall, Ziggy trotting behind me, calming now that the threat had receded. As I turned on the hallway light, Maddie appeared at the top of the stairs.

'What the hell's going on?' she said. 'Some of us are trying to get some bloody sleep up here.'

CHAPTER THIRTY-ONE

'What time was this?'
'I checked when I came back in. Around 2.30.'
'What exactly happened?' Morag Henderson was on the sofa opposite me. DS McBain was sitting beside her, a notebook open on his knee. Maddie was curled up on one of the armchairs, watching in silence. Henderson had so far pointedly not enquired about her presence.

I recounted in as much detail as I could what had happened the previous night. It seemed something of a blur. I was conscious I'd largely acted on instinct, adrenaline driving me on.

'You're sure he was carrying a firearm?'
'Definitely. I mean, I don't know if it was real or a replica, but I didn't imagine it.'

'I'm conscious this must have all happened quickly and in darkness. I want to be sure of the facts.'

'And you think I'm likely to be particularly suggestible given what happened to Lorna?'

'I need to make sure we're acting on accurate information, Mr Mellor.'

'No, fair enough. You're right. My first thought when I

realised someone was breaking in was that it must be the person who killed Lorna. But he was holding some kind of handgun. I'm sure of that.'

'He didn't shoot?'

'No. My impression was that he considered it then decided against. I'm not sure why, assuming he'd been prepared to use the gun in the house. Maybe he thought it would make too much noise outside, though there's only the farmhouse nearby. Or maybe he didn't feel sufficiently in control of the situation.'

'If he was a pro, that could be it,' Henderson said. 'He might have decided it was better to cut his losses rather than to take a further risk. I don't suppose you got his registration?'

'Sorry. At first the car was side-on to me. Then he drove off at speed without turning the lights on until he got to the bottom of the track so I couldn't make it out in the dark. The car was something anonymous. A Fiesta, I think. Dark-coloured, but I couldn't say much more than that.'

'Number would probably have been a ringer anyway,' McBain said morosely. He didn't look happy. I'd probably have felt the same in his shoes, given that an already challenging case had taken on another twist.

'Interesting that the dog reacted so strongly,' Henderson commented.

'That surprised me,' I said. 'Ziggy's a lovely old thing, but he's not usually the best guard dog. Too friendly. I'd never seen him behave like that before.'

'Makes me think he might have recognised your intruder.'

'And associated him with something bad? That was my thought, too.'

'Lucky you were sleeping down here,' Henderson said. For the first time, she turned and looked at Maddie. 'Did you witness any of this, Ms...?'

'Carson. Madeleine Carson. No, not really, I'm afraid. I'd

been wakened by Ziggy's barking and eventually came out to see what was going on. But by that time, it seemed to be all over and Jack was coming back into the house.'

Henderson nodded. 'You're just visiting?'

'Maddie's my ex-partner,' I said. There was no point in concealing any of this. If Henderson was interested, she'd find out anyway. 'She thought I might be in need of some company.'

'That's very solicitous,' McBain said.

'Actually, there's more to it than that. Maddie came up here because she thought her own life was under threat.'

It was the first time I'd taken Henderson by surprise. She looked from me to Maddie and then back to me. 'This isn't a joke?'

There was something in Maddie's expression I couldn't read. She didn't look entirely happy that I'd revealed her reasons for being here. 'Deadly serious. With the emphasis on the first word,' she said.

Henderson was still looking at me. 'You do seem to be a dangerous man to know, Mr Mellor.'

'So it seems. I've no idea why.'

Henderson tuned back to Maddie. 'You'd better tell me about it.' I could see McBain grimacing at the prospect of yet another complication.

Maddie told Henderson what she'd told me about the experiences in Glasgow. I couldn't tell from Henderson's expression how seriously she was taking Maddie's account. When Maddie had finished, Henderson said, 'And you feel sure these incidents are linked?'

'I can't be absolutely certain, obviously. But I'm pretty sure it was the same man.'

'You don't know why anyone would want to harm you?'

'Not remotely.'

'And you came up here to escape all that?'

'Which may not have been the smartest idea, as it turns out.'

Henderson had turned back to look at me. 'We don't get these kind of crimes up here. Not very often, anyway. Your arrival seems to have changed all that, Mr Mellor. I'm wondering why.'

'If I had the answer to that, I'd be the first to tell you. Especially now it looks as if I've been targeted too.'

'I'll be frank with you, Mr Mellor. We're not making the progress we'd like with the investigation into Ms Jardine's death. There are no obvious suspects, and we've so far identified no one with a potential motive for the killing. I keep coming back to you.'

'Are you still suggesting I was involved in her death?'

'I don't think so. Not in the way you mean, anyway. I can't imagine what motive you might have for killing Ms Jardine in that manner. But you somehow seem to be at the heart of all this. That's what's troubling me.'

'It's troubling me too. Especially after last night.'

She gazed at me for what felt like too long, as if she were somehow tapping into my thoughts. 'Is there anything you haven't told us, Mr Mellor?'

'I don't think so. Nothing pertinent to Lorna's death, anyway.'

'I see. And what about Sean Critchley's death?'

The question took me by surprise, and I knew I hadn't succeeded in concealing my reaction. 'Critchley?'

'Is there anything you haven't told us about Critchley's death?'

I hesitated. I hadn't previously told them about Critchley's visit to the cottage only because I'd thought it would give them another reason to put me in the frame for Lorna's murder. 'There's one thing I didn't tell you. Critchley came here.'

McBain glared at me. 'When I first interviewed you, you told me you'd had no contact with Critchley up here.'

'I'm sorry. It wasn't entirely a lie, but it wasn't the full truth either.'

McBain sighed. 'You do realise this is a murder enquiry, Mr Mellor.'

'It's an enquiry into the murder of someone who meant a lot to me,' I countered. 'I didn't intend to mislead you. I thought it wasn't relevant to Lorna's death.'

'It's probably better if you let us decide what might be pertinent to our investigation, Mr Mellor,' Henderson said. 'Tell us about Critchley.'

'I didn't have any contact with him up here. But he did visit the cottage. It was the night I first went for supper with Lorna. I came back to find the front door open. There'd obviously been an intruder but I couldn't see any sign of anything missing or any disturbance. It was only when I went upstairs to bed that I found he'd left me a note. Asking me to contact him. Just that and a mobile phone number. Signed Sean. At first, I couldn't even think of anyone I knew with that name. It took me a while to realise it must have been Critchley.'

'Do you have this note?'

'I'm sorry. I threw it away.'

'Did you try to make contact?'

'No. My first reaction was that I wanted nothing to do with Critchley. I hadn't known him well and I didn't much like what I did know.'

'Even though he saved your life?'

'That complicated things. But not very much. Critchley was very much part of a past I wanted to put firmly behind me. I wasn't happy that he not only seemed to have followed me up here, but had had the nerve to intrude into my new home.'

'You weren't curious about what he wanted?' McBain asked.

'Of course. I was intrigued by Critchley coming up here at all, and I couldn't begin to imagine what he might want from me. So I did some asking around among ex-colleagues. I'd thought he might make a return visit, and I wanted to be as well prepared as I could. No one could tell me very much. Then someone called me back to tell me that Critchley had been killed. That's all I know.'

'You have no idea what he wanted?'

'None at all. Maybe he thought I owed him one and had come up to call in the favour in some way. That would have been very Sean Critchley. But then I don't know why he didn't wait around for my return. My car was outside so it was obvious I wasn't away.'

'You'd had no other contact with him since leaving the force?' McBain asked.

'None at all. I'd only had very limited contact with him even before that.'

'Is there anything else you haven't told us, Mr Mellor?' Henderson said. 'No matter how trivial or irrelevant you might think it is.' There was a note of irony in her tone, but I suppose I deserved that.

'There's one other thing. Just from the other day.'

McBain sighed. 'Go on, Mr Mellor. What else haven't you told us?'

'It's probably nothing. But I went into Dingwall on Thursday. It was when Gregor McBride and Archie Kinnear were visiting.'

Henderson nodded. 'I heard there was a bit of a stooshie there. Pity McBride didn't think to consult with us before deciding to go walkabout. We might have been able to prevent that.'

'Aye, if only by telling him not to bother,' McBain added. 'Guy must have been looking for trouble.'

'He had his own hired muscle,' I said. 'Or at least Kinnear did. I nearly got on the wrong side of them. They looked as if they were about to assault someone so I intervened.' I couldn't see any point in mentioning Gus's name. 'Thing is, I knew one of them. Ex-cop called Kenny Taylor. Sacked for some kind of sexual harassment, I heard. We'd worked together briefly when I first joined. He recognised me, too. Knew I'd left the force, and seemed to know about the Danny Royce incident. He said something about keeping an eye on me.'

'But he didn't actually assault you?' Henderson asked.

'No. I thought he was going to but then he and his mate just walked away.'

'He threatened you?'

'There was an implied threat. I didn't know how seriously to take it. It felt like "I know where you live" stuff. I was just surprised he knew about me at all.'

'Police grapevine works in mysterious ways,' Henderson said. 'But we'll have a look at Taylor. See what he's been up to since leaving the force.'

'Anyway, that was it. Probably just a coincidence. But I'm finding it increasingly difficult to work out what might be relevant in this case.'

She nodded. 'The most relevant figure increasingly seems to be you. The fact that Critchley made efforts to contact you seems to put you even more firmly at the centre of the picture. It suggests his presence up here wasn't coincidental.'

'All I can tell you is that none of this makes any sense to me either. If I'm at the heart of this, I've no idea how I got there or what my role is.'

She nodded. 'I hope I can believe you, Mr Mellor. As for your intruder last night, we'll see what we can find on cameras in the local area. Given it was in the small hours, we may be able to identify the car on local cameras, but that may not give us much if the registration's fake. My primary concern is whether your intruder is likely to return.'

'That's rather my concern too. I've got a guy coming round to improve the security, but I don't know if that'll be sufficient if we really are dealing with a pro.'

'Do you have anywhere else you could go?'

'Nowhere. And even if I had I wouldn't be happy to be forced out of my home by something like this.'

'Your choice, Mr Mellor. We'll do what we can to keep you safe, but our resources are limited. Take care.' Henderson had already risen to her feet, and McBain was following her lead. 'We won't take up any more of your time today.'

She crossed to the door and then looked back. 'But you might want to keep thinking about why someone seems so very keen to position you at the heart of all this. If you have any ideas, let me know.'

CHAPTER THIRTY-TWO

After the police had left, Maddie headed back upstairs to get some more sleep. She'd been unable to sleep after the break-in, and we'd both sat up talking – or, more accurately, drifting into extended periods of not entirely companionable silence – until I'd felt it was late enough for me to call Morag Henderson. Henderson and McBain had turned up half an hour or so later, and she'd dutifully sat through our discussion. But two disrupted nights were telling on Maddie and I urged her to get some more rest. I was wondering what she might decide to do now, particularly as this place hadn't turned out to be the sanctuary she might have hoped. But there was no point in trying to make a decision until she was able to think clearly.

I was examining the damage to the front door when I saw Gus heading up the track towards the cottage. He was looking more serious and worried than I'd seen him. 'Morning, Jack. Hear you had some trouble in the night. Just had a wee visit from the police.'

It hadn't occurred to me that Henderson and McBain would call on Gus, but it wasn't surprising. He was the only other potential witness in the area, though I assumed he'd have been asleep. 'Sorry about that. I'd have called to warn you if I'd realised they'd head down to yours.'

'No worries. Couldn't help them anyway. Didn't see or hear a thing.' He peered over my shoulder at the door. 'Nasty business, Jack. What the hell's going on?'

'I wish I knew.'

'This stuff doesn't happen up here. First Lorna. Now this. I don't understand it.'

There was nothing openly accusatory in his tone, but I knew what he was thinking. It was as if I'd brought some kind of contamination with me. 'I've no idea what's going on, Gus. Even if someone wished me harm – and I've no idea who might – they'd have no reason to target Lorna.'

'Maybe they killed her to hurt you.'

I could tell from Gus's expression that he immediately regretted the words. He'd obviously expressed his sentiments more baldly than he'd intended. But he was right. It was a possibility I had to consider. It was an awful idea. That somehow, however unintentionally or indirectly, I might have been partly responsible for Lorna's death. 'I can't see that, Gus. All we'd done was have supper together a couple of times. And, yes, I'd hoped it might turn into something more serious, but we were a long way from that.'

'Aye, you're right. I'm scraping round for answers. I told police about Lorna's background. The rape, and all that. They took it all down, but I suspect they thought it was a stretch to link that to her murder.'

'Who knows? None of this makes any sense to me.'

He gestured towards Maddie's car. 'You've a visitor.'

I'd known this would be another awkward moment. 'Long story. Would you believe it's my ex-partner? I told her what had happened with Lorna. She insisted on coming up to help out.' I felt bad telling even this white lie to Gus, but I didn't want to talk about Maddie's real reasons for being here.

It wasn't clear how much Gus believed me or what he really thought. 'That was good of her.'

'I suppose it's helped a bit. And it was fortunate last night. If I hadn't been sleeping downstairs on the sofa, I might not have heard the intruder till it was too late.'

'That's true enough. Close call.' He was peering at the door, examining the damage. 'I'll get in touch with Grant. See if he can do you a running repair on that.'

'Thanks. I'd appreciate that. He's supposed to be coming at some point to do a full job on the security. Looks like I might need it.'

'I'll see if he can do it as soon as possible. He's got one or two jobs scheduled in for me over the next couple of days but I reckon this should take priority.' Gus straightened and turned to me, looking me straight in the eye. 'You think your intruder was the same guy who killed Lorna?'

I took a breath. 'It's a hell of a coincidence otherwise. The way Ziggy reacted suggested it was the same man.'

'But if he didn't kill Lorna to hurt you, why else would be want to kill you both?'

I had no answer to that. 'I've no idea. Maybe the killer thought I'd witnessed something, though I can't imagine why he might think that. Beyond that, I've nothing.'

'I asked the police if this might be some random lunatic. Someone killing for the hell of it. They reckoned that was unlikely and that they don't think there's any wider danger to the public, but again who the hell knows?'

'I'm sorry, Gus. Maybe it's time for me to move away. I feel as if I'm cursed, though I've no idea why.'

He shrugged. 'If this is some random killer that won't help, will it?'

'What about you?'

'I've a licensed shotgun. I normally keep it safely locked away. But for the moment it'll be in the bedroom with me. Just in case.'

'I don't want to put you through all this. I'm sorry.'

'Aye, well. We are where we are. It doesn't look as if there's much you can do about that. I'll get on the phone to Grant for you. In the meantime, stay safe.'

'And you.'

I watched as he trudged his way back down the track. Our parting had been amicable enough, but I felt that something had changed. I'd seen Gus almost as a father figure, or at least as the elder brother I'd never had. Now there was a barrier between us. Even if he didn't directly blame me for Lorna's death, he didn't trust me in the way he had. I'd brought trouble into his life, and I wasn't sure he'd forgive me for that. It was something else I'd lost, another potential future I might now never experience.

And I still didn't know why.

CHAPTER THIRTY-THREE

I tried to force myself to focus on the Kate Brodie case. Cameron Fraser would still pay me for whatever time I spent on the investigation, and it would provide me with something more constructive to concentrate on. I'd at least managed to come up with some information which didn't seem to have emerged from the police investigation, so I could give him something for his money.

Even there, though, I felt yet again as if I was heading into a cul-de-sac. The conversation with Heather Galloway had perhaps been a small step forward, but it hadn't provided the breakthrough I needed. I had no idea who Kate might have been planning to see before joining her friends in Cromarty, and I couldn't see any way of finding out. I had some fragments of new information, but no way of pulling them together into anything coherent.

It was time I updated Fraser on the latest developments. This time the call rang out to voicemail, and I left a brief message asking him to call me back.

I was expecting a lengthy wait, but the phone rang a few minutes later. Whatever else he might be, Fraser was certainly responsive.

'Jack,' he said. 'Sorry I missed your call. I was finishing a call on the landline but I'm free to talk now. I believe you've had some further trouble.'

I wondered if his preceding call had been from his police contact. 'Someone tried to break into my cottage last night. Someone with a firearm.'

'This is becoming intriguing, Jack. Why would anyone want to harm you?'

'I've no idea. But then I've no idea why anyone would have wanted to harm Lorna Jardine either.'

'It must be concerning. Do you think this intruder is likely to return?'

'I've honestly no idea. I suspect not immediately. The risk would be too great. But the thought that there's someone out there who wants to kill me isn't exactly reassuring.'

'If there is anything I can do, Jack, let me know. I do have some resources at my disposal to address threats like this. I like to make sure those who work for me are kept safe.'

I had no idea what he meant, and I wasn't sure I wanted to find out. 'Thanks. That's appreciated. I'll see how it goes.'

'Was this what you were calling to tell me? I wondered if you might have had second thoughts about continuing with our investigation.'

'Not at all. In fact, I've a potentially new piece of information. I had another call from Heather Galloway, Kate Brodie's neighbour, and she told me something no one else appears to have mentioned. That Kate had spent time in the Highlands and had some contacts up here.'

There was a moment's silence. 'Does she know who?'

'Unfortunately not. Galloway apparently mentioned it to the police at the time, but they didn't seem interested.'

'That does seem to be a recurring theme.'

'Morag Henderson was pretty sure they did nothing with the information. It would have potentially opened up new lines of enquiry. But I'm not sure how far it gets us unless we can identify the contacts. The other question, if she did know people up here, is whether she might have made a detour to see someone on the Friday night. That would explain why she didn't go straight to the house in Cromarty. If so, it must have been someone based relatively close by. Is there anyone you can think of?'

'I'm not aware of anyone, I'm afraid.'

'I did wonder if she might have been coming to see you?'

'Me? Why would she have been coming to see me?'

'I don't know. Perhaps she was seeking some advice or support. Some business proposition, maybe.'

'I'm afraid you're wide of the mark, Jack. I didn't know Kate well at all. I'd met her a couple of times through Archie. But I'd not had any contact with her at all in recent years. I can't think of any reason why she'd have wanted to see me. I don't know if she'd have even known where I lived.'

Another dead end then. 'It was just a thought. None of her other friends have mentioned anyone else she knew up here, but I haven't asked that specific question. That's probably my next step.'

'Good luck with your enquiries, Jack. You seem to be making some progress.'

As always, he ended the call with no formalities. I'd been surprised by his reaction to my news. He'd been much warmer and more positive than I'd expected. Yes, I was making some progress where the police apparently hadn't, but only because I was taking seriously what Kate's friends were telling me. I was no closer to discovering what had happened to her.

Ziggy was growing restless, keen to get out of the house. I'd taken him for a short walk before the police had arrived, but he needed more exercise. Perhaps he even needed to work out whatever emotions had been stirred in his canine head by the events of the night. Fair enough, I thought. I had an idea how he must be feeling.

I delayed a few moments sending a blind-copied email to those of Kate's friends who had responded to my initial query, asking whether any of them knew if Kate had had any friends up here in the northern Highlands. I wasn't optimistic about receiving any positive responses, but it was worth a try.

The walk with Ziggy took longer than I'd planned. I'd felt uneasy leaving the front door unsecured, particularly with Maddie asleep in the house, but there wasn't much I could do about that till Grant McLeish had fixed it. I'd intended to walk to the top of the hill to keep the house in sight, but Ziggy had different ideas. As soon as I took him off his lead, he raced away up the hill, while I trudged more slowly behind him.

Once I reached the summit, I was reluctant to proceed further, but Ziggy was tearing away down into the next valley. I let him run for a while, dissipating the energy that had built up through that long morning, throwing sticks for him to chase and return to me. In the meantime, I kept my eye on the scene behind me, watching to see no one was approaching the cottage.

When Ziggy appeared finally to have exhausted himself, I reattached his lead, allowing him to trot ahead of me as we descended the track together. It had remained a fine day, the late-morning sun still low in the clear sky, an icy breeze stirring the shadows across the hillside.

As I reached the cottage, I saw a white van approaching from below. Grant McLeish, I guessed. He pulled up outside the cottage as I reached the door. I waited for him to emerge then gestured towards the damage. He gave a low whistle. 'Someone keen to get in.'

'Someone who didn't care about making too much noise or damage,' I said. 'Which was maybe fortunate.'

'Aye, Gus was telling me. You really think they wanted to kill you?' He gave an involuntary shudder and glanced over his shoulder, as if concerned my intruder might still be in the vicinity.

'That's the way it felt, anyway.'

'Hard to believe in a place like this.'

'Tell me about it. Do you think you can do something with it?'

'I can do a temporary job for the moment, so you can lock the door. I've prepared a quote for the full work to make this and the back door more secure, if you wanted to go ahead with that.'

I glanced at the written quotation he'd prepared for me. It seemed more than reasonable in the circumstances. 'I think I'd better.'

'I'll get this patched up for the moment. Will need to get a few bits and bobs for the full work, so I'll make a start on that tomorrow. Gus asked me to give this priority over the work I'd had scheduled for him.'

'I'm very grateful to both of you. It's unnerving not even being able to lock my own front door.'

He nodded slowly. 'I can imagine. Mind you, until now, I'm not even sure I'd considered it necessary.'

CHAPTER THIRTY-FOUR

I'd already had a couple of responses from Kate's friends. Both said that they couldn't recall Kate ever mentioning any acquaintances in the Highlands, and they'd no knowledge of her ever spending any time in the region. The second added that Kate had never talked much about her personal life, particularly in recent years.

The impression I had was that Kate hadn't been an unfriendly or unsociable person, and she'd been well-liked by those who'd known her. But she didn't seem to have participated in the sharing of personal revelations that normally helps cement close relationships. Perhaps that had just been the person she was or perhaps it was connected with the nature of her work for Archie Kinnear, but it felt like something more, as if she'd had an almost pathological need for secrecy. So what was it she wanted to hide?

And what friend or associate could she have had in the Highlands? It was someone who wasn't known to her other friends. So where might Kate have first encountered this person? Work was a possibility, perhaps, though that was an area I couldn't explore without risking alerting Archie Kinnear to my interest. Every tiny step forward left me even more frustrated. It felt almost as if, through her privacy and secrecy, Kate had connived in her own disappearance.

That idea had been nothing more than a casual thought that had slipped into my head and should have slipped straight out again. But somehow it lodged there a moment longer than it should have done, and after that I couldn't quite get it out of my mind. The possibility that, somehow, Kate had conspired to enable her own vanishing.

I didn't mean that literally, even though that had been one possibility considered by the police. What I meant, I supposed, was that because she'd been so secretive about her personal life, she might have unwittingly made it easier for someone seemingly to remove her from the face of the earth. If she'd revealed more about her acquaintance in the Highlands, there would have been more leads for the police to pursue. So was it possible that her silence had been deliberately encouraged or even enforced by someone?

Expressed in those bald terms, it sounded far-fetched. But I couldn't quite dislodge it from my brain. Why would someone be secretive or evasive about their personal life? Kate might have been a naturally reticent person, someone shy and reluctant to be the centre of attention. But the way others described her didn't fully support that portrayal. She was seen as sociable, outgoing, good company. In some cases, her friends had hardly even noticed how little she revealed about herself.

If that wasn't the explanation, what else might be? Someone might keep quiet about their private life because there were parts of their life they'd prefer not to be made public – actions that were illegal, unethical or simply embarrassing. From what Cameron Fraser had told me about Archie Kinnear, at least some of those might have been potential factors. If these actions involved some other person, that person might also be keen to ensure that they remained private.

It was really nothing much more than an idle thought. But once the idea had taken shape, I couldn't shake it off. I knew from experience that when a thought lodges in my head like that, it's worth taking notice. Almost without realising it, as I'd been sitting there, I'd drifted into that semi-dissociated state that had sometimes served me well in the force. Those moments when it felt as if I'd almost stepped outside myself, outside my own head, as if I could observe my own thoughts dispassionately. It was an ability – if that's the right word – that had benefited me in surveillance situations when I'd felt as if I could not only observe my surroundings but also, in a way I can't really describe, observe my own interactions with those surroundings.

I can't express it more clearly than that. I'd experienced it once or twice in investigative situations as well, typically when I'd been trying to piece together information or evidence that didn't quite seem to fit. Just as my conscious self was becoming lost in the mire, this odd dissociated self seemed to offer a different, more remote perspective that perceived links or patterns invisible to closer sight. My subconscious brain seemed to draw in ideas and make connections that I'd otherwise have overlooked.

It's probably no more than an illusion, a way of the brain finding different ways to approach problems. I'd experienced it most commonly when I'd been tired or under stress. I supposed I was both of those at present.

Even so, perhaps there was something there worth considering. Perhaps Kate had had some reason to keep quiet, and maybe someone had had an interest in encouraging her to do so.

Immediately on the heels of that came yet another thought.

If someone had encouraged Kate to keep quiet, then what action might they be prepared to take if Kate was no longer willing or able to maintain her silence? And what further actions might that person be prepared to take to ensure that Kate's secret, whatever it might have been, remained buried?

I had nothing to support any of these suppositions. I was simply trying to give some shape to what had begun to feel like an increasingly amorphous mystery. I forced myself to take a mental step back. Up to now, I'd been approaching the question of Kate's disappearance in an essentially neutral way, without really considering what might have lain behind it. There were really only three possibilities. Kate might for some reason have chosen to disappear, she might have suffered some kind of physical accident or psychological breakdown and perhaps taken her own life, or she might have come to harm at someone else's hands. The first or second of those weren't impossible, but felt unlikely.

That left the third possibility. If some third party had been involved, it was either someone who'd acted randomly and opportunistically, or someone who'd had a motive for their actions. Given the circumstances of the disappearance – particularly the fact that her car had been left tidily in the Inverness back street – the first option seemed unlikely. Which brought me back to my first thought. If I assumed Kate had been killed, the murderer might have had any number of possible motives. But it felt as if the most probable one was to ensure her silence.

Looking back now, this whole line of thought seems impossibly tenuous. I don't think I was even taking it very seriously myself. It was just an attempt to marshal my thoughts into some kind of coherence. But it was beginning to make a bizarre kind of sense. Kate seemed to have always compartmentalised her life, choosing which titbits to share with which audiences. Somewhere in one of those compartments might lie the answer to this conundrum.

I'm not sure I was thinking particularly rationally by that point. I'd glorified my state of mind as dissociation, as I'd sometimes done in the past, but maybe it was never any more than the kind of unconstrained thinking that accompanies exhaustion and stress, the point at which your brain takes control of itself, a more logical version of what happens as you're drifting off to sleep.

It probably didn't matter much. It was at least a train of thought I could pursue. If Kate had been killed to ensure her silence, then what kind of secret might she have been carrying? Was this something she'd recently discovered, or a secret she'd been concealing for some time? If it was the latter, why would she choose to reveal it now?

I was stumbling into yet another cul-de-sac. Even if my suppositions were right, I couldn't see any way of verifying them. None of this was anything more than unsubstantiated guesswork.

But my mind was racing on. I'd had another thought. If Kate had been killed to ensure her silence, perhaps that was true of others too. Perhaps that was why Sean Critchley had been killed. Perhaps it was why Lorna Jardine had been killed. And perhaps it was why someone wanted to kill me.

That would imply that I knew something worth silencing. The reality was I knew bugger all, or if I did know something I didn't understand what it was or why it might be significant.

I was going round in circles, creating a narrative from my own imagination to compensate for the lack of hard evidence. But my brain couldn't let it go. Up to this point, I hadn't seriously envisaged any link between Lorna's death and that of Sean Critchley, other than the coincidence that they'd both known me. But what if that hadn't been coincidence, and their killings had been in some way linked to my investigation into Kate Brodie's disappearance?

It was an intriguing thought, but again not one that took me very far. It was conceivable Critchley might have come here to share some information, but I couldn't imagine how he might have known I was looking into the Brodie case. On the other hand, Critchley had a track record of knowing things that were useful to him, and he had no shortage of sources. That left the question of Lorna. She hadn't even been aware I was looking into the Kate Brodie case. What could she possibly have known about Kate Brodie? It wasn't impossible that she might – after all, she'd known Cameron Fraser as a client in the past – but it didn't seem likely that she'd known anything worth killing for.

I had to remind myself I was building an edifice of supposition on almost no foundations, but it did at least feel as if this was a narrative that might make some kind of sense. I picked up my phone and dialled Morag Henderson's number.

This time she took a little longer to answer. When she did, I heard her saying, presumably to someone with her, '...Probably ought to take this. Sorry. Just crack on. I won't be a minute.' Then to me: 'Hi. Can you bear with me? I'll find somewhere quieter to talk.' I suspected that she'd deliberately allowed me to overhear her apology to her colleague so I'd realised she wasn't alone.

After a few moments, she said, 'Sorry. Can talk now.'

I was surprised she'd even taken my call. I thought she probably wouldn't be best pleased once she discovered my half-baked reason for calling her. 'If you're in a meeting, we can speak later. It's nothing urgent.'

'To be honest, I'm glad to escape for a few minutes. We're trying to push on with the Jardine and Critchley cases and I'm just getting endless balls-ache about budgets and overtime and you name it.'

'You're sure you're okay to talk to me? I don't want to cause you any difficulties.' It seemed to me she was taking a risk in having any contact with me at all.

'I deal with a lot of informants,' she said. 'We all do. You must have done.'

'Yes, of course, but—'

'It's a judgement call but it's mine to make. And I hope I've made the rules very clear, particularly in respect of the ongoing investigations into the two killings.'

'Understood. Though that probably means you won't be prepared to answer the question I wanted to ask you.'

'Try me.'

'Okay, in general terms then, have you come across any apparent links between Lorna Jardine and Kate Brodie?'

There was a longer silence than I'd expected before Henderson responded. When she did, all she said was, 'Bloody hell.'

'Sorry?'

'Are you psychic or something?'

'Maybe something,' I said. 'But not psychic. I don't understand.'

'Look, I'm not telling you any of this but you may have opened up a very interesting line of enquiry. You've answered a question that's been nagging at me all afternoon.'

'I mean, glad to be of help, but—'

'As I said this morning, we've been making frustratingly slow progress with our investigation into Lorna Jardine's killing. And Sean Critchley's, for that matter. Both seem like pro jobs and neither has an obvious motive. Critchley made his fair share of enemies, but none that we can easily tie to his murder. As for Lorna Jardine, well, we've identified no motive at all. So, in the absence of any other leads, we've been working painstakingly through whatever material we do have. Which in Lorna

Jardine's case means her laptop and desktop, her tablet, all her papers and files, and anything else we've been able to find.'

'And you found something?'

'One of the things we found was Lorna Jardine's desk diaries for the past couple of years. They're not particularly informative for the most part. Just times and dates of business meetings. Mainly online or face-to-face meetings with clients. A handful of personal things. The Hogmanay party you mentioned. The supper with you. But it doesn't look as if she had much of a social life. There were only two or three names we haven't yet been able to identify. One of those recurs several times across the year, every three months or so, but the most recent entry was on a date that rang a vague bell with me, but I hadn't been able to remember why. They're all slightly odd entries because there's no time or detail specified. The last one was in the evening section of the page. And they're also odd entries because they're the only ones that don't give a name. All the entries say simply "KB".'

It was my turn to be silent. Finally I said, 'As in Kate Brodie.'

'I might have made the connection eventually, but it would have taken me longer if you hadn't mentioned her name just now.'

'And the date of the last entry?' I said.

'Exactly. When you mentioned the name, I realised why that date seemed familiar. It was the Friday Kate Brodie disappeared.'

CHAPTER THIRTY-FIVE

At first, I was simply baffled, my head struggling to make sense of what Henderson had said. 'So it was Lorna that Kate was going to see on her way to Cromarty?'

'Obviously, I can't be sure of that. Maybe it's just a coincidence. Perhaps she knew someone else with those initials. It's possible they don't even refer to a person.'

'But if she'd been the person Kate was planning to see, why wouldn't she have come forward with that information?'

'That's the question, isn't it?'

I couldn't think of an immediate response. If Kate had been planning to visit Lorna that evening, there was surely no good reason why Lorna wouldn't have volunteered that information to the police.

'And the second question,' Henderson went on, 'is what prompted you to ask me about links between Kate Brodie and Lorna Jardine in the first place?'

It took me a moment to work out what she was asking me. I'd been so taken aback by what Henderson had told me that I'd almost forgotten why I'd phoned her. If nothing else, the diary entry seemed potentially to validate the ideas that had been running half-formed through my mind. 'It was nothing more than a hunch really. Or not even that. I'd been sitting here trying to make some sense of everything that's been happening.'

'Good luck with that.'

'That's the point, though, isn't it? Everything seems so disconnected and random. Kate's disappearance. Lorna's killing. Critchley's murder. The attempt on my life.'

'As I've pointed out already, there is one obvious link between all those events.'

'I know, but again that's the point. I seem to be in the middle of all this, but I've genuinely no idea how or why, so my first thought was to dismiss it as a coincidence. Something that looks like a pattern because I happen to have some connection with the different parts of it, even though the actual connections are random. I couldn't see any way of joining the dots between, say, Kate, Lorna and Critchley.'

'And now you can?'

'Not really. But I was thinking. What if it isn't coincidence? What if there is some real link between the different parts of this? That set me thinking about what an oddly secretive person Kate seemed to be, and whether she'd had some reason for that reluctance to talk about her private life.'

'Such as what?'

'Again, I don't know. But maybe something she feels guilty or ashamed about. Perhaps for some reason she'd finally felt the need to speak out about something, and that's why she was silenced.'

'With respect, there's a hell of a lot of maybes in this scenario.'

'I know, and it was nothing more than idle speculation. But then I wondered if Lorna and Sean Critchley might have been killed for the same reason. Because they had some knowledge that was potentially threatening to someone out there.'

'I know how you lot down south ran investigations. We're usually looking for something a lot more substantive in terms of evidence.'

'Except that we do now have something which seems more substantive. A potential link between Kate Brodie and Lorna.'

'I'm not going to get carried away. It's a set of initials in a diary.'

'If the entry was for any other day, I'd agree.'

Henderson was silent for a moment. 'But, to go back to your original question, the answer is that, apart from this diary entry, I'm not aware of any other connection between the two women.'

'Have you been looking for one?'

The question came out rather more bluntly than I'd intended, and I was relieved when she laughed. 'No, you're right. We haven't. Kate's initials and the date rang a bell with me because of my involvement in the original investigation, but that wouldn't be true of most officers working on the case.'

'Perhaps it would be worth having another look?'

'Are you telling me how to do my job, Mr Mellor?'

'I wouldn't dare.'

'Very wise. But you're right. Given the diary entry, it probably is worth us trying to identify any possible connections. I say this very begrudgingly, but thanks. It may come to nothing but it's a potential lead.'

'Maybe a lead in both investigations,' I suggested.

'Don't push it, sunshine. I've already said thanks once.'

I ought to be feeling pleased with myself, I thought as we ended the call. It had been largely inadvertent, but I'd helped provide Henderson with a potentially very significant piece of information. Even so, the development had left me more disturbed than gratified. If Lorna had been expecting a visit from Kate Brodie on that Friday night, I couldn't understand why she wouldn't have given that information to the police.

I couldn't envisage that Lorna might have been involved in harming Kate in any way. But maybe the answer was more straightforward. If Lorna had been the last person to see Kate alive, for whatever reason, perhaps she'd simply wanted to avoid putting herself at the centre of the police investigation. That wouldn't have been a noble act, but it was perhaps an understandable one. I'd seen myself how DS McBain had initially been only too keen to focus on a readily available suspect for Lorna's killing, and it was something I'd witnessed often enough as a serving officer.

It would be disappointing to discover that Lorna had behaved in this way, but I had to remind myself that she'd never claimed to be a paragon of virtue. There was a danger I might idealise her now she was gone, whereas the truth was I hardly knew her.

'You're looking thoughtful.'

Maddie was standing in the doorway watching me.

'That's because I was thinking. Did you get some more sleep?'

'Slept like a log actually. Didn't think I would with so much on my mind. I'd probably have slept longer if it wasn't for your guy working on the front door. He's not the quietest.' As always, she somehow managed to imply that this was my fault.

I'd been so engrossed by my conversation with Morag Henderson and then by my own reverie that I'd barely noticed any noise that Grant McLeish might be making. There wasn't actually much, other than the occasional whizz of his electric drill, but that wouldn't stop Maddie complaining about it. 'I couldn't leave the front door in that state.'

'Particularly not if there's someone out there who wants to kill you. I can see that. By the way, I think I gave him a bit of a shock. Your guy at the door, I mean. Didn't expect him to be there when I came down the stairs, so I left him gawping rather.'

As on the previous day, she was wearing my dressing gown, apparently with little underneath.

I bet you did, I thought. If Maddie left men gawping, it was rarely accidental. At least I'd mentioned Maddie's presence to Gus, but there'd no doubt be more gossip doing the rounds. 'Have you made any decisions?' I said. 'About what you're going to do, I mean.'

'Give me a chance. I've only just woken up. I'll go and have a shower and get my brain in gear. If you have a coffee waiting for me when I come down, that would be perfect.'

I'd never really been able to decide whether Maddie's infuriating behaviour was simply a reflection of her personality, or deliberately intended to wind up anyone who had the misfortune to be sharing a space with her. 'I'll make you some coffee,' I said wearily.

'And maybe a bit of breakfast? Although I suppose it's lunch now, isn't it?'

'A late lunch,' I pointed out. 'I'll see what I can find.'

She disappeared back into the hall, no doubt distracting Grant McLeish again in the process. After a few minutes, I dragged myself to my feet and followed her. McLeish was crouched by the front door doing something to the frame.

'How's it going?'

'More or less done the basics. I'm going to see what I can do to reinforce the door and the frame. It'll be a quick fix for the moment, but it should make it harder to crowbar open, particularly if I add a couple more deadlocks. If you want me to, I'll do the same for the back door.'

'That would be great, thanks. I'm not sure that our friend's likely to return immediately, but I'd rather be as secure as possible.'

I could tell he was desperate to ask me about Maddie, but I wasn't sure I had the mental energy to embark on another explanation. No doubt Gus would tell him soon enough. 'I'm making some coffee,' I said. 'Would you like one?' It seemed the safest way to move the conversation on.

'Aye, why not.'

I left him to it and made my way through to the kitchen. As I made McLeish's coffee, I reflected on what to do about Maddie. There wasn't any obvious answer. In the end, the choice would have to be hers, assuming I could manage to tolerate her presence for a few more days. I'd probably feel safer sleeping downstairs anyway, so that wasn't really a consideration.

The other question was whether Maddie's experience fitted into this whole narrative. If I was correct that Lorna and Critchley had been killed because of something they knew, why would anyone want to silence Maddie? The only potential connection I could think of was through Martin, particularly if he had been doing some business with Critchley.

There was only one person I could think of who might be able to give me information on the seamier side of Scottish business. I didn't feel up to another conversation with Cameron Fraser just yet, but I texted his mobile number: *Not urgent, but wondering if you'd come across a businessman called Martin Garfield. Based in Glasgow. Probably not important, but his name cropped up.* That was vaguer and more enigmatic than I'd have liked, but I couldn't tell Fraser why I'd an interest in Garfield.

I wasn't expecting a quick response and I'd assumed the answer would be in the form of a return text, almost certainly in the negative. But almost immediately the phone rang in my hand. I looked at the screen.

Cameron Fraser wanted to talk.

CHAPTER THIRTY-SIX

As usual with Fraser, there were no preliminaries. 'Martin Garfield. Why are you interested in Martin Garfield?'

There was something in his tone that warned me to consider my response carefully. 'It's a long story, and I'm not sure if there's any link with Kate Brodie.'

'Why do you think there might be?'

I told him about Maddie's unexpected small hours arrival, and the supposed threats on her life. 'It's another bizarre coincidence, alongside what happened to Lorna and to Sean Critchley. But, other than the fact that Maddie's my ex, I couldn't see any connection with Kate Brodie. So I was scraping around to see if I could identify any other links. It occurred to me that Garfield might have a business link to you or to Archie Kinnear.'

'I'm not sure this is what I'm paying you to investigate, Jack.' There was an undertone in his voice which sounded like an implicit threat. I didn't feel particularly happy about that.

'I'm happy to do this in my own time,' I said. 'Given that someone apparently tried to kill me last night, I do have something of a personal interest.'

There was a moment's silence as if Fraser was considering what I'd said. 'I take your point, Jack. And the truth is that I do know something about Mr Garfield.'

'I understand he's some sort of businessman.'

'Sort of, yes. He's never done any business with me, I'm pleased to say.'

'But with Archie Kinnear?'

'I understand Garfield's been trying to make himself part of Archie's inner circle. He's been taking on a few jobs for Archie and is looking for more. In particular, Garfield's keen to become part of Archie's inner team working for Gregor McBride on the Scottish development projects. I don't know that Archie trusts him enough to allow that yet, but then Archie doesn't really trust anyone. Garfield's doing whatever he can to ingratiate himself so he may well get there, but Archie will keep him dangling for a while. Archie likes to keep people dangling.'

'From what little I know of Martin Garfield none of that entirely surprises me.'

'This is all most interesting, Jack, but I don't see how it can have anything to do with Kate's disappearance. I don't see where Garfield fits into that.'

'Neither do I yet. But there's something else.'

'Go on.'

I hadn't been sure whether to tell Fraser about my conversation with Morag Henderson. It felt like a breaking of confidence. On the other hand, Henderson hadn't explicitly bound me to silence. It was possible Fraser could shed some light on why Kate might have wanted to see Lorna. 'We may have discovered who Kate was planning to see that Friday night. I think it might have been Lorna Jardine.' I told him about my conversation with Henderson, and about the entry in Lorna's diary. 'Do you know any reason why Kate might have wanted to visit Lorna? How did they know one another?'

During the whole of this conversation, Fraser had seemed uncharacteristically lost for words. The silence now was the longest so far. Finally, he said, 'I don't know how Lorna Jardine would have known Kate. But she certainly knew Archie.'

I remembered the story Gus has told me. I hadn't made any connection between the unnamed Glasgow businessman and Archie Kinnear. 'She worked with him as a trainee accountant in Glasgow?' I said. 'Before she moved up here.'

'Once again you surprise me, Jack. You really are very skilled at this.'

I couldn't work out if he was being sincere or ironic. 'Just a lucky guesser.'

'I'm a little surprised she told you the story.'

'She didn't. I don't know if she would have done, but she never had a chance. She'd once told Gus about it. Gus told me after her death. I imagine he's also told the police. But Gus didn't know she was talking about Archie Kinnear. Neither did I, till just now.'

'I'm surprised she told anyone. It's not a story that reflects well on her.'

'Really? I'd have thought the only person it reflected badly on was Kinnear.'

'I don't think Archie behaved well. He was probably leading her on more than he acknowledged, but she was old enough to make her own choices.'

I'd never exactly envisaged Fraser as a feminist, but I couldn't believe what I was hearing. '"Leading her on" is an odd way to describe rape.'

'I think we're talking at cross purposes, Jack. There was no rape. That was confirmed at the time.'

'So it was hushed up,' I said. 'That doesn't surprise me.'

'I don't think so. Or not in the way you mean.'

'So what's your version of the story?'

'My version, Jack, is what I saw. This was in my final period working with Archie, not long before we decided to go our separate ways. I met Lorna a few times. She was only a trainee but she was bright and had done some good work for us under the supervision of one of the partners. She was an ambitious young woman. Perhaps a bit too ambitious for her own good.'

'In what way?'

'She was keen to get on the right side of Archie. He was a big deal at the time. He'd just started working with Gregor McBride so that was attracting some publicity. One of the many reasons I ended up falling out with Archie. I wouldn't trust McBride any further than I could throw him – which given the size of the man is no distance at all – and I thought he was high risk in business and reputational terms. But it had helped to raise Archie's profile, and Lorna definitely had her sights on him. He's a smart man, but he's also a silly old fool where young women are concerned. She took advantage of that.'

I'd heard versions of this story so many times. It didn't matter how much the man might be a predator or that there was a power imbalance. It was always the woman's fault. 'That's what Kinnear told you.'

'It's what I witnessed, Jack. I'm sure you don't want to hear this, but she took advantage of him. She was happy to do whatever it took to win him over. And I mean anything, including sleeping with him. She was basically a gold-digger. I'm sorry to be so blunt. But you ought to know.'

'I don't believe that. That wasn't the Lorna I knew.'

'Ach, well, she was badly burned by it. I hope she learned her lesson. She was maybe a different person afterwards.'

I still didn't accept a word of this, but it was presumably what Fraser believed. 'She seemed very different from anything you've described.'

'I can't make you believe it, Jack, and I can understand why you don't want to. But it's true. Not that Archie was remotely blameless. He was only too happy to encourage her advances at first. Elderly man flattered by the attentions of an attractive younger woman. But Archie's not stupid, especially where money's concerned. He'd begun to suspect Lorna's motives, perhaps because I'd been asking him some pointed questions about what she was up to. Believe me, Archie can be ruthless. He tried to cut her out of his life completely, just like that. She didn't give up easily. She harassed him, calling him outside work, sending him photos. You can imagine what kind of images. And then she told him she was pregnant with his child. Then when it was obvious that wasn't going to work, she came up with the rape story. I think she thought she could blackmail him into paying her off.'

'So what happened?'

'You don't try to blackmail Archie Kinnear. He went to her employer, told them what had been going on. He made it clear to them that he was happy to involve the police if anyone doubted his word.'

I bet he was, I thought. If the police had to choose between the conflicting testimonies of Archie Kinnear and a young trainee accountant, who were they most likely to believe? None of this was persuading me of the accuracy of Fraser's account.

'You were right in a sense,' Fraser went on, 'in that it was all hushed up. Archie was one of the company's biggest clients, and they weren't going to get on the wrong side of him. The last thing they wanted was for the police to be involved. Lorna was sacked, though she was allowed to present it as a resignation. Between you and me, I think Archie paid her off as well, and may have helped secure the job up here. I don't know if she really was pregnant. If she was, he probably sorted that out for her too. But he made it clear that if she troubled him again, he'd destroy her.'

'Sounds a real charmer.' I wondered how much of this version even Fraser really believed. People change, of course, but I couldn't see Lorna as the kind of gold-digger Fraser had depicted. The account she'd given to Gus sounded much more plausible. Even so, the doubts sown by Fraser's version had tainted my memories of Lorna. I found myself resenting Fraser for that.

'She chose the wrong person to threaten,' Fraser responded. 'The wrong person to get involved with at all, some might say.'

'In any case, none of that explains how Lorna might have come to have known Kate Brodie,' I pointed out. 'It's hard to imagine they met through Kinnear.'

'I can't help you with that,' Fraser said. 'It's possible they might have met at one of Archie's bashes.'

'Roy Brodie told me about Kinnear's parties. Pretty wild affairs, I understand.'

'There was a time when Archie was known for them. Mainly for clients, business associates, that kind of thing. And, no, Brodie's right. We're not talking demure cocktail evenings. Let's just say that Archie had a reputation for procuring whatever his clients might want, from drugs to sex, if it helped him win business. All very discreetly, of course. Most of the guests wouldn't even have realised. But it was another point of difference between us. I'm no prude, but there are limits and Archie often went well beyond them. Anyway, at the point when Archie was being seduced by Lorna, it's possible he invited her to one of those parties. I've no recollection of it, though. Kate was sometimes there though she made sure to steer clear of anything questionable. She was happy just to turn a blind eye. I can't think of anywhere else where their paths might have crossed. Maybe you and Henderson have got it wrong. Maybe the initials didn't refer to Kate at all.'

I didn't bother to argue the point. The coincidence of the

initials and the date seemed too remarkable, particularly now I knew there was a link at least between Lorna and Archie Kinnear. How that link might extend to Kate, I didn't know, but I wasn't prepared to dismiss the idea. Fraser ended the call in his usual peremptory manner, but I wasn't sorry about that. I wasn't sure what response I could have offered. He'd seemed solicitous enough, but I'd been left with a sense that, whether deliberately or not, he'd deftly inserted a stiletto into my heart and then given it a delicate twist.

I didn't believe his account for a moment, but I wondered now whether Lorna would ever have trusted me enough to tell me her version.

CHAPTER THIRTY-SEVEN

'You don't seem to have made much progress with that breakfast.'

Maddie was standing in the kitchen doorway, now fully dressed, watching me with what looked like amusement. It occurred to me to wonder how long she'd been standing there, and how much she'd overheard of my conversation with Cameron Fraser.

'Sorry. I got a bit tied up.'

'Sounded like it. Who was that?'

'Cameron Fraser. The guy who's paying me to carry out this research stuff.'

'Pretty intense discussion from the bit I heard.'

'Long story,' I said. I was tempted to tell her everything, including Cameron Fraser's version of what had happened to Lorna, simply because I wanted to talk to someone about it. But Maddie would be the worst person to share that story with.

'Which you clearly don't want to tell me.'

'In all honesty, Maddie, I really don't.' I pushed myself to my feet. 'What do you fancy to eat?'

'What have you got?'

'Not much. More ready meals. Some bacon.'

'Bacon sandwich would be fine.'

'I reckon I can stretch to that. I'll get that going while you can make us both coffees.' I felt as if I'd already imbibed more than enough caffeine that morning, but I'd need some stimulation to get through another conversation with Maddie.

While I focused on frying the bacon, Maddie filled the kettle and spooned coffee into the cafetière, her body language suggesting she resented even this mild request to do something for herself.

'Have you decided what you want to do yet?' I said.

'Are you throwing me out?'

I thought about that. Much as I'd have liked to, I couldn't really do it yet. If there really was some threat to her life, I couldn't leave her to deal with that on her own. The question was whether she'd be safer here or elsewhere. 'Not yet. But I'm wondering how you feel about last night?'

'It didn't exactly feel welcoming. But I assume you were the intended target.'

'Thanks. But what if we both were? And even if I was the target, I wouldn't imagine that any potential witnesses would be safe.'

She offered no immediate response. She'd already have thought about this herself.

'For what it's worth, I don't think we're likely to see an immediate return of our friend from last night. If he's a pro, he'll see it as too risky. He'll wait a while or try some other approach.'

'Funnily enough, I don't find that entirely reassuring. But I take your point. I'd prefer to stay, Jack. There's nowhere I could go that would make me feel safer.'

'Let's play it by ear, then. You can't stay here forever, but another day or two won't make much difference. If nothing's changed by then, we'll have to think about making other plans. But there's one thing you ought to know.'

'Which is?'

'One of the things Cameron Fraser told me was that Martin's doing business with Archie Kinnear.'

'Archie Kinnear? Name rings a bell but can't remember why.'

'Maybe through Martin. Kinnear's a big-shot business type in Glasgow. He was also Cameron Fraser's former business partner. He's been doing business with that guy Gregor McBride in the US, and Martin's apparently been trying to inveigle his way into Fraser's inner circle.'

Maddie gave a low whistle as she carried the two mugs of coffee across to the table. 'Gregor McBride. That's the guy who stood for President a couple of years back? That would presumably be a pretty big deal. What's McBride's interest in Scotland?'

'Development. He already owns a couple of upmarket resorts here. He wants to open more, including one just down the road from here. The Highlands are "an untapped playground for the wealthy" supposedly. You can imagine how that goes down with the locals. He'll face a lot of opposition, but he seems to have a knack for overcoming that. By brute force if necessary.'

'You sound as if you care.' She gave me a slightly mocking smile.

'I do, as it happens. I've seen the people round here. People like Gus. This isn't a playground. It's homes, communities. And people are being driven out of those communities – if not directly through eviction, then indirectly through increasing property prices.'

'They probably see you as an incomer yourself, you know?'

'I'm sure they do, and they're not wrong. Doesn't stop me caring about them.'

She shook her head sadly as if pitying my naivety. 'That does give us another link, though.'

'That was why I asked Fraser if he knew Martin. I was trying to see if there was any link between you and the killings up here, anything that might tie you into this other than the fact that you'd once been with me. Anything that might provide an explanation for the attempts on your life.'

'It's still pretty tenuous, though, isn't it? And it doesn't explain why anyone would want to kill me.'

'I've no idea. None of it makes much sense to me, but we've got too many links now for it to be purely coincidental.'

'I suppose.'

I carried the sandwich across to her and she bit into it eagerly. She hadn't eaten since the previous evening. I'd had something earlier, but was beginning to wish I'd made one for myself. My appetite seemed finally to be returning.

'And there's another link.' I'd initially not been intending to tell Maddie what I'd discovered in my conversation with Morag Henderson. In line with Fraser's instructions, I hadn't so far told her anything about my investigation into Kate Brodie's disappearance. But as we'd been talking, it occurred to me that, if her life was really at risk, she deserved to know the whole story. Or at least as much of it as I could tell without breaking my agreement with Cameron Fraser or betraying Lorna's memory. 'You remember Kate Brodie? The young woman who went missing a year or so back?'

'I remember the news stories.'

'She was Archie Kinnear's daughter.'

She nodded. 'That was probably why his name was familiar. Not sure Martin ever talked about him, but I remember him being mentioned in the news coverage of her disappearance. What about her?'

'I've been doing some digging into the case.'

For the first time, she looked interested. 'Why do you want to know about that? Is this part of your work for Cameron Fraser?'

'Not directly,' I said vaguely. 'Just something that intrigued me.'

She looked sceptical. 'That right? You may need to get out more, Jack.'

'It's a long story. But one of the mysteries of the case is how Brodie could have gone missing between the last sighting of her car near Inverness and her intended destination in Cromarty. As far as anyone knew, she didn't even have any reason not to have driven straight there.'

'And you think she didn't?' A glaze of boredom had returned to her eyes. 'This is fascinating stuff, Jack.'

'You might find the next bit more interesting. It looks as if Brodie might have been planning to call on someone on her way to Cromarty. And I've an idea who that someone might have been. I think it might have been Lorna Jardine.'

'Really?'

I described my conversation with Henderson. 'We may be completely barking up the wrong tree,' I concluded, 'but the combination of the initials and the date would be another big coincidence. The question is how Kate might have known Lorna. Lorna had had some dealings with Kinnear when she was a trainee in Glasgow – he was a client of the firm she worked for – but there's no obvious reason why she'd have had contact with his daughter.'

Maddie was still chewing on her sandwich. 'I mean, it's another intriguing coincidence, I guess. But I can't understand what it's got to do with the rest of this. What did Henderson think?'

'You mean did she take me seriously or dismiss me as an obsessive who was coming up with wild paranoid theories?'

'I wasn't going to put it in those terms, and I accept there's a lot going on here, but you're actively looking for answers. There's a risk you may be seeing patterns where they don't really exist.'

'And Lorna's death has probably unbalanced me more than I realise? Yes, I know. Don't you think I've considered all that, Maddie?'

'You may have considered it, but you might not be the best person to reach a conclusion. I want to be sure that, if there is a threat to either of our lives, we're looking in the right direction and not chasing shadows.'

'Of course I can't be sure of any of this. But it was Henderson who mentioned the diary when I asked about possible links between Lorna and Kate. She seemed to be taking it seriously.'

Maddie frowned. 'But I don't see where I fit in. Why were you talking to Henderson about Kate Brodie anyway? How could Lorna Jardine's murder be connected with Brodie's disappearance?'

I realised I'd made a potential mistake in mentioning my conversation with Morag Henderson. She was already taking a professional risk in talking to me about the Brodie case. Any discussions we had about that needed to be in the strictest confidence.

'I've been trying to make some sense of all of these apparent connections. I wondered if there could be any link between Lorna's death and my probing into Brodie's disappearance. To be honest, I was expecting Henderson to say she wasn't aware of anything. Which is probably what she would have said if she hadn't been mulling over the diary entry. Even then I suspect she wouldn't have told me anything if I hadn't caught her off guard.'

'I'm surprised she was happy for you to call her in the first place.'

'I don't know if she was. She gave me her number in case anything else occurred to me in respect of Lorna's death. She probably wasn't expecting me to call with random questions. If I hadn't inadvertently given her what might turn out to be a useful lead, she'd probably have told me to bugger off.'

'So what is it you're saying? That Lorna Jardine was killed because she knew something about Brodie's disappearance?'

'It's possible, isn't it?'

'I suppose. But why kill her now?'

'I don't know. Maybe because someone heard that I was probing into the Brodie case and that Lorna and I were getting closer. Perhaps they were afraid she might tell me what she knew.'

'But if she was prepared to tell you, why wouldn't she have told anyone before now? Why wouldn't she have told the police?'

'I don't know, Maddie. I don't know if there's anything in this at all. I've no more idea what's going on than you have.'

I think I might have lost my temper if she'd asked any more, particularly about Lorna. Luckily, we were rescued by the appearance of Grant McLeish at the kitchen door. 'I've done what I can with the front door,' he said. 'Are you happy for me to have a go at the back one?'

'Go ahead. I'll make you another coffee.' It was the distraction I needed from Maddie. I was starting to wonder how I'd manage to tolerate her even if she stayed only for another day or two.

I busied myself at the sink while McLeish got on with

whatever he was planning to do to the door. Maddie finally took the hint and returned to the living room.

'Hope I've not driven your friend out,' McLeish said. He was clearly fishing for me to tell him more.

'She's not my friend,' I said. 'She's my ex.'

'Ah,' he said, in a tone that suggested this explained everything.

'She's here for a day or two. Supposedly to provide some emotional support.'

'Well, that's a nice gesture. Especially from your ex.'

'You'd think so, wouldn't you?'

He grinned at me, though there was no obvious humour in his eyes. 'No, mate, I wouldn't. I really bloody wouldn't. In your shoes, I'd just be wondering what she wanted from me.'

CHAPTER THIRTY-EIGHT

The rest of the day passed uneventfully. I took Ziggy out for a long walk, partly as a reason for getting out of the house. I asked Maddie if she wanted to come, knowing full well she'd say no. More than anything I needed some space. I was well aware that my irritation with Maddie was as much a result of my own stresses as it was of her behaviour. I didn't exactly feel scared – though there were good reasons why I should – but I did feel tense, waiting for the next thing to happen.

I didn't even know if I was taking a risk heading out on to the moors. The only advantage I had up here was that I could see anyone approaching from some distance. But I was conscious I only had an hour or so before it would be beginning to grow dark.

I felt better as soon as I was outside. Ziggy was as lively as ever, racing up the hill ahead. This time I followed him down into the next glen. I wanted to put some distance between me and everything that had been happening. Ziggy and I tramped on for another half hour or so. The weather had remained fine, and the landscape was at its winter finest. I was content to keep walking, drinking in the pure chill air. I'd left Gus's land by now and I thought back to our conversation a few days before, wondering who might own the earth I was now striding over.

Regardless of who owned the land, a few days before this would have been a scene of unalloyed joy, a place where I'd known I wanted to stay for the rest of my life, even if my relationship with Lorna had never progressed beyond friendship. It had genuinely begun to feel like home. Now, I was wondering quite how long I'd actually remain here.

Everything felt tainted. Mostly of course by Lorna's death. But also by Sean Critchley's intrusion into the cottage and his subsequent death. Then by last night's break-in and its possible implications. Even, at a more trivial level, by Maddie's unexpected arrival, by my increasing estrangement from Gus. Above all, I was tormented by the thought that I might somehow have brought all this on myself. If all this was in some way connected to Kate Brodie's death, then perhaps my probing on Fraser's behalf had triggered this mess.

Was that why Fraser had insisted I keep his involvement quiet? Had he known that this might be the outcome? Had I and the people around me been set up as fall guys, allowing Fraser to dig into Brodie's disappearance without sticking his own head above the parapet? It was quite possible. I guessed anything was possible with Fraser. Lorna had told me right at the start that he always got what he wanted.

The smart move now might be to cut my losses and extract myself from all this. I could walk away, move away from here. Not necessarily back to Glasgow, but to somewhere else where I could leave everything behind.

But I knew I wasn't going to do that. Not now. I had too much invested, emotionally and psychologically, and I couldn't see I'd much more to lose. Other than my own life, of course, but I wouldn't be safe no matter what I did. And I wasn't sure how much I really cared.

The sun had disappeared below the horizon, and the twilight was darkening, shadows thickening across the landscape. I called for Ziggy who obediently came bounding up to me, and we made our way back to the cottage. By the time we reached the front door, it was almost dark, the first stars showing in the clear sky. Grant McLeish had given me the keys to the new locks before I'd left, and had shown me what he'd done to reinforce the door. I didn't know if it would be sufficient to keep out a determined intruder, but it would delay anyone long enough to give me ample warning. The lock turned smoothly, and I stepped inside.

From the hallway, I could see McLeish working on the rear door, a radio playing quietly beside him. I could also hear the sound of Maddie's voice, presumably talking to someone on the phone, her voice too low for me to make out what she was saying. I closed the front door behind me, waved an acknowledgement to McLeish and entered the living room.

Maddie's phone was sitting on the low table in front of her. She looked up as I entered. 'How's the outside world?' she said.

'Refreshing,' I said.

'You mean cold.'

Ziggy seemed to share her view. He trotted over to the wood-stove and flopped himself down beside it. 'Both, I guess.' I gestured to the phone. 'Talking to someone?'

The question clearly took her by surprise, and there was a noticeable pause before she responded. 'Just my mum. I wanted to check she was okay, and let her know that I was.'

By the time she'd walked out on me, I'd become more adept at spotting when Maddie was lying to me. She was a skilled liar, but there were occasional tics in her body language that gave her away once I'd learned to recognise them. I had no doubt she was lying to me now. The question was why, and who she'd really been talking to. There was no point in challenging her. She'd double down and we'd end up in a shouting match. 'How is she?'

'She's fine. A bit bemused that I'd made such a rapid exit. I told her I needed some time to myself after leaving Martin. I also wanted to check that she'd had no visitors asking for me, but apparently not.'

My guess was that she'd really had this conversation with her mother at some point while I'd been out, but it hadn't been the call she'd ended on hearing me enter the house. If you're going to lie, keep it as close as possible to the truth. In my experience, Maddie had always followed that adage.

I was left feeling awkward in her presence. She knew I knew she was lying, but neither of us was able to say anything. 'I'll go and see how Grant's doing with the door,' I said. 'Coffee?'

'I didn't think I'd ever say it, but I'm probably over-caffeined already. I'm not sure I'm going to sleep well tonight whatever happens, but it won't help if I'm wired to the limits.'

Grant McLeish rose to his feet as I entered the kitchen. 'Just about finished. I've done what I can for the moment, but I'll come back once I've got the materials to do a more thorough job. That's assuming you still want it?'

'More than ever,' I said. 'What do I owe you for this?'

'Pay me when I've done the lot. I'll do it all for what I originally quoted.'

'You've done a great job. I feel safer already.'

'I hope so.' He nodded thoughtfully. 'Because you do seem to be a man who attracts trouble.'

CHAPTER THIRTY-NINE

I cobbled together something for us to eat for supper, reflecting that I'd need to do a further supermarket shop in the morning. The provisions I'd bought to get me through the following few days had already been depleted by Maddie's presence. So much seemed to have changed in the few days since Lorna's death. I'd expected to be lost in a daze, unable to come to grips with the magnitude of what had happened.

But it hadn't felt like that, partly because dealing with Maddie had kept me occupied, but also because of the nuggets of information I'd stumbled across in the meantime, the growing sense that Lorna's death and Kate Brodie's disappearance were linked in some way I couldn't yet begin to understand. I was also recognising how little I'd really known Lorna. I'd constructed a fantasy future with her without the slightest real understanding of her past.

After we'd eaten, Maddie and I returned to the living room. We'd polished off most of the single malt the previous evening, so I'd dug out a couple of bottles of wine for us to share over supper and afterwards. I didn't want to drink too much tonight in any case. I wanted to be sufficiently alert if anything happened during the night.

Maddie seemed in an odd mood. Her state of mind was usually obvious enough and generally resulted in similar patterns of behaviour, always with Maddie at the centre. She could be needy, provocative, manipulative, or even straightforwardly abusive. Sometimes she offered some permutation of all four, but you were rarely left in any doubt that it was all about Maddie.

Tonight felt different. She seemed remote, withdrawn, as if her mind was somewhere else entirely. There were points in the evening when she'd barely even responded to my questions or comments, let alone initiated any conversation of her own. She seemed lost in thought, as if concerned about something she didn't feel able to discuss with me. I wondered if it might be linked to the mysterious phone call earlier.

I tried to draw it out of her, giving her the chance to talk if she wanted to. 'You're very quiet tonight.'

'Am I? I was thinking, I suppose.'

'What about?'

'About what I do next. About whether my life really is under threat. About what I do if it is. I know I can't stay here forever, Jack, so I'm wondering what I should do instead.'

These were all perfectly reasonable answers, and all the things that she really ought to be thinking about. But, as with her responses about the telephone call, I didn't believe a word of it. I knew she was lying to me or at least not telling me the whole truth, She might well be thinking about all of these things, but they weren't at the forefront of her mind.

'Have you come to any conclusions?'

'Not really. Let's see what happens tonight, if anything.'

The vagueness of her response convinced me I'd been right. Whatever happened tonight was unlikely to make much difference to her thinking or to mine for that matter. If someone did succeed in shooting one or both of us, I supposed any future planning might become irrelevant. But otherwise we were likely to be left with the same uncertainties.

Perhaps Maddie was simply worrying about the night ahead and what might or might not happen. Again, that would have been reasonable. But we'd discussed that earlier and she'd seemed oddly untroubled by the prospect. I didn't think that was just bravado. Maddie didn't usually miss an opportunity to dramatise a situation.

As the clock approached 10pm, the limited small talk we'd managed to sustain had more or less disappeared entirely. Maddie yawned theatrically and said, 'I'm going to head off to bed now. Sorry if I've not been my usual scintillating self. There's a lot to think about.'

'No worries. I've not exactly felt the life and soul of the party either. I need to get some sleep. Hope we get an undisturbed night.'

'Me too.' She was gazing at me as if she wanted to say something more, but in the end she pushed herself up from the sofa. 'Goodnight, Jack.'

I waited till she'd left the room before pouring another glass of the wine. We'd inevitably moved on to the second bottle, but there was about half left. I'd been intending to stick that in the fridge for use tomorrow or in cooking, but I felt in need of some further emotional reinforcement.

Something was wrong. I didn't know what, but I could sense it in Maddie's behaviour. If you'd asked me why I felt that, I couldn't have begun to offer an explanation, but I felt it strongly nonetheless. It was something about the way she'd behaved, particularly in those last few moments before retiring to bed. Something in her tone of voice, in her expression, that seemed oddly familiar.

It took me another moment to work out what it was, but then I had no doubt. The emotion was something akin to pity, perhaps even contempt. It wasn't a display of sympathy, more a regret that she'd ever chosen to be involved with someone like me. A loser. A beta male, if not someone even further down the alphabet. I'd detected it at various points in our relationship, generally when something was going wrong in my life – a failed bid for promotion, a case that had gone awry, even some minor domestic problem. Another woman might have offered some sympathy in those moments, but not Maddie. Her only sympathy was for herself, that she'd somehow made the error of falling into a relationship with me.

I'd seen that expression, heard that tone, most frequently in the months before she finally walked out. The months when she was having an affair with Martin. I'd seen it most clearly in the moment when she'd finally told me she was leaving me. She'd shown no guilt or shame in her own behaviour. All she'd felt was pity for the man who, in her eyes, had driven her to behave that way.

That was exactly what I'd felt just now, and I wondered what might have prompted it. Perhaps she was thinking about how much I'd lost through Lorna's death, or how much my life had changed and then crumbled since leaving the police. But I didn't think it was only that. I'd not detected that expression previously in the time she'd been here. It was as if something more had changed, something she knew about but I didn't. Something that meant I was yet again to turn out the loser, even more than I had already.

I made a point of ensuring that the front and back doors were fully secured before retiring to bed myself. Grant McLeish had done a pretty decent job of improving the robustness of the doors and frames, as well as installing some solid locks. I checked that the doors were locked and then hesitated. My initial inclination had been to leave the keys in the locks. I had a vague recollection from my days with Maddie that the lock on our flat in Glasgow couldn't be opened from the outside if one of us had accidentally left the key in the lock inside. One of countless sources of irritation between us.

Now, though, suspicious of Maddie's intentions, I had second thoughts. I gathered up the various keys and slipped them into my pocket. Then I returned to the living room and lay down, fully clothed, on the sofa.

I still didn't seriously expect the previous night's intruder to return so soon. But after the way Maddie had behaved I had something more to worry about. I wasn't expecting to get much sleep.

CHAPTER FORTY

I was right about the lack of sleep. I spent the first hour or so lying awake, thinking about what Maddie might be up to. I was trying to recall how she'd behaved when she'd first arrived. My instinct was that even then she'd been displaying the telltale signs that should have told me she was lying, but I honestly couldn't recall. I'd been feeling too self-absorbed even to think about it, and too taken aback by her unexpected arrival to focus on how she was behaving.

The question was how much of her story I could believe. It had never entirely made sense. Maddie was certainly the impulsive type and I could easily envisage she might have made the decision to drive up here without stopping to think about it. I'd never thought of her as easily frightened – she was much more likely to be the one doing the frightening – but as Martin's partner she'd have mixed with some questionable company so perhaps she'd genuinely thought she was under threat.

But, looking back, she'd seemed less scared or worried than I might have expected. Right from that first night, for good or ill she'd essentially been the Maddie I remembered. She hadn't seemed cowed or unnerved by what she'd supposedly experienced. At the time, if I'd considered it at all, I suppose I'd assumed she was putting on an act, maintaining the familiar Maddie façade. That wouldn't have surprised me. I'd be the last person she'd want to reveal her real feelings to.

I found myself running through these questions as I lay there in the darkness. I had no answers, only an increasing number of questions. Outside, the weather had changed again. The day's clear skies had become clouded as the evening fell, and I could now hear spatters of rain being tossed against the window by a rising wind. Inside the house I could hear nothing but the rhythmic sound of Ziggy's sleeping breath.

I must eventually have slipped into at least a shallow sleep, because when I eventually stirred enough to check the luminous dial on my watch, it was almost 3am. At first, I thought I'd woken of my own accord, my anxiety keeping me on the surface of consciousness. I could hear the rain falling outside, but that and the brush of the wind seemed too low-key and unchanging to have disturbed me.

Then I heard something else. A faint movement in the hallway. I'd left the living-room door ajar to be sure of hearing any sounds from out there. As I rolled over to look towards the doorway, a faint flash of light crossed the gap between the door and the frame.

Moving as silently as I could, I made my way across to the door. I was certain that no one could have entered the house without my hearing them. Apart from the firmly locked doors, the only other possible entry routes were the two windows in the living room and the window in the kitchen. All the windows were locked, and I'd have heard any sound of breaking glass.

That left only one possibility.

There was a light switch for the hall to the right of the living-room door. I reached carefully round and turned on the hall light, keeping back from the full glare for long enough to allow my eyes to adjust to the brightness. Then I stepped into the hall.

Maddie was bent over by the front door, a heavy-looking flashlight in her hand. She was blinking from the sudden light, staring angrily at the door.

'Was there something you wanted, Maddie?'

She straightened up and gazed at me in fury. It was only then that I registered that, while she was holding a flashlight in one of her hands, she was also holding some kind of handgun in the other. She'd made a half-hearted attempt to conceal it behind her when I'd first stepped into the hall, but now she held it forward, pointing it towards me.

'I don't know what this is all about, Maddie,' I said. 'But put the gun down. You've no idea how to use it. You'll probably end up breaking your wrist.'

'You really think that?' She smiled. 'You don't spend any time living with Martin Garfield without being taught how to look after yourself.'

'Now that I can believe. Martin taught you everything he knew?'

'I've still got a lot to learn. But, yes, Martin's teaching me more than you can begin to imagine.'

'I thought you'd walked out on Martin?'

'You really believed that, didn't you? Fell for it all. Anyone tell you you're the perfect mark?'

'You did. Countless times. If not in quite those words. What's this all about, Maddie?'

'What has it always been about? It's about you. You being a sap. You being used by everyone, usually at the point where you think you're being most clever.'

'I don't know what you're talking about.'

'Story of your life, Jack. Out of the loop. Uninformed. Being played for a fool.'

I'd had enough of this. I didn't know what was going on, and frankly at that moment I didn't much care. All I cared about was the prospect of Maddie with a gun. 'Give me the gun,' I said. 'Before you hurt both of us.'

'Only one of us is going to get hurt. And it won't be me. I'd like you to open this door, Jack.'

'Are you going away finally? I can't say I'm sorry. And this time it's definitely goodbye and not *au revoir*.'

'I'm not going anywhere, Jack. Not yet. I want you to let someone in.'

'Now why would I want to do that? I'm guessing any friend of yours out there isn't going to have my best interests at heart.'

'Because if you don't, I'll shoot you anyway. If you do what I say, there's a possibility we can come to an arrangement.'

'What the hell are you talking about? What arrangement?'

'It's not mine to make,' she said. 'Open the door.'

'Who's out there?'

'If you let them in, you'll find out, won't you? Can I suggest you stop buggering about and open the fucking door.'

Maddie was holding the gun unnervingly steadily. In any case, this was a tiny enclosed space and Maddie was standing only a few feet from me. If she fired in here, she'd struggle to miss me, regardless of how limited her skills might be. I couldn't spin it out any longer. I pulled the keys from my pocket and held them out for her. She shook her head. 'I'm not that dumb, Jack. You don't really think I'm going to turn my back on you?'

'I was always a trier,' I said. 'Okay, let me have a go.'

We moved past each other in the narrow hallway, Maddie keeping the gun firmly trained on me. I waited till we were level, just inches from each other, then reached out and grabbed her wrist. I could see her finger tightening on the trigger, but I could also see the uncertainty in her eye. I gave her wrist a sudden sharp twist, and she winced and dropped the gun. I caught it deftly in my other hand.

'One little tip, Maddie,' I said. 'If you're going to threaten someone with a gun, turn off the safety catch first.' I did so with an ostentatious click, still pointing the gun in her direction.

'You wouldn't shoot me,' she said.

'I'm not sure if you realise quite how pissed off I am right now, Maddie. Trust me, it wouldn't take a lot to make me pull this trigger. Don't give me even half a reason.'

The smart thing would have just been to call the police there and then. But I was long past doing the smart thing. I just wanted to know what the hell was going on, and I didn't much care about the consequences. Gesturing for Maddie to step back, I turned to the door and, as quietly as I could, I slipped the various keys into the locks and turned each one. As well as the additional lockable bolts that McLeish had provided, there were two old-fashioned bolts. Keeping a close eye on Maddie behind me, I reached up to slide back the upper one, then did the same with the other. Then, holding the pistol in front of me, I opened the door.

I had no idea who or what to expect. A blast of chill damp air hit me in the face. I blinked, and realised that the man standing immediately outside the door was Martin Garfield.

It was only then that I realised how thoroughly I'd been set up.

CHAPTER FORTY-ONE

'About bloody time,' he said. 'Is this place always this bloody cold and wet?' He gestured to the gun. 'What kind of welcome is that?'

'The only kind you deserve. The one you were presumably saving for me.'

He held up his hands. If I'd taken him by surprise, he was showing no sign of it. 'It's not like that, Jack. We're on the same side. Or at least I hope we will be.'

'I'm not on anybody's bloody side. Certainly not yours. I'm tempted just to shoot you right now.'

Garfield was staring at me, his eyes unblinking. 'But you're not going to. Because you want to know what's going on. And I'm the only one who might be able to give you a clue. Are you going to invite me in?'

My first thought was that it had been Garfield who'd tried to break in the previous night. That it was Garfield who'd killed Lorna. If so, I wouldn't have had any compunction in killing him there and then. But I noted that Ziggy wasn't reacting to Garfield's presence in the way he had to the previous intruder. He'd come into the hallway behind Maddie, but was just passively watching us. In any case, I didn't think professional killing was really Garfield's style. He wouldn't have the bottle and he wouldn't risk getting his hands dirty. He'd leave that to others. 'Why not? I could do with a bedtime story.'

I stood back and gestured for him to come past me into the hall, tensing myself in case he should make any kind of move. He raised his hands, indicating he had nothing to hide. 'In there.' I gestured towards the living-room door, shutting the front door behind me, keeping the gun trained on Garfield throughout.

I followed him into the living room. Oddly, I wasn't feeling particularly scared. More than anything, I was feeling angry. I'd had more than enough of these unwanted fragments of my past turning up here uninvited. I was damned if I was going to be frightened by Martin bloody Garfield.

I waved him towards the sofa. 'Sit down.'

I sat myself down on one of the armchairs. He sat down on the sofa opposite me, pushing aside the duvet I'd been sleeping under. 'You've a big mouth, Mellor. It's got you in trouble before. It'll get you in trouble again.'

'I'll take that risk.'

'Your choice. But maybe you should think about the impact on others. Sorry for your loss, incidentally.'

Maddie had entered the room ahead of Garfield and seated herself quietly on the other armchair. I looked across at her, but she was avoiding my eye. 'What do you know about that?'

'You're tougher than I expected, I'll give you that. I thought you'd have taken the hint long before now.'

'I don't understand.'

'Maybe you're not tough after all. Maybe you're just dumber than we realised.'

'Obviously. I certainly don't know what the hell you're talking about.' I was still pointing the gun in his direction, toying with it casually. I could see that Garfield kept glancing at it nervously, as if worried that I might shoot him by accident. I could have assured him that, if I did pull the trigger, it would be entirely deliberate.

'And yet you've got this reputation as the great detective. The man with the intuition. The guy who gets results against the odds.'

I'd no idea how he knew all this. It wasn't something I'd ever shared with Maddie. She knew what my job involved but she'd never had any interest in the detail. I don't think we ever talked about any of the cases I was involved in, not even in the most general terms. In any case, it was all bollocks. I'd worked hard. I'd got lucky a few times. That was all it amounted to.

'It might have escaped your notice but I'm not doing that anymore.'

'Still sticking your nose in, though.'

This was the first clue he'd given me. Whatever Garfield was up to, it had something to do with the investigations I'd been conducting for Cameron Fraser. The idea struck me like a blow to the stomach. I had already begun to suspect that Lorna's death was connected to my enquiries, though I'd been struggling to join the dots. I was being inescapably drawn to the conclusion that, however inadvertently, I'd somehow contributed to her murder.

'I don't know what you're talking about.'

'You keep saying that. You don't seem to know much, do you?' He paused. 'Why are you up here, Jack?'

'Why not?'

'You've had an interesting few months, haven't you? You walk out on a supposedly successful police career for reasons no one can quite fathom. Then you decide to leave the big city behind for the arse-end of nowhere. Nobody seems to know how the fuck you're going to make a living. Then, presumably as a hobby, you decide to start probing into the disappearance of Kate Brodie.'

'I hadn't realised you had such an interest in what I was up to.'

'Let's say it was drawn to my attention.'

There was a sound from behind me. A faint growl. Ziggy seemed to have finally recognised that this latest guest wasn't entirely welcome. I called him to me, and stroked his head, trying to calm him. He was obviously unhappy at Garfield's presence but seemed prepared to accept him as long as I was.

'Did you kill Lorna Jardine?' I wasn't even sure I wanted to know the answer, but I couldn't stop myself asking.

'That's an interesting question. What reason do you think anyone would have to kill her?'

'I've no fucking idea. She'd never hurt anyone.'

'You still don't know, do you? You still haven't got it worked out. Mr so-called Intuition.'

'That doesn't answer my question.'

'For what it's worth, I didn't kill her. Well below my pay grade.'

'But you know who did?'

'I'm guessing someone was paid to do a job. One of Archie's thugs. But I wouldn't waste your sympathy on her.'

I had to force myself not to react. I'd achieve nothing by losing my temper before I'd learned some more. 'She was worth ten of you.'

'You reckon? Why do you think Kate Brodie went to see her on that last Friday night?'

'How do you know about that?'

'More to the point, how do you? Another case of that famous intuition of yours?'

'Something like that.' I wasn't sure where Garfield was

leading me, and I wasn't at all sure I wanted to follow, but I couldn't help myself. 'So why did Kate Brodie go to see her?'

'Because she'd been helping Kate for months.'

'Helping her in what way? How did she even know Lorna?'

'How do you think? Through Archie Kinnear.'

'That's the only connection I'm aware of. But I don't see how they'd have got to know each other.'

'They knew each other because they were both working for Archie.'

He was enjoying this. Keeping me dangling, knowing I desperately wanted to know the truth even if I didn't want to face whatever that truth might turn out to be. 'Okay, I'll bite. So what kind of work was Lorna doing for Kinnear?'

There was a prolonged silence before Garfield finally responded. 'That's the part I don't know,' he said. 'Not yet. That's what I've come up here to find out.'

CHAPTER FORTY-TWO

My first inclination was simply to laugh. 'You really are full of shit, aren't you, Garfield? You turn up uninvited. You get your girlfriend to wave a gun ineptly in my face. You spout a load of crap and innuendo. But you still don't have a clue what's actually going on.'

If Garfield had been the one holding the gun, he'd probably have happily pulled the trigger at that moment. I don't know what he'd been expecting or planning when he'd turned up here, but it was clear none of this was going quite the way he wanted. 'What I know,' he said, 'is that Archie had been paying a pretty substantial retainer to your precious Lorna for months, maybe years. She was providing some service in return for that payment, even if it was just keeping her mouth shut. The interesting thing is that over the last year – pretty much since Kate's disappearance in fact – he'd increased the payment substantially.'

'How do you know all this?'

'Where Archie's concerned, I make it my business to know as much as possible.'

'So what are you suggesting? That Lorna was somehow

involved in Kate's disappearance? I don't believe that.' Even as I spoke, I was all too conscious of my previous speculation about the reasons why Lorna might have been killed.

'I'm not suggesting anything. I'm just telling you some facts. Here's another one for you. Kate Brodie was pregnant.'

'What?'

'She was pregnant. At the time of her disappearance.'

I shook my head. 'That must be bollocks. Surely it would have been reported at the time?'

'Only if anyone knew about it. As far as I know, the only people who were aware, other than Kate herself, were Archie and a couple of his inner circle.'

'Including you?' I said sceptically.

'Very much not including me at that point. I've got a lot closer to Archie since. But, like I say, I make it my business to know stuff. I overheard enough conversations. She was pregnant.'

'So who was the father?'

'I don't know exactly, and it's possible she didn't either. My guess is it happened at one of Archie's famous parties. You might have heard about those. Archie had a reputation for providing anything his guests wanted. Anything.' He was silent for a moment, allowing me to think about the implications of what he'd said.

'You mean that might have included his own daughter. That's insane.'

'Kate was very much her own woman. She wouldn't have done anything unless she wanted to. And, in fairness, even Archie wouldn't have done it for just anyone. They'd only have done something like that for his most important client.'

'Gregor McBride.'

'McBride was present that night. He's been to Scotland several times since he and Archie began working together. He's over here now, as I believe you're all too aware. So, yes, it seems likely. Maybe the price they felt they had to pay to seal the deal.'

'Including allowing him to father her child?'

Garfield shrugged. 'Maybe. But I'm wondering if that was just Kate on a frolic of her own. Perhaps she thought it would provide some additional leverage over McBride.' He paused. 'Or possibly she saw it as bringing together two empires. McBride has no other children. Maybe Kate thought she could get herself a stake in his business.'

I'd no idea how far I should believe Garfield. He was painting a different, and much more cynical picture of Kate Brodie than any that had appeared in the media at the time of her disappearance. But then perhaps, in the end, she had simply been her father's daughter.

'All I know for sure is that Kate was planning to keep the baby. From what I knew of her, that wouldn't have been just because her maternal instincts had kicked in.'

'So what does this have to do with her disappearance? And with her meeting Lorna on that Friday night?'

'I don't know. That's why I'm here. But Kate went to see Lorna Jardine that night because she was pregnant.'

'What was she expecting Lorna to do? She was an accountant not a midwife.'

'I've no idea. Kate would have been only a few weeks pregnant at that point.' He paused. 'How much do you know about Jardine's background?'

I hesitated. My memories of Lorna had already been tainted by the account Cameron Fraser had given me, whether or not I chose to believe it. The last thing I wanted was to hear Garfield's version of those events, but I knew he was going to tell me. 'I've heard various stories,' I said. 'Some positive. Some less so.'

'If I were you, I'd go with the less positive ones. You might have thought butter wouldn't melt in her mouth. Archie wouldn't have agreed.'

'I'm not sure I need Archie Kinnear's opinions on anything.'

'Not that he treated her well. But she took advantage of him and then tried to screw him over.'

'I was told he raped her.'

'Maybe he did. I've no idea. Archie's capable of almost anything. All I know is Jardine became pregnant and it's likely Archie was the father, whatever the circumstances. He paid her off, moved her up here, and arranged the termination of the pregnancy. I don't imagine he did that out of the goodness of his heart. There's never been that much goodness in Archie's heart to begin with. He paid her to keep quiet, and he kept on paying her till the day she died, the payments increasing after Kate's disappearance.'

'Wouldn't that have been risky in itself?'

'If you're thinking that the police will be able to link the payments back to Archie, that won't happen. Nothing will be traceable. Archie knew what he was doing. He wanted some continuing leverage over her. She'd probably have kept quiet anyway, because she was terrified of him, but Archie preferred the mix of carrot and stick. More humiliating for her, apart from anything else.'

None of this was anything I wanted to hear. 'Why are you telling me all this?'

'I've come up here to try to find the last piece of the jigsaw. You didn't have to be part of that.' He gestured towards the gun, which I was still pointing in his direction. 'You chose to interfere.'

I nodded towards Maddie, who'd been watching our exchange in silence. 'Except that Maddie was trying to let you into my house. I've no reason to trust your good intentions.'

He shrugged. 'Believe what you like. I've no reason to harm you.'

'So you say. But whatever this is about, it's not in your interests to leave any loose ends.' I glanced across at Maddie. 'I don't know if Maddie's considered this, but perhaps you'd have killed both of us. The only question is whether you'd actually have had the bottle to do it.'

'Lucky for you that you'll never find out, then. But Maddie knows me better than that. As for why I'm telling you all this, since you've chosen to involve yourself, I just thought you ought to know what you've been taking on. You've even managed to trouble Archie. Not much, but enough.'

'At least I've achieved something in life, then.'

'Even if your life is shortened as a result? As for your friend Lorna's role, you need to understand that Archie's a master manipulator. He could take you out at midnight and convince you it's noon.'

'Like all abusers.'

'Maybe so. I've seen how he controls people. He could easily have got Lorna Jardine dancing to whatever tune he wanted. But I don't know what tune that might have been. I don't know how he felt about Kate's pregnancy. I doubt whether that had been part of the original plan, or something that Kate herself had cooked up. I don't know whether Gregor McBride was aware of the pregnancy or how he might have felt about it. Maybe Kate had tried to be too smart and had become an inconvenience. That might be why she disappeared.'

'You think Kinnear might have harmed his own daughter?'

'I think Kinnear's capable of almost anything. If it came to a choice between his daughter and his business interests – well, I know where I'd put my money. I don't know why Kate had arranged to meet Lorna Jardine, but I suspect it was something Archie had set up. Whatever its supposed purpose, the effect of the detour was to take Kate off-piste, as it were. Once she left the A9 there'd be few police cameras or CCTV so she'd be difficult to track. Maybe the aim was simply to lure her to Jardine's cottage.'

'And Lorna would have been aware of this?'

'I don't know. It's all just speculation. But she must have known something. If it was a set-up, I assume she'd have gone along with it because she was scared of Archie, or maybe scared of losing his money. I don't know, and I don't know what happened after Kate arrived at the cottage. Whether she went inside, or if she was picked up outside. Most likely your friend did nothing more than turn a blind eye.'

A few minutes before I'd wanted to punch Garfield. Now I felt as if all the life had been sucked out of me. I didn't know if he was lying or telling the truth. 'So what happened to Kate?'

'That's the real question, isn't it? And, as I said, it's the one I don't yet have an answer to.'

'How come you've got answers to all the rest? How do you know all this?'

'I've been slowly working my way into Archie's inner circle. The small group he trusts to handle his dealings with Gregor McBride. I'm not his closest confidant, but I'm close enough. Over the last couple of years, I've made it my business to get as near to him as possible. I've made money for him. I've done favours for him no one else would. I've even dug him out of a few holes. He's a smart guy but he's getting on and his judgement isn't always what it was, especially in his dealings with McBride.' He shook his head as if feeling real sympathy for the old man. 'There would have been a time when he wouldn't have revealed anything. Anyone who worked for him would have known only what they needed to know. I coaxed some of this out of him. Sometimes he's told me things without even realising he's doing it.' Garfield shrugged. 'Or maybe he does realise it and wants to get some things off his chest before it's too late. If so, I'm happy to sit in the confessional.'

'But you're seriously saying that Kinnear might have harmed his own daughter?'

'Something happened to her up here, and I've little doubt Archie was behind it.'

'I still don't understand why you're telling me this. Or why you're here at all.'

Garfield smiled, as if this was the point he'd been leading up to all along. 'I'll come to that in a minute. But you might be better off asking yourself a different question.' He paused, clearly for effect, the smile still plastered across his face. 'You might be better off asking yourself quite why *you're* here.'

CHAPTER FORTY-THREE

Garfield was clearly a smart guy. Smarter than I'd assumed. But I was growing tired of him stringing me along, talking in riddles. 'What do you mean?'

'Do you think you're up here by accident?' He shook his head. 'You've been played, Jack. Every step of the way. By both sides. Right from the moment Danny Royce supposedly stumbled across you in his bloody garden.'

'Royce was tipped off.' It wasn't even a question. I guess I'd known that all along. It had all been too bloody neat.

Garfield tapped his hands together in mock applause. 'That's why Critchley was conveniently on hand. It gave him the justification he needed to top Royce. Immediate threat to life and all that.'

'Why would Critchley want to top Royce?' I asked the question almost wearily. I didn't know what the precise answer would be, but I had little doubt about Critchley's motives.

'Critchley, like a number of your former colleagues, was on Archie Kinnear's payroll. Royce had become an irritant to Archie, trying to muscle in on his territory.' Garfield smiled.

'But that wasn't the only reason. Archie also wanted you out of the police.'

'Me? Why did he give a fuck about me?'

'I don't imagine he did. But you were becoming a pain in the arse. You'd already come dangerously close to shopping a couple of Archie's cronies in the force. And not even for corruption. Just for not being woke enough to meet your high standards.' He laughed. 'Like Al Capone being convicted for tax evasion. Archie had engineered it so you'd have been disciplined for neglecting your duties that evening.'

'I didn't neglect my duties.' As I said the words, I wondered again if they were actually true. I'd had my own doubts about how diligent I'd been. I should never have allowed Royce to take me by surprise. Even at the time, I suspected I'd most likely become the scapegoat for a failed operation. I hadn't realised that someone actively wanted that to happen. At least I knew now what Kenny Taylor had been talking to me about when he'd threatened me in that Dingwall back street.

'Doesn't matter, does it? They'd have made it stick. But you made everybody's lives easier by walking out. Which surprised us. And made us wonder what your motives might have been.'

'My motives were simple,' I said. 'I was sick to death of the whole bloody thing.'

'Not because you were working for Cameron Fraser then?'

'What? I wasn't working for Fraser or for anyone.'

'But you're working for Fraser now?'

I didn't respond. Fraser had told me to keep his involvement confidential. I didn't doubt Garfield knew full well I was working for Fraser, but I wasn't about to provide confirmation.

'Don't worry. Your secret's safe with me. But are you seriously saying you weren't on Fraser's payroll back then?'

'I wasn't on anyone's payroll.'

'That's even funnier. You were doing his work without even being paid for it.'

I wanted to ask him what he meant, but the truth was I knew. All those little useful anonymous tips, the informants who passed on useful intelligence. Even at the time, it had seemed a little too easy, but I'd been only too happy to ascribe it to my own skills. I wondered now how many of them might have related to Cameron Fraser's rivals.

'Don't get me wrong,' Garfield said. 'You must have been a decent detective. I wasn't joking about the intuition thing. From what I hear, you had a knack for it. Feed you enough titbits and you'll pull them together into something coherent. The perfect unwitting tool.' Garfield placed a not particularly delicate emphasis on the last word. 'That was why he decided to bring you up here.'

'He didn't bring me up here.'

'You think? So it was coincidence that someone drew your attention to this place?'

I thought about that. I remembered the guy who'd told me about the cottage, the relative of Gus's. He'd made a big effort to tell me about the virtues of the place, and I'd no doubt made it clear I was looking to go somewhere remote. 'No one brought me up here. It was my own choice.'

'I suspect if you hadn't bitten, Fraser would have found some other way of enticing you here. Maybe some kind of job offer. But Fraser prefers to stay behind the scenes if he can. Partly to ensure deniability if anything goes wrong. Partly because he likes toying with people. In that respect, he and Archie are the same. Probably why they got on so well, and why they fell out so spectacularly.'

'Why would Fraser have wanted me up here in the first place?'

'He wanted someone to start digging into Kate Brodie's

disappearance. Archie's already becoming yesterday's man, even if he doesn't quite know it yet. If he's not lost his touch, he's losing it. It's hard not to laugh. He really thought he'd hit the big time when he tied himself up with Gregor McBride. That was why I was so keen to get close to him. But the whole thing's turning into a disaster.'

'I'd have thought McBride and Kinnear were made for each other.'

'On paper, maybe. But that's the problem with Gregor McBride. Most of it's only there on paper.'

'How do you mean?'

'I mean that most of his supposed wealth is just an illusion. He's leveraged up to his eyeballs, drowning in debt he ultimately can't afford to pay. His whole chain of businesses is just a giant Ponzi scheme, forever chasing the next big thing in the hope that this'll be the one to bail him out.'

'So how come he's still trading?'

'It's like they say. If you owe the bank a thousand pounds, it's your problem. If you owe them millions, it's theirs. But the rumour is that the banks are losing patience with him, starting to look at calling in their debts. He's stiffed a few too many people, including Archie Kinnear. Archie stands to lose a fortune if this Scottish deal goes tits up. I'm not sure Gregor McBride is even bright enough to realise how much crap he's in, but Archie is beginning to find out and he's already panicking.' He smiled and pulled his mobile phone out of his pocket. 'Look at this. I managed to secretly film this clip of Archie and McBride's last meeting over here, just a few days ago.' He thumbed the phone for a moment, then passed it to Maddie to hand to me. 'No audio, but you'll get the idea.'

The clip apparently showed McBride and Kinnear engaged in a stand-up row. They were both tall, imposing figures, though Kinnear was clearly in much better physical shape. He looked like a man I wouldn't want to tangle with, but even so I had the sense that McBride was having the better of the argument, his finger jabbing repeatedly into Kinnear's chest, his face so close to Kinnear's that he was almost spitting on him. The look on McBride's face went beyond anger. There was something manic about it. This was a man capable of anything, a man accustomed to bending others to his will.

'That's Archie confronting – or trying to confront – McBride about the lack of funding. McBride doesn't even care. He probably doesn't even really understand what Archie's saying. He's just going to chew Archie up and spit him out, the way he's done with everyone else.' Garfield looked up at me. 'You'd need a heart of stone not to laugh.'

I could see nothing humorous about the image on the screen. I felt as if McBride was haunting this place, a malicious absent presence corrupting everything. 'What does any of this have to do with Kate Brodie? Or Cameron Fraser for that matter?'

'Because the McBride shitshow gives Fraser an opportunity to screw Archie Kinnear over once and for all. Once Archie's out of the picture, the winner can take it all. And Cameron Fraser wants to be the winner.'

'What about you? I thought you wanted a piece of Kinnear's empire.'

'I did, and I still do. That's why I'm here. I'm not going to try to take on Cameron Fraser. He's like Archie was ten or fifteen years ago. Very smart, utterly ruthless and as slippery as a snake. For the moment, I'd much rather be inside his tent pissing out.'

I thought about what Fraser had said about Garfield in our earlier conversation. 'Why would Fraser trust you if you've been so close to Archie Kinnear?'

'He'll trust me if I give him enough insider gen about Archie's empire, particularly if I can also tell him what's really going down with Gregor McBride. If the Scottish deal goes under – which I reckon is almost certain, especially if Archie's not there to steer the ship – there's a real opportunity for someone to step in and pick up the pieces for a song.'

I thought about Cameron Fraser's earnest tributes to the virtues of the local community, and wondered quite how sincere they'd been. 'I imagine he'll need some persuading that it's legit. Fraser's not a soft touch.'

'I didn't imagine he would be. But I can give him whatever he needs, and it's all solid stuff.'

It sounded to me as if Garfield was playing a dangerous game, but that was his business. 'So you've got it all sewn up then. Why are you here?'

'To find the last piece of the jigsaw. What happened to Kate Brodie. That's the information Fraser really wants. He has an idea that Archie Kinnear was behind her disappearance, and I'm sure he's heard just how much shite Archie's in with McBride. But even now Archie's got powerful friends, and Fraser will struggle to bring him down without something really substantive. That's why he employed you.'

I wasn't intending to rise to the bait. 'Why would he want to use someone like me if it's so important to him?'

'His sources told him you had a gift in that direction. He wants complete deniability in all this. Fraser's not scared of Archie or even of Gregor McBride – he's got enough power of his own – but if anything goes tits up he doesn't want his fingerprints all over it. If he's paid you a retainer, check where the money came from. I'm willing to bet you'll find no traceable link to Cameron Fraser.'

I already knew he was right about that. 'Still doesn't explain what I'd be able to do for him. I'm just an ex-cop with no resources.'

'You underestimate yourself. Wind you up and point you in

the right direction and you uncover things. Which is what you've done. Enough to get Archie even more rattled. Which is what Cameron Fraser was banking on. He knows the state Archie's in now. He knows how much Archie's worried about the fall-out from his deal with McBride. There'd have been a time, maybe even only a few years ago, when none of that would have troubled Archie. He thought he was invulnerable. If some problem arose, he'd get it dealt with. If he lost money, he'd win it back again and more. But the old Archie's slipping away. It's been sad to watch. The only enemy he couldn't beat was time. Even before he got into bed with McBride, he'd made mistakes. Some bad business deals. Bits of his empire chipped away. Lost some supposedly loyal people who could see the way the wind was blowing. It was probably why he signed up with McBride in the first place, though he must have had reservations. He saw it as one last chance to secure his legacy, whereas it's more likely to be what brings him down. He's not exactly a scared old man quite yet, but he's heading that way.'

'He must really have lost his touch if he's been rattled by me.'

'You're just the latest problem. He's at the stage where he's desperately fighting fires. Acting without thinking things through. And he's going for the wrong targets. He heard you were digging into Kate's disappearance. He initially decided to use Lorna Jardine to get closer to you. He panicked when he heard you'd had that little altercation with his hired muscle the other day. He was afraid you were getting too close and she might let slip too much. So he had her dealt with.'

I had no idea whether I could believe any of this. The thought of Lorna acting as an informant to Archie Kinnear was sickening. Maybe that was the only reason she'd got to know me in the first place. 'If he was going to kill someone, why not just kill me?'

'I'm guessing because he thought you were too close to Cameron Fraser. Fraser's methods are more subtle than Archie's but he makes sure he's well protected and he has a reputation for looking after his own. It might have been different a few years ago, but these days even Archie would think twice about taking on Fraser directly.'

I had no idea how much of this I could believe. 'What about Sean Critchley? Where does he fit in?'

'Like I said, he'd been on Archie's payroll. He was another one who'd seen where things were heading and wanted out. He'd actually headed up here with a packet of juicy information about Archie's empire, hoping to do some sort of deal with Fraser.'

'The same as you, then.'

'At a much lower level. The material Critchley had was small beer. I doubt it would have impressed Fraser much. But again Archie got worried. Had someone tail Critchley. Critchley realised he was being followed and made himself scarce.'

'Why did he come here? How did he even know where I was living?'

'Critchley was like me. He made it his business to know things. That's how he came to have the dirt on Archie. I don't know, but he may have come here because you were the only person he knew and thought he could trust up here. He was looking for somewhere to hide away.'

I thought about that. I'd always thought Critchley was little more than a scumbag, the worst kind of bent cop. Even so, the thought that he might have come here to seek my help and that I'd ignored him was an uncomfortable one. 'So why didn't he stay and wait for me?'

'My guess is he was followed here. The fact that he was visiting you would have worried Archie even more. He'd have assumed Critchley was intending to pass on some information to you, probably intended for Cameron Fraser. I'm only guessing, but maybe it wasn't coincidence Lorna Jardine had invited you for supper that night. It made it easy for Archie's people to pick Critchley up. It looks as if they spent some time trying to – well, let's say persuade him to tell them what he knew before they topped him.'

I could feel the bile rising in my throat. I didn't want to believe Garfield – and maybe I'd have been right not to – but what he was telling me made a horrific kind of sense. And every word of it overturned what I thought I'd known about Lorna.

'You can't know any of this for sure.'

'Not all of it, no. Maybe I've got some parts of it wrong. But I do know how worried Archie was, particularly after Lorna Jardine's death. He realised too late he'd screwed up. If he'd been prepared to trust her, she could have been his spy in the camp. So he wanted someone else who could play that role.'

I looked over at Maddie who'd been sitting listening to all this in silence. The penny had finally fully dropped. 'You sent Maddie.'

'Brilliant, wasn't it? Maddie knows you inside out. She knew full well that if she turned up here unexpectedly with some convoluted sob story, you wouldn't throw her out. You're a soft touch.'

'So you've been feeding everything I'd told you back to Martin here? And all that stuff about walking out on him and the threats to your life were all bollocks.'

'I'm sorry, Jack.'

'The big consolation for you is that nothing of what you told Maddie made it back to Archie. I kept telling him what he wanted to hear, which was that following Lorna Jardine's death you were making no progress.'

'Part of this was about protecting you, Jack,' Maddie said.

I didn't believe that for a moment, but there was no point in arguing. 'So what about last night? What was that all about, if Kinnear doesn't think I'm a threat?'

'That's another reason I'm here. It's all coming to a head. Archie's had even more bad news about his dealings with McBride. That's why McBride's been over here. He blusters and shouts, but all Archie's seeing are more delays in funding, more threats of foreclosure from the banks. And Archie's increasingly the one on the rack for it, his reputation and authority disappearing along with most of his money. It's driving him over the edge. The paranoia's taken over. He doesn't trust anyone now. Including me.'

'From what you've said, he's right not to trust you,' I pointed out. 'Doesn't this mess up your plans to walk away with material you can use to bargain with Cameron Fraser?'

'Do you think I didn't get that stuff out long ago? Archie's already screwed. He just doesn't know it yet.'

'So what did bring you here? To rescue Maddie?'

'Maddie's hardly the type who needs rescuing. She could have left any time she wanted. No, the plan was just to use this place as a bolt-hole for a few hours. I knew we could depend on your hospitality.' He gestured to the gun, which I was still pointing in his direction. 'Mind you, you could have been more welcoming.'

'Or I could have been dead. I've no reason to trust you.'

Garfield held up his hands. 'I didn't force you to get involved in any of this. It's been your own choice. And it's still in your hands. You can stop waving that gun around, leave me to finish the job with Archie, and I won't trouble you again. But I'm happy to involve you if you prefer. You can make it easier for me to gain access to Cameron Fraser.'

'I've no influence with Fraser.'

'Can we drop this pointless pretence that you're not

working for him? Even Archie worked that out in the end. That's why he thinks you're dangerous. When he thought you were some lone wolf sticking your nose into his business, he wasn't too troubled. But now he can't be sure how much Fraser knows. Hence your visit last night.'

'I've still no influence with Fraser.'

'I'm not expecting you to provide me with a bloody reference. But you could make an introduction. I'm hoping that by then we might have something that will really make him want to see me.'

'Which is?'

'A better idea of what happened to Kate Brodie.'

'You said you didn't know what happened to her the night she visited Lorna.'

'I don't. But Archie does.'

'So what are you planning to do? Waterboard him to get the information?'

'It's a tempting thought. But I'm hoping it'll be easier than that. Archie's coming up here today.'

'Up where?'

'That's what I want to know. As far as I'm aware, there are only two things that link Archie to the Highlands. One is that Cameron Fraser moved back up here after their big bust-up. The other is Kate Brodie. It was a sudden decision, and these days Archie doesn't make many sudden decisions. I've stuck a GPS tracker on his car. There was probably a time when he wouldn't have fallen for something as basic as that, but that's where we are.'

'So why do you think that's going to reveal anything about Kate Brodie? There could be a hundred reasons why he's coming up here. Maybe he's planning to confront Cameron Fraser.'

'Archie's driving himself. He never does that these days,

even when he's driving around town. He pretends it's a status thing but it's really old age. If he's decided to make a four-hour drive on his own, he doesn't want anyone to know what he's up to. I've been listening to what he's been saying in the last few days. That's another area where his powers are waning. He's talking too much, and that's become worse as he's grown more worried about the mess he's in. I think he's worried that, on top of all his other troubles, there's some potentially incriminating evidence about Kate that's still traceable. He's coming up here to try to deal with it.'

This sounded like the longest of long shots to me, but I supposed Garfield knew much more about Archie Kinnear than I did. 'So what's your plan?'

'My understanding is Archie's setting off early. I'm going to keep track of where he's heading so I can be waiting. That was why I was so keen to take advantage of your hospitality. It's a bloody sight warmer in here than out there.'

'I'm all heart,' I said. I still thought it was more likely that if I hadn't intervened, Garfield would have been only too happy to silence me and probably Maddie too. I'd wondered if he might try to jump me, regain control of the gun, but he probably knew his chances were low. I had several inches and a good few pounds on him. I was in better shape, and more accustomed to looking after myself. None of which meant I should relax my vigilance. 'So what's your plan?'

'Just to play it by ear. Follow Archie to wherever he's going, find out what he's up to, and take it from there.'

It didn't sound much of a plan to me, and I wasn't sure Garfield really had the skills even to do that much. 'I'm coming along. You've clearly no idea what this might involve. You need some backup. At least I've got the right skills. I was a surveillance specialist, and I've been trained to handle a gun.' I held up the pistol just in case he might have forgotten about it.

I saw Garfield exchange a glance with Maddie. Maybe they'd known all along how I'd respond. Perhaps that was why Garfield had come here in the first place. Because he needed the support that he'd have been too proud to ask for. But Maddie knew me all too well. What was the word she'd used? Quixotic.

'Your choice,' Garfield said.

'Entirely. And I'm not asking you. I'm telling you. I'm coming. Apart from anything else, I'm invested in all this, financially and emotionally. Whatever the truth about Lorna Jardine's life, Archie was responsible for her death and I won't allow him to get away with that. On top of that, I want to know what happened to Kate Brodie.'

'I'm not arguing, Jack. We could all come out of this as winners.'

I stared at him. The last thing I felt like at that moment was any kind of winner. Even if we came through this safely and I was able to give Cameron Fraser what he wanted, I'd already lost everything that mattered. There was no response I could offer. Finally I said, 'Sounds like we're in for a long night. I'll go and make some coffee.'

CHAPTER FORTY-FOUR

Garfield had the application for the GPS tracker on his phone and was keeping an eye on it. I moved into the kitchen, still keeping the gun in my hand, ostensibly to make the coffees but mainly because I needed time to myself. Garfield's account of the events that had brought us to this point had left me with far more questions than answers, and I'd no idea how much credence to place in his version. But it had undermined any certainties I might have had, and left me doubting my own role in this. Was it really possible I'd been played all along, and that none of this was accidental or coincidence? That most of what I'd assumed about Lorna was untrue, and that I'd directly contributed to both her and Sean Critchley's deaths?

I didn't want to believe any of it, but Garfield had no strong reason to lie. Not about all that, at least. Unless this was another charade. Maybe Garfield was actually still working for Archie Kinnear, and all of this was nothing more than a ruse to lure me into a trap. But that made no sense, either. If Kinnear had wanted to kill me, he could have done so without all this complication. He'd had a good go the previous night, and it wouldn't have been difficult to come up with another opportunity.

Mostly, though, I was left with the sense that everything had been an illusion. That the control I'd thought I'd had on my life had been non-existent. That the place I'd thought was a remote paradise was as snake-ridden as the urban life I'd left behind. That the future I'd imagined for myself was haunted by the ghost of mine and others' pasts. That nothing was real, and nothing much was left of me.

The kettle boiled. I left it a moment and then poured the hot water over the ground coffee. Behind me, I heard the kitchen door open. I didn't turn round, but I picked up the gun from the work surface where I'd placed it while I dealt with the kettle.

'I'm sorry, Jack,' Maddie said.

'What are you sorry for? You've done nothing. Well, except lie to me. But I'm used to that.' My words sounded more bitter than I'd intended, but I didn't really care.

'I'm sorry for you, mainly. You've been used.'

'Again, that's not exactly a new experience.'

'Martin's not as bad as you think, you know.'

I finally turned to face her. The door was open behind her but I didn't care whether or not Garfield overheard. 'He's a gangster working for gangsters. Smarter than most, but the ones who get to the higher levels usually are. Whether he's as smart as he thinks he is is another question. Even if he does eventually manage to claw his way to the top, there'll be someone behind looking to drag him down. Just like he's doing with Archie Kinnear.'

'Do you think he doesn't know that?'

'No, I don't. He's like all of them. He thinks he's invulnerable till he discovers he isn't. You should get out, Maddie. While you can.'

'And come back to you?'

'Christ, no. That's the last thing either of us wants. But for your own sake you should get away from Garfield.'

'Even if I wanted to, it's too late. I'm in much too deep.'

'Your decision. I'll bring the coffee through.'

'Martin wanted you to know that Kinnear's made a move. Heading north.'

I glanced at the clock on the kitchen wall. Not yet four. 'Early start.'

'Kinnear's always an early riser, according to Martin. But Martin thinks he's keen to get up here before daylight.'

'Deeds best done in darkness? Seems likely.'

I followed her back into the living room bearing the tray of coffee and mugs, the gun in my pocket. I didn't think I was likely to need it now – at least not with Garfield – but I wasn't about to take any chances. Garfield was staring intently at his phone, as if he wanted to track Archie Kinnear's movements mile by mile. 'Left about ten minutes ago. So we've three hours or so.'

'Depends where he's going,' I pointed out. 'The Highlands is a big place.'

'My instinct is that it's somewhere in these parts.'

He was probably right. If Kinnear really had had his daughter killed, the killer wouldn't have wanted to travel far with the body. There were plenty of remote spots round here where the body would have been unfindable. But that raised the question of what kind of evidence Kinnear might be concerned about. Perhaps the body had been hidden less well than he'd have liked. But would an elderly man be capable of doing much about that?

I didn't much care. If Garfield was on some wild goose chase, that was his problem. I just wanted to know what had happened to Kate Brodie and what Lorna's role had been. What

I'd told Garfield was true. I was invested in all this. Not so much financially, attractive though Cameron Fraser's pay-off might be. But, emotionally, I did want to discover the truth. And if Archie Kinnear had been responsible for her disappearance and Lorna's death, I wanted him to face justice.

But I also knew Garfield might be dragging me into something utterly unpredictable. He seemed to have had no plan beyond waiting to see what Kinnear was up to. He couldn't be sure Kinnear really was coming here, or that he was travelling alone. Even if he was coming by himself, he might have arranged to meet some accomplice. I didn't even know if he was right about Kinnear's motives for making this trip. The more I thought about it, the more half-baked this all seemed. Archie Kinnear might be an elderly man, maybe well past his best, but everything I'd heard about him suggested he wasn't someone to underestimate.

Even so, I wasn't going to back out now. It was too late and, like Maddie, I was too far in. What did I really have to lose, anyway? I had no future worth thinking about. I didn't want to stay up here, and I couldn't envisage going anywhere else.

Garfield was still staring fixedly at his phone. Maddie was managing to look both bored and anxious.

I gestured towards Garfield's phone. 'How's he doing?'

'Still heading in this direction.'

We spent the next couple of hours in the same way, Garfield glued to the screen of his phone, Maddie curled up on the sofa, her body language suggesting she might be expecting a physical blow. I disappeared periodically into the kitchen to replenish the coffee, partly because I suspected we might benefit from the caffeine, partly to give myself something to do. Garfield was doing his best to appear nonchalant but the tension was palpable.

So far, Archie Kinnear was behaving as Garfield had

predicted. He'd continued on the A9 past Perth, heading up through the Cairngorms National Park towards Inverness. He'd made good progress, presumably encountering little in the way of traffic, although he'd stuck to the speed limit all the way. I didn't imagine Archie Kinnear was particularly law-abiding, but I guessed he wasn't keen to either be stopped or to be caught by the A9's speed cameras. It occurred to me to wonder whether Kinnear might be using fake plates. This was a man of considerable resources who'd probably want to ensure that his trip up here was untraceable.

That thought led me back to Garfield, and I wondered how cautious he'd been. He struck me as a smart man who was likely to act more impulsively than was good for him. I was increasingly feeling that I was being led into something beyond my control.

After another half hour, Garfield finally looked up. 'He's approaching Inverness. I think we need to start getting ready.'

'What does that involve exactly?' I asked.

'Are you okay to drive?'

I hadn't expected that. 'Do I need to?'

'I need to concentrate on the tracker. We don't want to risk losing him. And if he spots us there's a risk he might recognise my car. He won't know yours. Anyway, you know the roads round here better than I do.'

I wasn't sure if Garfield might still be looking to pull some stunt, but I couldn't really argue with the logic. I'd also feel more in control if I was driving. 'If you say so.'

'Let's get ourselves going, then. He's not that far away. We need to be able to follow whichever way he goes.'

I went to fetch my coat. The rain had stopped but it would be damp and cold outside. Garfield pulled on his own waterproof jacket, his eyes fixed on the phone screen.

Maddie said, 'I'm coming too.'

Garfield stared at her. 'You're staying here.'

'Fuck off, Martin. I'm as deep in this as you are. Deeper than Jack. You don't think I'm just going to sit here like the obedient little woman worrying what the fuck might be happening to you both.'

'For fuck's sake, Maddie—'

'You haven't got time to argue with me. I'm coming.'

'It's your funeral. Just make sure you do what I tell you.' He turned to me, and I could see the anxiety in his eyes. 'We can't afford to fuck this up.' He looked back down at his phone. 'He's still heading up in this direction.'

Maddie and I followed Garfield out into the chilly night. The sky had cleared and was heavy with stars, the pale smear of the Milky Way stretched out above us. Apart from the faint brush of the wind against the trees, the darkness was silent.

I could feel the weight of the gun in my coat pocket, but that seemed the opposite of reassuring. I don't think I'd ever felt more tense in my life.

CHAPTER FORTY-FIVE

Once we were in the car, I said, 'So what do we do?'

'He's still on the A9. What are his options?'

'The first question is what he does when he gets to the roundabout at Tore. He might continue along the A9 up to the Cromarty Bridge or turn off towards Dingwall. If he really is heading up here, he's more likely to do the first.'

I started the engine then headed slowly down the track to the road, stopping some yards back from the junction. I could see Lorna's cottage to our left, unlit and empty. I turned off the headlights and left the engine running. 'There's no point in going any further yet. Let's see which route he takes, then we'll have a better idea.'

We sat in silence, Garfield intent on the pale glow of the screen, Maddie curled up on the back seat. Finally he said, 'He's stayed on the A9. Heading this way.'

'Next question is what he does after he's crossed the Cromarty Bridge. If he continues on the A9, he's still heading this way.'

We continued like this, Garfield occasionally showing me the screen, until there seemed little doubt that Kinnear was heading in our direction. Was it possible he was heading towards Lorna's cottage? I found it hard to believe there'd be any evidence left in there that hadn't been discovered by the police. At the same time, they'd had no reason to search for anything that wasn't straightforwardly related to Lorna's killing. I didn't imagine they'd examined the garden, for example.

A few moments later, there was a wash of car headlights from somewhere further down the hill. 'This is it,' Garfield said. 'Let's see what he does.'

I had no idea what might happen next. The lights appeared and disappeared as the car below navigated the narrow winding road, but they were coming closer.

I was expecting Archie Kinnear's car to pull to a halt outside Lorna's cottage, but instead it continued up the road into the hills. I moved to start the engine but Garfield placed a hand on my arm to stop me. 'Give him a few minutes. We're not going to lose him with the tracker, but I don't want him to have an inkling we're here. How well do you know that road? Are you going to need to use your headlights?'

The prospect of finding my way along this narrow road without headlights wasn't an attractive one. On the other hand, neither was the idea of Kinnear discovering our presence prematurely. 'I can give it a go with sidelights if we take it slowly.'

'I'd prefer that. Even if we're some way behind him, there's a risk he'll catch a flash of the headlights.'

We waited a few more minutes then Garfield signalled for me to move. My eyes had adjusted to the darkness and driving with the sidelights was easier than I'd feared. There was little risk of encountering other traffic, so the biggest challenge was the twists and turns of the single-track road.

I had no idea where Kinnear might be heading. As far as I could recall, there was little up here other than a few farm buildings. There were some residential houses but not for some distance. Kinnear was a couple of miles ahead of us, still moving, and we caught occasional flashes of his headlights against the sky. He was moving faster than we were, but driving cautiously so there seemed little risk of losing him.

Finally, Garfield said, 'He's turned off to the left. Though there's no road shown on the map.'

'There are no other roads for the next few miles,' I said. 'Must be some sort of private track.'

'Slow down. We need to keep an eye out for it.'

I decreased the speed still further. 'Any sign?'

'We're just about at the point he turned off.' Garfield was peering intently through the windscreen. 'There. That looks like it.'

It took me a moment to see what he meant. It was barely more than a gap between the trees, a rough track leading away into the darkness. I turned cautiously into it, hoping that the surface was solid. 'You're sure about this?'

'Not remotely. But it looks to be where he turned off.'

The first stretch of the road was little more than a rough track, and I kept my speed very low as the car bounced over the uneven terrain. Then, just ahead of us, I saw a tall wire fence, clearly marking the boundary of some territory. There was a set of double metal gates in front of us which had been left open. I'd driven along the road past here countless times but never spotted the fencing or guessed that there was anything here but woodland.

Beyond the fence, the track became firmer and smoother. My guess was that the rough entrance was intended not to be conspicuous to any passers-by, but we were clearly now on someone's private land. Most probably Archie Kinnear's. Another expanse of land which had been quietly acquired without the local community becoming aware.

'Continue slowly till I tell you to stop,' Garfield said. 'I don't want to get too close in the car. We'll have to do the last part on foot.'

He was sounding less confident and more nervous than he had back at the house, as if he'd only now realised what he was taking on. I followed his instructions, and, when he told me to stop, I pulled off the road, finding a spot between the trees. The landscape here was thick woodland but there was open moor ahead of us. There was no means of fully concealing the car, but there was a further dip in the hillside ahead which should prevent Kinnear from spotting us. The wind was stronger and blowing towards us, so I was hopeful he wouldn't have heard our approach.

Garfield climbed out of the car, closing the door quietly. Maddie and I followed him.

'You sure you wouldn't prefer to stay in the car?' I said to Maddie.

'Miss out on the boys' games, you mean. Bugger that. I'm part of this now.'

'For fuck's sake,' Garfield said to me. 'You should know better than I do. There's no arguing with her. As long as she doesn't screw it up, she can do what she likes as far as I'm concerned.'

'You two are made for each other,' I said. We began the walk up to the brow of the hill, moving slowly and cautiously. I was listening out for anything that might provide a clue to Kinnear's position or to what he was doing, but there was nothing but the buffeting of the wind. According to the tracker his car was parked about half a mile ahead of us.

We reached the top and looked down. Ahead of us was a small but imposing building, lights showing in its lower and upper windows. My guess was that it had once been some kind of hunting lodge, presumably part of a larger estate. It had clearly been recently renovated and adapted to create an attractive residence, which managed to combine classical elegance with some clever modern touches. The kind of place that only a substantial amount of money could create. Kinnear's car was parked in front of the building.

I wondered if Kate Brodie's body had simply been dumped here somewhere, on the assumption that no one was ever likely to come looking in this remote spot. The question was why Kinnear had become worried now. Perhaps he was concerned that, if the police discovered the link between Kate and Lorna, they might start to pay more attention to this area.

We moved closer. In the darkness, it was difficult to discern much beyond the silhouette of the building, punctuated by the light from the uncurtained windows. We stopped a few yards back from the house. I couldn't imagine we'd be visible in the darkness, but I still felt uncomfortably exposed. I wanted to know where Kinnear was and what he was up to.

Garfield tapped me on the arm and pointed. The nearest window opened on to what was clearly a reception room of some kind. There was a sofa, a couple of armchairs facing away from us, and several expensive-looking cabinets around the walls. The room had a slightly anonymous air, like the lounge in an upmarket chain hotel.

At first, I thought the room was empty, but then I realised what Garfield was pointing to. There was someone sitting in one of the armchairs, almost concealed from us. I could see only a hand, tapping impatiently on the arm of the chair.

'Is that Kinnear?' I whispered to Garfield. 'He looks as if he's waiting for something.'

'Something or someone.' Garfield glanced nervously behind him. If some other visitor turned up, we'd be sitting ducks.

I turned to look at Garfield and Maddie, wondering what we should do. I didn't know what Garfield had been expecting, but I'd assumed he had some sort of plan in mind. He remained rooted to the spot, staring past me into the room, a spectator waiting for the next act of a drama he didn't fully understand. Maddie was shifting impatiently from foot to foot, clearly wanting something to happen.

And then, quite suddenly, it did. The figure in the chair climbed to his feet and I realised it wasn't Kinnear after all. It was a man who was immediately recognisable, though I'd previously seen him only on film or from a distance.

Gregor McBride.

'What the hell's he doing up here?' Garfield whispered. It was clear now that this was playing out very differently from any scenario he'd imagined.

We watched as McBride left the room. It was another few tense minutes before he returned. To my surprise, he wasn't alone. He was almost literally dragging another figure behind him, someone who seemed barely able to walk and who stumbled on entering the room. It was clearly a woman, but initially all I could really see was a skinny, almost emaciated body dressed in a stained T-shirt and worn tracksuit trousers. The face was concealed by an unkempt mop of black hair that hadn't been washed in a long time.

Then the woman turned and my throat grew dry. I wanted to turn away and blank out the sight, but I knew it would remain imprinted on my vision and in my head.

Behind me, I heard Maddie whisper, 'Christ almighty.'

CHAPTER FORTY-SIX

I would have given almost anything to turn away, climb back in the car, drive as far as possible. Anything rather than having to intervene in this. But I knew I had no choice. Whatever I might prefer, I couldn't walk away.

Garfield's nerve seemed to have deserted him. Whatever he'd been anticipating, it clearly wasn't anything like this. He'd geared himself up for a fight, some straightforward physical risk, perhaps the sordid aftermath of some past crime, but instead had found himself staring at a living hell. I had no idea what to do, but it was clear I wouldn't be able to rely on Garfield for any leadership.

I pulled the pistol from my pocket. I felt uncomfortable carrying it, even though I'd been trained to handle firearms. But I didn't want to enter that house, especially in the current circumstances, without some means of defending myself. For the moment, I kept the safety catch on.

Without waiting to check whether Garfield was following me, I moved towards the front door of the house. I'd expected it to be locked so that we'd have to find some other means of entering, but when I pressed gently on the handle the door opened. I stepped in the brightly lit hallway, allowing a few moments for my eyes to adjust to the glare. I was moving as silently as I could, wondering how to deal with whatever might happen next. I could hear movement, some kind of banging, in the adjacent room. I glanced back. Garfield had finally followed me and was standing uncomfortably in the front doorway, Maddie just behind him.

I took another step forward and peered through the doorway into the reception room, holding my breath. More than anything I wanted not to look, to turn my head away, but I couldn't afford to give McBride any advantage.

The woman was crouched in front of the sofa, her arms wrapped tightly around her body. She was desperately thin, unkempt, her hair long and matted. Her face and arms were a deathly white and covered with deep purple bruising. Her eyes were dark and hollow, staring vacantly into space. She seemed beyond being terrified, even with McBride's ungainly figure looming above her. More than anything, she looked worn out, as if she wanted only to bring things to an end. As I watched, he raised a hand and struck her across the face.

At first, I wondered if we'd found Kate Brodie, although the emaciated woman in front of me looked very different from the elegant figure I'd seen portrayed in the media at the time of Brodie's disappearance. It took me another few moments to decide that, whoever this poor creature might be, she definitely wasn't Brodie. She was probably only in her teens, and was whimpering in a language that wasn't English.

I drew the pistol from my pocket and held it in my hands. I hoped that McBride wouldn't be able to see I hadn't released the safety catch. I took another two steps forward. McBride had his back to me and hadn't registered my presence. Although the woman had been facing me, she hadn't seemed to see me before that moment. Her eyes had been glazed and unfocused. Now, finally, her eyes momentarily flickered in my direction.

It was hardly even a movement, but it was sufficient to alert Gregor McBride. He turned, his body tensing. I imagine that in his day he'd been a hugely imposing, burly figure, but he was long gone to seed. I held the gun firmly in both hands, and did my best to keep my voice steady. 'Let her go.'

He stared at me uncomprehendingly as if simply baffled by my sudden presence in the room. Finally, he said, 'Who the hell are you?'

'Just let her go.'

McBride was looking past me at Garfield and Maddie, who had now gathered behind me in the doorway.

'Just hand her over,' Maddie said. 'We'll take care of her.'

McBride remained motionless, his expression suggesting he had no idea what to say or do. There was no trace of guilt or embarrassment in his face. Just the kind of disgust and disdain I imagine he'd have shown to anyone who tried to prevent him doing whatever he wanted. 'What the fuck is this? Why are you even in this fucking house? This is private fucking property.'

I gestured towards the woman. 'Is she just your property too?'

'She sure as hell isn't yours. You think I'm scared of you? You're not going to shoot.'

He was wrong, I thought. At that moment, I could have pulled the trigger, killed him comfortably in cold blood for what he'd done to that young woman. Before I'd entered this room and witnessed the state of her, I wouldn't have thought myself capable. Now I knew I wouldn't hesitate. Keeping my hands steady, I released the safety catch. 'Try me.'

I know now that I should have simply done it, whatever the consequences might have been. But I'd delayed a moment too long. From behind me, a guttural Glaswegian voice said, 'What the fuck is this? Some kind of fucking house party?'

I turned round to see Archie Kinnear standing in the doorway behind Garfield and Maddie. I hoped that Garfield might try to stop him, at least buy me a few more seconds to reach the woman, but Kinnear pushed past him, moving faster than I'd have believed possible for a man of his age. Unlike McBride, he was clearly a man who'd kept himself in shape. He grasped my wrist, twisting my arm so that the gun was pointing away from McBride towards the wall. He twisted harder and I thought he was going to break my arm.

He was stronger than I'd ever imagined. I had no choice but to release the pistol. It fell, skittering along the carpet towards Garfield. Garfield tried to make a lunge for it, but again Kinnear was too quick. He kicked the gun away, sending it to rest against the far wall. If this was a man with diminishing powers, I wouldn't have wanted to cross him in his prime.

'Who the fuck do you think you are?' he said. 'Breaking into my house. Shouting the fucking odds. Cameron Fraser won't protect you now.' He stabbed a finger towards Garfield. 'And of course you're here. Another slimy bastard on the make. You seriously thought the two of you could bring me down? I'm Archie fucking Kinnear.'

I tried to keep my voice steady. 'The only plan was to find out what's happened to your daughter. And what the hell else might be going on here. This woman clearly needs protection.'

Kinnear stepped forward until his face was inches from mine. 'Whatever's happened to my daughter, it's none of your fucking business, son. And neither's this woman. I do what I like. With her, and with everyone. It's all just fucking business. That hasn't changed, whatever some people might think.' He glared at Garfield and then, as if untroubled by our presence, walked over to pick up the pistol.

I took my chance, throwing myself bodily on to Kinnear. I succeeded in taking Kinnear by surprise, and he toppled sideways, unable to maintain his balance. He dropped to his knees, and I was on top of him, hammering with my fists at his head and body.

Garfield finally responded too, throwing himself at Kinnear's legs, trying desperately to support my efforts. Kinnear slumped to one side, and for a moment I thought we'd succeeded in overcoming him. Too late, I realised what he'd done. We'd driven him towards where the gun had come to rest. He'd grabbed it and was pointing it at Garfield's head. 'Unlike your friend here, I won't hesitate. Get off me and get yourselves over there.' He nodded his head towards where the woman still lay.

I had no doubt Kinnear would carry out his threat. He'd kill Garfield and then he'd shoot me and Maddie. He probably would anyway, but at least if we obeyed him now we might buy ourselves another opportunity to stop him. Maddie had already moved over to the sofa and was trying to lift the terrified woman to sit beside her. Garfield and I moved over to join them.

Whatever might be happening here, there was nothing else we could do. This was Archie Kinnear's show now. Perhaps it always had been.

CHAPTER FORTY-SEVEN

Gregor McBride was staring at Kinnear as if he couldn't believe what was happening. 'What the hell is this, Archie? I didn't sign up for this kind of fuck-up.'

'And I didn't sign up to be ripped off by some Yankee shyster,' Kinnear said. 'And yet here we seem to be.'

McBride slumped back down into one of the armchairs. 'What the hell are you talking about?'

'You know exactly what I'm talking about,' Kinnear said. 'Or maybe you don't. I've never known how much you believe your own fucking mythology. The reality is that you're just full of shit.'

McBride started to rise from his chair. 'You don't talk to me like that.'

Kinnear pointed the gun directly at McBride. 'I thought you were such a big fucking deal. I thought you were the one who was finally going to take me into the big time. I did everything I could to make sure you were on-side. Pandered to your every fucking whim, the way everyone always fucking has. All you've done is just sucked me dry to feed your own ego, just like you have everyone else.'

McBride stared up at him as if he hadn't understood a word of what Kinnear had said. 'So what are you going to do now, smartass?'

'I'm going to start tidying up. Salvage as much of my fucking business as I can.' He gestured towards the woman on the sofa. 'I came here to tidy up a few loose ends. Ends I'd left dangling because you'd insisted I should. Even now you couldn't keep your fucking hands off, could you? I knew it wouldn't take much to get you up here.'

'You told me—'

'I told you what you wanted to hear. Everyone always does. But I brought you here to make sure you were fully implicated. If you don't keep quiet about this, we'll both be fucked.' He waved his gun towards me. 'As for the rest of you bastards, you've just complicated things. Cameron Fraser's little lapdogs.'

'You can't deal with all of us,' I said.

'You reckon? Maybe think about how successful you were just now. I could shoot all of you before any of you got near. Anyone fancy a go?'

He stepped forward and grabbed the woman's thin, already bruised wrist, pulling her down on to the carpet in front of McBride. I half rose to try to stop him, but he simply jammed the gun in my face. I sank back down on to the sofa. I'd no idea how I could help this woman even alive, but I'd be no use at all to her dead.

Kinnear had taken a step back and was pointing the pistol directly at the woman's head. I never knew if he was intending to kill her there and then, but I'd little doubt he was more than capable of doing just that. I had no idea why he'd want to, or what exactly was going on here. But I could see from Kinnear's expression that, in his head, this was no longer a living person, a human being. She was nothing more than an inconvenience. An embarrassment. Incriminating evidence.

For an absurd moment, it occurred to me that the only consideration that might make Kinnear hesitate was the prospect of the woman's blood soiling this pristine room. More incriminating evidence. Except that I already had a suspicion that this building, however much it might have cost, wouldn't survive the night. Kinnear was wiping the trail behind him, taking McBride along with him.

I still had no idea what had been happening here, but it was clearly nothing good. All I knew was that I couldn't allow Kinnear simply to shoot a defenceless terrified woman without at least making an attempt to stop him. This time, I simply ignored the gun and threw myself from the sofa. In that moment, I don't think I even thought about my own safety or the likely consequences of my action. I simply wanted to do something, anything, to stop Kinnear.

The suddenness of my action gave me a brief advantage, but I knew immediately that it wouldn't be enough. This time, Kinnear had remained stubbornly on his feet, and it took him only seconds to regain his equilibrium. His hand came apparently from nowhere and grabbed me round the throat. A moment later, the barrel of the gun was jammed firmly under my chin. 'Anybody ever told you you're a fucking pain in the arse? I'm having a bet with myself as to how much of your brain's going to end up on the ceiling.'

There was nothing more I could say or do, except wait for Kinnear to pull the trigger. I thought back to that moment in Danny Royce's garden, months before, when I'd been in the same position. It turned out that all Sean Critchley had done was buy me a short respite. Just long enough to destroy my life more completely.

'For Christ's sake. Why do you always have to make everything much messier than it needs to be?'

Kinnear was still grasping my throat, and I couldn't see

where the voice had come from or who had spoken. But it was someone who hadn't been in the room before now. A woman's voice, icily calm and controlled. Kinnear pulled the gun away from my throat, and threw me to the ground. 'Bastard had it coming,' he said.

'No doubt, and in other circumstances I'd probably happily pull the trigger myself. But we had a plan and we need to stick to it. We've only got a limited window for this.'

I was finally able to twist my body over to see the speaker. She was standing in the doorway, looking untroubled by everything that had just occurred. I still had no idea what was going on, but I had little doubt that the woman in the doorway was Kate Brodie.

'We've still got to deal with these bastards.' Kinnear waved the gun in an arc that was presumably intended to encompass me, Garfield, Maddie, as well as the woman still lying on the floor.

'They're a complication,' Brodie said, 'but nothing we can't deal with. We just need to be systematic. There've been too many fuck ups already. Bring them through here.'

Kinnear gestured for the three of us, along with the young woman, to follow Brodie down the hallway. The woman seemed to be struggling to walk, but Maddie and Garfield were supporting her. I wondered about making another attempt to stop Kinnear, but I'd lost the element of surprise. He'd shoot me and the rest of us without hesitation now.

We followed Kate Brodie along the hallway into a room on the left. We'd passed what was clearly a kitchen, so I assumed this was going to be another reception room, similar to the room we'd just left.

But it was something far more disturbing.

It took my brain a moment to adjust to what I was seeing because I'd encountered nothing quite like it in a human context. It was a dormitory of sorts, I suppose, with beds lined up against the two walls. Only a couple of the beds were occupied, both with young women of a similar age to the woman stumbling between Garfield and Maddie. Both women were gazing at us in apparent terror and incomprehension, and both looked skinny and undernourished. Something in their expression suggested to me that they were sedated in some way. After a moment, I realised that both of them were secured by a strap fixed to the wall beside the beds. These were, in the most literal sense, captives.

I gazed around the room in horror, scarcely able to take in what I was seeing. I didn't know exactly why these young women, seemingly little more than children, were being held like this, but it wasn't difficult to guess at the possible reasons. I'd remembered now what Cameron Fraser had said about Gregor McBride's businesses being largely staffed by illegal, typically people-trafficked migrants. I assumed that most of those wouldn't be living in quite these conditions – though little about McBride would surprise me – but I imagined that what I was seeing here was simply an extreme point on that same spectrum.

Kinnear shepherded the four of us into a corner of the room, holding the gun unwaveringly. Then he pulled the woman away from us, handing her over to Kate Brodie. Brodie led her to one of the beds, taking a moment to secure the woman's wrists to the strap by the bed.

I had no idea what to do. If we could co-ordinate our actions, we might somehow succeed in overwhelming Kinnear, but I didn't give much for our chances. If we made any move, he'd shoot immediately and I suspected he was capable of taking out all three of us before we could offer any real resistance. Even as I was thinking this, I realised that Brodie had also produced a handgun from somewhere, cradling it gently in her hands. I'd no idea if she really knew how to use it, or if it was nothing more than a prop to terrorise the young women. But I guessed that if you were Archie Kinnear's daughter you'd have picked up a few skills on the way.

In those few minutes, my mind was racing uncontrollably, trying to make sense of events in the brief time I might have left. I was wondering about Kate Brodie's pregnancy. Nearly a year had passed since her disappearance, so either the pregnancy hadn't continued to full term for whatever reason or there was a baby somewhere. Was that why Brodie had been hidden away up here? But that made no sense. We weren't living in a nineteenth-century novel. Archie Kinnear's daughter was presumably well enough off to do as she pleased. But there was also the question of parentage. If Garfield was right and McBride was the father, had he somehow been responsible for Brodie's concealment up here?

Whichever way I turned it, I couldn't make sense of the picture. There was still something missing. Some final piece of the jigsaw.

It probably didn't matter much now, anyway, unless we could find some way of dealing with the two firearms trained on us. The room we were in was clearly designed to be secured from the outside, with hefty-looking locks on the solid doors. The only windows in here were positioned high on the walls, and were narrow and barred. My guess was that this room, like the rest of the house, had been constructed with a specific purpose in mind. The house had probably been built as a venue for some of Kinnear's famous parties, though I guessed it had never actually been used. Or perhaps this had been intended as one of the more exclusive attractions in McBride's infamous development. Either way, it seemed that something had disrupted the original plan.

Whatever the background, it wasn't difficult to guess how

Kinnear had been planning to deal with this mess. Simply burn the place to the ground. Our arrival had complicated matters, but that was probably still Kinnear's intention. The bodies would be found, but my guess was that there'd be nothing to link this place directly to Archie Kinnear. If anything, the ownership would be linked to Gregor McBride's convoluted network of international companies. Whatever else Kinnear might be, he was no fool. He'd always have had an escape route prepared.

As if to confirm my thoughts, Kinnear nodded to Gregor McBride. 'I want you to watch this, McBride. See how a real businessman does things. All planned and thought through long ago. Then quick, ruthless and no bullshit. No flying by the seat of your pants. And you're completely tied into this now. Whatever's happened, and whatever happens now, you're implicated. This place belongs to you. It's all in your name. Even the fucking baby's yours, for what that's worth. We can prove the paternity. And you can either accept that graciously, or we can claim that the sex was non-consensual. Either way, we can take you to the cleaners if you don't play ball. So you've got two choices. Either you work with us, and we use your influence and contacts to get us out of the crap, or we all go down together.'

For a moment, Gregor McBride simply looked baffled by what Kinnear was saying. Then, to my surprise, he walked slowly forward until he was standing immediately in front of Kinnear, seemingly oblivious to the gun inches from his chest. 'You don't do this, Archie. Not to me. Nobody does this to me.'

'Is that right?' Kinnear said. 'The truth is, you're nothing. You're a has-been who was never much of anything in the first place. So shut the fuck up.'

I'd never seen anything like the expression on McBride's face. I had the same thought I'd had when I'd first watched the film of him at Gus's party. McBride was a man who should have simply been ludicrous, but there was something about him, something almost inhuman, demonic, that transcended all that. In that moment, he looked more than merely furious. He looked incandescent, vengeful. He looked like someone who'd never be stopped. Not even by someone as ruthless as Archie Kinnear.

I expected Kinnear to shoot but he seemed to hesitate. He didn't exactly look scared or intimidated by McBride, but he seemed taken aback, as if he'd suddenly realised he'd taken on more than he'd expected. He took an involuntary step back and raised the pistol. 'Back off, old man. I don't want to have to kill you too, but I will if there's no other choice.'

McBride seemed hardly to hear the threat. He seized Kinnear's wrist, easily twisting the gun to one side. I expected Kinnear to resist – I'd discovered myself how unexpectedly strong he was – but he seemed almost unable to respond as McBride forced his way forward, pushing the pistol away from his own body. It was as if this wasn't a battle of physical strength but one of sheer force of will. For a moment, I had the sense that McBride's ungainly body was simply a clumsy vessel for something darker and less human.

Kinnear stumbled, momentarily losing his footing. McBride's burly body was obstructing my view and all I knew was that, suddenly and shockingly, the gun was fired.

I'd assumed Kinnear had shot McBride in the struggle. But it was Kinnear who fell back, blood pouring from a gaping wound in the centre of his chest. McBride straightened and stepped back as Kinnear slumped to the ground in front of him. Kinnear was still gripping the gun in his hand, and it slipped from his fingers only as he finally hit the floor.

Kate Brodie stepped forward and, clasping her pistol in both hands, pointed it towards McBride. McBride was gazing at her as if he had no idea who she was or why she was there. She raised her arms as if preparing to fire, but somehow I knew she'd never pull the trigger. I felt she sensed the same inner darkness I'd glimpsed moments before.

McBride just stared at her for a moment, then reached and simply plucked the gun from her hand. She made no obvious effort to resist. McBride stared down at the gun for a moment, then handed it to me. His face was impossible to read. 'I guess you'd better call the police,' he said. 'And maybe an ambulance. Though the bastard's well beyond that now.'

Almost as if nothing had happened, he turned and left the room. I hesitated a moment, then turned to Kate Brodie. I'd expected she might show some final bravado, but she simply looked lost. The ruthless assertiveness she'd demonstrated while shepherded into this room had drained away like the blood from her father's body. It seemed almost as if a spell had been broken, as if she'd suddenly returned to consciousness and realised what she'd been involved in.

'If you try anything,' I said to her, 'anything at all, we'll strap you to one of these beds and leave you in here. I might even be tempted to burn the whole place to the ground myself.' I nodded to Maddie and Garfield to release the three young women. They looked terrified and baffled as Maddie ushered them out of the room. I raised the pistol towards Kate Brodie, and then Garfield and I escorted her back through to the living room.

Maddie had gathered the three young women on the sofa. They were really little more than children, I saw now, though given their emaciated condition it was difficult to be sure of their exact ages. Garfield led Kate Brodie to one of the armchairs, then stood over her. She looked in no state to try anything, but she was clearly not someone to be underestimated.

McBride was sitting in one of the armchairs. I'd expected that he might try to organise some sort of cover-up for this mess, but he seemed oddly untroubled. Perhaps this was simply how he'd lived his life, uncaring of the chaos he was leaving in his wake, knowing someone would clear it up, that he would still somehow come out on top. I'd no idea whether he really would be able to walk away from all this, but somehow I thought he probably could.

I watched him as I dialled the emergency services. He looked now like nothing more than a harmless old man, gazing blankly into space, barely aware of his surroundings. But I knew what he'd done, and I knew what he was capable of doing. And I knew he scared the hell out of me.

The room had fallen silent as I dialled. It was only then, in the moment before the call connected, that I realised that, from somewhere in the house, I could hear the sound of a baby crying.

CHAPTER FORTY-EIGHT

'The good news,' Morag Henderson said, 'is that you're fully in the clear. The Fiscal's accepted your account of events.'

I could do with some good news, I supposed, though I didn't much care what the Procurator Fiscal's office had decided. If they'd thrown the book at me, it wouldn't have made much difference to how I felt.

We were sitting in a dark corner of the bar where we'd intended to meet originally. The meeting that had never taken place because of Lorna's death. I was struggling to get to grips with everything that had happened since.

'In any case,' Henderson went on, 'we've bigger fish to fry. Including unravelling Archie Kinnear's business empire. There's a lot emerging there now he's no longer around to keep a lid on it. Including his links with Gregor McBride.'

'What's happening to McBride?'

'He'll be heading back to the US. Your account confirmed that Kinnear's death was an accident resulting from McBride's attempts to defend himself and the rest of you. We tried to hold him in connection with the abduction and detainment of those young women, but he's denied all knowledge. Claimed he had no idea why Kinnear had taken him up to the lodge that morning and no knowledge anyone was being held there.'

'That's bollocks,' I said. 'He knew full well they were there. He'd been there before. Why the hell would he have gone up with Kinnear otherwise?'

Henderson sighed. 'I know. And we might well have been able to build a forensic case against him. But Kate Brodie wouldn't play ball. We've got her bang to rights on people trafficking and modern slavery charges. It looks like she's been playing that role for a long time as part of Kinnear's businesses. That lodge was just the latest example. A place for entertainment for Kinnear's special guests, apparently. We're still working through all their links but there's a whole network of illegal migrants underpinning Kinnear's business – money laundering, sex workers, you name it. But she's insisting that was just her and Kinnear, and that McBride had no part in it.'

'Why would she say that? McBride must have been involved. They'd have been providing staff for McBride's development.'

'If you want my honest opinion, she's either been paid off or frightened off. Most likely both. McBride's got some powerful friends. The National Crime Agency are liaising with the FBI on some of that, but I don't know how far they'll get. Probably no further than they got last time.'

'The last time?'

'The reason why Brodie "went missing", in the first place.'

'I've been wondering about that.'

'The NCA's apparently been investigating Brodie's activities for a while, in conjunction with various other international agencies. Brodie had always been pretty smart and kept her own hands largely clean, but she and Kinnear were concerned the investigation was getting too close for comfort.'

'Another area where Kinnear might have lost some of his touch.'

'Quite possibly. He certainly didn't want the investigation going anywhere near him. So we suspect he called in a few favours. Brodie supposedly went missing. A few senior officers in Glasgow back-pedalled on the investigation. Evidence was concocted that suggested she'd taken her own life. It didn't suit anyone to challenge that conclusion too strongly.'

'She couldn't have expected that to hold forever, though. I mean, she couldn't spend her life hiding away in some remote corner of the Highlands.'

'She didn't need to. She and Archie had always had exit plans if things started to go pear-shaped. A discreet private jet out to somewhere with no extradition treaty. The original plan would have been to wait a few months for the dust to settle, then for Brodie to slip quietly away. The pregnancy delayed that. She hadn't wanted to risk leaving immediately so she decided to wait until the baby was born. Kinnear had organised fake passports and documentation for both her and the child, so ultimately it would just have been another layer of camouflage. No one knew Kate Brodie had a child. I suspect the plan would have been to use the baby to exert some leverage over Gregor McBride. Probably with Brodie running some far-flung bit of his business empire. He has interests in some interesting parts of the world.'

'What's happened to the baby?'

'Taken into care at the moment. Longer term, I'm not sure. It may depend on McBride. It seems as if he really is the father. Poor wee thing.'

I assumed she was referring to the baby rather than McBride. 'Strikes me McBride never does anything he doesn't want to.'

'Maybe. But one reason we didn't push the investigation

here is that we were under pressure to allow McBride to return to the US. He's being investigated there on a range of potential fraud charges. We're liaising with the FBI in respect of his dealings with Kinnear and others here. The lodge itself seems to be owned indirectly by one of the companies associated with McBride's development, but again he just says he left all that in Kinnear's hands. Maybe we'll be able to untangle that eventually, but I'm not pinning too many hopes on it.'

'I suspected Kinnear was intending to torch the place and us with it,' I said. 'I'm guessing he always had an exit strategy.'

'Seems likely. There was a load of petrol in a shed at the rear of the house.'

I was silent for a moment, thinking about that and about what might have happened without McBride's unexpected intervention. 'Good luck with all that. I won't hold my breath about McBride going down. He strikes me as invulnerable. Destroys everyone around him then walks away.' I thought back to those moments in the lodge after Kinnear's death. The emptiness in McBride's eyes, the sense that he was channelling an evil I couldn't begin to fathom.

'His luck must run out eventually. That's what I tell myself.' She paused. 'You should know we're also having a close look at your friend, Martin Garfield.'

'He's no friend of mine.'

'Yet you went after Kinnear with him?'

'Only because I thought it might be the only chance we got to find out what had happened to Kate Brodie. Even if the outcome wasn't what I'd expected.'

She took a sip of her beer. 'You succeeded there, right enough. Pity you didn't involve us earlier, though.'

I'd thought a lot about that in the intervening weeks. Henderson might have been right. If the police had been involved the outcome could have been different. The truth was it hadn't even occurred to me until too late. I hadn't been thinking clearly that night. But then I hadn't been thinking clearly for a long time. 'There are lots of things I could have done differently.'

'Maybe it's for the best,' Henderson said. 'At least you helped save those poor young women. Though poor young girls might be more accurate.'

'Christ. Though I imagine there were plenty more like them who are beyond hope.'

I hesitated. I'd been putting off asking the question that really mattered to me, but I had to broach the topic eventually. 'What about Lorna?' I asked. 'What was her role in all this?'

There was a long silence before Henderson responded. 'We don't know exactly. We've found nothing in writing, as you'd expect. But we think she was acting as Kinnear's agent up there. Brodie obviously couldn't leave the lodge, and they couldn't risk anything being delivered there. So it may be that Lorna took food and other supplies up there as needed.'

Henderson had offered this information tentatively, as if it was no more than a theory, but her tone suggested that the police had evidence to support what she was saying. She was simply trying to spare my feelings.

I didn't even want to think about Lorna, but I was left wondering again about Archie Kinnear. His seemed a much more mundane, sordid form of evil than McBride's, but it was still more than capable of corrupting others. Kate's ex-husband had described him as no more than a small-time thug, a bully with big pretensions. I wondered how much McBride had been able to manipulate Kinnear's existing qualities – his greed, his ruthlessness, his overweening ambition – to further feed McBride's own inner darkness.

I still couldn't really process everything that happened that night up in the hills, and some of it I'd simply blanked out, perhaps to help preserve my own sanity. The moments up to the shooting were indelibly burned into my brain, but everything after that was a blur. I'd called 999 and then sent a message to Henderson to confirm our location. I told her only that we were with Gregor McBride, that Kate Brodie was alive and Archie Kinnear dead.

McBride had sat silent and motionless in one of the armchairs, seemingly oblivious to what was going on around him. Garfield and I stood guard over Kate Brodie. Maddie had gone to track down the crying baby, and the three young women sat bewildered on the sofa.

It had seemed an eternity until the emergency services finally arrived, two marked vehicles, blue lights pulsing, then an ambulance, and finally Henderson and McBain in separate cars. I was in no state to give them anything more than the briefest of explanations, but I must have managed some kind of coherent account.

When Maddie, Garfield and I had finally made our way outside into the first light of a chilly morning, I'd never felt so glad to drink in the clean fresh air. I can't remember anything after that. We left the police and paramedics to deal with Brodie and McBride, and they were organising support to take care of the baby and the three women.

They must also have arranged for us to be taken back to the cottage. The next clear memory I have is waking up on the sofa much later in the day. It was sometime around 4pm. Garfield and Maddie had slept upstairs but were already up, drinking coffee in the kitchen. None of us had felt like talking.

After that, there'd been days of giving statements, answering questions, trying to provide a clear account of what had happened that night, why we'd been there in the first place, and exactly what it was we'd known about Archie Kinnear and Gregor McBride. I played a straight bat, being as honest as I could in the face of the seemingly endless questions. Henderson finally accepted that any incoherence in my responses was a result of my confusion rather than because I had anything to hide. I presume she'd reflected that in her report to the Procurator Fiscal. Whether Garfield and Maddie had responded in the same way, I'd no idea. I'd had no contact with them since that night.

'What about Cameron Fraser?' I asked now.

'I was going to ask you that,' Henderson said. 'He's not part of our investigation. There's no reason why he should be. I've had no contact with him.' She paused. 'Has he paid you for your part in this?'

I shook my head. 'I told him I didn't want his money. Not now.' That wasn't the whole truth. I had told him that, but a day or two later a substantial sum had appeared in my bank account. I had no way of paying it back. In the end I donated it to a charity helping survivors of modern-day slavery.

With Kinnear dead and McBride and Brodie under investigation, the proposed Scottish developments had supposedly been halted. Even so, Gus had told me gloomily that there were rumours of some third party taking over the project, quietly snatching up the land and the planning rights for a bargain price. I wondered again whether Cameron Fraser's supposed love of his community would really outweigh his greed and opportunism. I didn't have much doubt about the answer.

'And what about you?' Henderson said. 'What are you going to do now?'

It was a good question, and I'd had no ready answer. My first thought was that there was simply nothing left for me. I'd lost Lorna, and my memories of her were tainted and confused. I had no friends up here, and nothing to look forward to. I'd no desire to work for Archie Kinnear and there were no other job prospects on the horizon.

But none of that was the real problem. I felt as if, at least for the moment, there was simply nothing left of *me*. Everything I'd believed about myself had been either untrue or meaningless. I'd been played for a fool right from the start by powers I hadn't even known existed. I'd contributed, however inadvertently, to the deaths of Lorna and Sean Critchley.

That was pretty much what I'd said to Morag Henderson.

To my surprise, she'd laughed. Sympathetically rather than mockingly, but she clearly hadn't taken my answer seriously. 'You've been through a hell of a lot,' she'd said. 'Now's not the time to be making decisions. Give it a month or two. If you want a job, there's no reason you couldn't rejoin the police. You've got an unblemished track record. If you didn't want to rejoin as an officer, there are civilian roles you could consider. There'll always be opportunities for someone with your experience.' She'd paused. 'And if you're short of friends, well, I'm always open to someone buying me a pint. One day, I might even tell you about my own background.'

I hadn't been sure how much she'd meant it, but her matter-of-fact response had been enough at least to drag me out of the real depths of my self-pity. She was right. I had savings. I still had the income from the Glasgow flat. I was fit and well, and had options open to me. I didn't need to make any urgent decisions.

Gus had said he was happy for me to remain in the cottage. At first I hadn't been sure if he'd really meant it. Though he'd never said it, I wondered if Gus had decided I was bad luck. For a dark moment, I'd even wondered if Gus himself had been part of the conspiracy to lure me up here. But in the end I'd had little doubt that his involvement had been as unwitting as mine, and that he sincerely wanted me to stay.

Above all, I still had Ziggy. Lorna had had no next of kin, and I'd no intention of letting anyone else look after him. So there he was, at night, nuzzling up to me in the cottage, by day bounding gleefully along on the hillside.

On the morning after my meeting with Morag Henderson, I'd woken early as usual. My sleep had improved, and I was no longer experiencing the half-remembered nightmares that had repeatedly woken me in the small hours after that night in the hills. Instead, I was generally disturbed now only by Ziggy snuffling up to the bed, letting me know he was ready for food and a walk.

I made my way downstairs, filled the kettle and topped up Ziggy's food bowl. Ten minutes later, refreshed by my first coffee of the day, I took him outside. It was still dark, but the clear sky was lightening in the south-east. It looked set to be a fine day. We tramped together up to the top of the hill, and then I let Ziggy off his lead and left him to race away with his customary enthusiasm. I could only admire his sheer unalloyed pleasure as he headed first down into the darkness of the next glen, then up and past me back towards the cottage. It was as if he was heading deliberately towards the imminent sunrise.

I could learn from Ziggy, and his ability to live only in the moment. After all, the darkest times had already passed. I needed only to struggle on, find a way of starting again, work back towards some as yet unknowable future, Ziggy no doubt still bounding energetically ahead of me. Winter was passing and some kind of spring would come. The sun was rising.

All I had to do was wait for the light.

ALSO BY ALEX WALTERS

Winterman

Human Assets

THE DI ALEC MCKAY SERIES

Candles and Roses (Book 1)

Death Parts Us (Book 2)

Their Final Act (Book 3)

Expiry Date (Book 4)

For Their Sins (Book 5)

A Parting Gift (Book 6)

ACKNOWLEDGEMENTS

Thanks as ever to all those who made this book possible, particularly to Peter Buckman for his plotting suggestions, and of course to Helen for her ideas and her patience and support through endless re-readings.

And thanks as ever to all at Bloodhound Books for their work on the book – especially Betsy, Fred, Tara, Ian and Abbie for their input and support.

ABOUT THE AUTHOR

Alex has worked as a consultant and advisor in numerous organisations across the UK and internationally, including police forces, prison and probation services and other parts of the criminal justice system. He is the author of numerous crime novels with series set in Mongolia, Manchester and the Peak District. His DI Alec McKay series, published by Bloodhound Books, is set in the Scottish Highlands where Alex now lives.

A NOTE FROM THE PUBLISHER

Thank you for reading this book. If you enjoyed it please do consider leaving a review on Amazon to help others find it too.

We hate typos. All of our books have been rigorously edited and proofread, but sometimes mistakes do slip through. If you have spotted a typo, please do let us know and we can get it amended within hours.

info@bloodhoundbooks.com

Printed in Great Britain
by Amazon